WITCH

WITCH

The Bone Chilling
True Story of US Murderer
BROOKEY LEE WEST

GLENN PUIT

EBURY
PRESS

1 3 5 7 9 10 8 6 4 2

This edition published 2012
First published in 2012 in UK by Ebury Press, an imprint of Ebury Publishing
A Random House Group company
First published in USA by The Berkley Publishing Group,
a division of Penguin Group (USA) Inc in 2005

The Random House Group Limited Reg. No. 954009

Addresses for companies within the Random House Group can be found at
www.randomhouse.co.uk

A CIP catalogue record for this book is available from the British Library

The Random House Group Limited supports The Forest Stewardship Council
(FSC®), the leading international forest certification organisation. Our books
carrying the FSC label are printed on FSC certified paper. FSC is the only
forest certification scheme endorsed by the leading environmental organisations,
including Greenpeace. Our paper procurement policy can be found at
www.randomhouse.co.uk/environment

Printed and bound by CPI Group (UK) Ltd, Croydon, CR0 4YY

ISBN 9780091947286

To buy books by your favourite authors and register for offers visit
www.randomhouse.co.uk

This book is dedicated to my late grandfather, Glenn Edick, and my mother, Dolores Hicks, who currently lives in upstate New York. Without you two, who knows where I'd be.

Author's Note

In the spring of 2001, I was assigned to cover the criminal case of Brookey Lee West for Nevada's largest newspaper, the *Las Vegas Review-Journal*. I had no inkling at the time that the assignment would prompt a tumultuous, three-year personal odyssey—some would say obsession—to document the most remarkable criminal case I've ever come across in my journalism career.

West was a successful technical writer who seemed to have it all when she was arrested in Vegas on charges she killed her own mother. Following her arrest, authorities detailed a suspected crime spree spanning two decades and two states, and when it was over, two were dead, one was missing and at least two others were victimized in frightening acts of violence.

The seeds of the mayhem, according to Las Vegas authorities, can be traced to the occult, and more specifically, witchcraft and Satanism.

In 2003, I met with Brookey Lee West at the Southern Nevada Women's Correctional Center in North Las Vegas, and despite an avalanche of evidence against her, she denies all of the accusations. For the record, she denies being a witch, a Satanist or a killer. I'll let you decide on each of those issues.

In 2004, I spent nearly two days with West discussing her life in tape-recorded interviews, and she is an enigma of a human being. To this day, after three years of researching her life, I still haven't quite figured her out, and many of the police officers who investigated her for a decade in California and Las Vegas will tell you the same thing.

But there are three things I can say about West with absolute certainty. First, she is extremely intelligent. She is not your typical criminal defendant. Second, West has a history of mental illness—she herself will tell you as much. And third, she had a truly horrible childhood. In my humble opinion, it was her mental illness and her upbringing that played a huge role in determining why she ended up where she is today.

Before we get to West's story, however, I need to give you a primer for what is coming. For you to fully comprehend the contents of this book, you have to understand Brookey Lee West's family, and to do that, you must familiarize yourself with the basic players in the West clan.

West's mother is Christine Smith. Her father is Leroy Smith. Her brother is Travis Smith, and her stepmother is Chloe Smith,* i.e., Leroy Smith's second wife. If you can keep West and these four family members straight in your mind, you should have no problems following the complex series of events documented in this book.

I used the standard news-gathering principles in putting together *Witch*. The book is based on two years of interviews with dozens of witnesses and approximately 3,000 pages of law enforcement and court documents gathered in Nevada and California through open-record laws. Unlike other true-crime books, you will find no re-created conversations in *Witch*. The quotes in this book came either from my inter-

views with witnesses or from the police reports, although I
have edited some quotes for the sake of clarity and brevity.

For a handful of witnesses in the book, I was obligated
to use false names, or pseudonyms, to protect their privacy.
Each pseudonym is noted by an asterisk. However, I used
false names very, very sparingly. I used them only for witnesses who were the victims of a violent crime and who requested anonymity, or for those who are the subject of
allegations made by West herself, and the veracity of those
allegations could not be verified in any other independent
way.

Otherwise, if someone gave a statement to the police in
the Brookey Lee West case, then their name is in this book.
Their comments are, by law, a matter of public record.

It is also important for you to understand that the contents of this book are not meant to demean the legitimate
Wiccan following in the United States. There are hundreds
of thousands of people in the United States who identify
themselves as Wiccans or witches, and they do not use the
craft for evil.

Special thanks go to: Brookey Lee West, who was kind
enough to meet with me so her side of the story could be
told; literary agent Jim Cypher, who helped make all this
possible; Samantha Mandor, my editor at Berkley Books;
the *Las Vegas Review-Journal*'s editors, who gave me my
chance at the big time in the news business nearly a decade
ago; former Clark County, Nevada, district attorney Stewart Bell, who granted my massive records requests; Nevada
prosecutor Frank Coumou, who guided me through the
mass of paperwork; Clark County deputy public defender
Scott Coffee, who is a true professional and a hell of an attorney; former Tulare County, California, homicide detective Daniel Haynes, who was kind enough to meet with me
although he still cannot discuss facts surrounding the slaying of West's husband; Las Vegas homicide detective Dave

Mesinar; the Indiana State University journalism program in Terre Haute, Indiana; and all the other witnesses who gave their valuable time. I especially want to thank my wife, Tina. Only she knows what I've been through in making this dream a reality.

1

> *Give me your blessing; truth will come to light; murder cannot be hid long.*
>
> —William Shakespeare, *The Merchant of Venice*

The downtown corridor of Las Vegas is a sinner's paradise.

In the shadows of the Las Vegas Strip, a tourist can slip a cabbie $20 and, within minutes, be smoking a rock of crack bought from a dealer in the city's projects. On Fremont Street in the center of downtown, streetwalkers troll in front of run-down weekly-rent motels, copping sex acts for cash at all hours. Or a $50 bill to a bouncer at most of the city's strip clubs will secure a hand job from a voluptuous stripper in a back room.

While other cities boast fine arts and entertainment, Las Vegas prides itself in its industry of flesh. It even advertises it. "What happens here, stays here," the Las Vegas Convention and Visitors Authority said in a recent national television advertisement aimed at luring tourists to Southern Nevada.

At the city's casinos, greed is the game. Customers fill up on free alcohol and throw away their cash at the gaming tables. The casino offers credit when the money is gone, and the legalized loan-sharking not only helps gamblers chase their lost money, it helps makes Nevada the nation's suicide capital, where destitute drunks and drug addicts routinely take fatal plunges off casino parking garages.

The sex. The alcohol. The drugs. The gambling. They blend together, forming an economic juggernaut that draws some thirty-five million out-of-towners to Vegas annually. They pack flight after flight into the city's McCarran International Airport, where jumbo jets line up in the southeast Vegas sky like huge mechanical birds descending upon Sodom.

But there is another side of Vegas few tourists see.

Within a few hundred yards of the downtown corridor begins a massive, rolling expanse of residential development that houses the Las Vegas Valley's 1.6 million residents. The most pristine portion of the city is about fifteen minutes from the Strip in northwest Las Vegas, where upscale homes sit at the base of the towering, rusty brown Sierra Nevada mountains to the west. Life here is a world away from Sin City—it is suburbia, an existence of stucco homes, grocery stores, libraries and golf courses.

Soccer moms whisk their kids to and from $15,000-a-year private schools in luxury sport utility vehicles. Casino workers take their families to church on Sunday. Gaming executives and Vegas lawyers find refuge from the city's twenty-four-hour hustle in their ultra-exclusive gated country club communities.

Murder is a rarity here.

Las Vegas police dispatch received the call at 1:31 p.m. on February 5, 2001. On the phone was Bill Unruh, general manager of Canyon Gate Mini Storage on West Sahara Avenue in northwest Las Vegas.

Unruh was calling to report a terrible smell floating in the air at the business.

"People were complaining about it," Unruh said. "It

started getting worse and worse. You'll never forget it. The smell."

Unruh, sixty-three, keeps a watchful eye over Canyon Gate, an expansive, two-story storage facility sitting in the middle of suburbia. Las Vegans can rent storage sheds to stash their excess belongings at Canyon Gate for twenty dollars a month. Kitty-corner to Canyon Gate is a luxury 24 Hour Fitness gym, where BMWs, Jaguars and Hummers fill the parking lot. Down the block a few hundred feet is a series of upscale shopping complexes catering to the Vegas rich.

Unruh told police the smell at Canyon Gate was so pungent he and coworker Greg Stoner made like makeshift bloodhounds and trailed the smell to the second floor of the business. They tracked the stench to storage unit #317, a tiny, five-by-five-foot storage locker rented by a woman named Brookey Lee West. West could not be reached despite repeated phone calls to the number she listed on her Canyon Gate rental sheet.

"My manager and I went out there, and we found the unit where it was smellin' the worst, and we cut the lock," Unruh said.

Under a cool, cloudless winter sky, the men rolled open the white door to unit #317, and a sickening odor rushed out in a thick, invisible fog.

"We opened up the door, and the smell hit us," Unruh said. "That's when I said, 'This is not one for us. It's for the police.'"

The men peered into the storage unit and noticed boxes and boxes of shoes lining the interior of the shed.

"Shoes, and there was a potty in there for older people to use for a bathroom, for anybody that's crippled or anything like that," Unruh said.

The men noticed something else, too. A large green plastic garbage can was in the back left corner of the storage shed.

It was leaking.

"We noticed a green plastic trash can with blackish fluid coming out of the sides and the bottom," Stoner wrote in a police statement.

Unruh and Stoner scrambled back to Canyon Gate's main office and dialed 911. Patrol officers arrived and knew immediately from the smell something was dead and decaying inside unit #317. The officers contacted dispatchers and asked for Detective Todd Rosenberg and sergeant Jim Young of the Las Vegas police General Assignment Detail to respond to the scene.

"As soon as you entered the storage building, it was an unmistakable smell of decaying flesh," Young said.

Young, forty-three, is a detective with a shock of grayish-brown hair, and Rosenberg, thirty-nine, is a clean-cut, brown-haired Indiana native with a wife and kids at home. Together, Rosenberg and Young have a combined quarter century of experience working the night shift on the General Assignment Detail for Vegas police. It is a grisly endeavor, encompassing the investigation of seven hundred death scenes annually in Las Vegas and the surrounding desert of unincorporated Clark County, Nevada.

"When you get to the scene, all you know is somebody is dead," Young said. "You don't know whether it's natural death, accidental, homicide or suicide, so you have to figure it out."

Their job is to determine whether a death is suspicious or not and whether homicide detectives need to conduct further investigation. On average, approximately 140 of the death scenes general assignment detectives investigate each year in metropolitan Las Vegas and the surrounding desert turn out to be murders.

Rosenberg and Young arrived at Canyon Gate in their unmarked Crown Victorias and were directed by patrol to unit #317. They smelled the odor, too, but at first, they were not convinced this was necessarily a dead-body call.

"Just two weeks earlier, we were called to another storage shed across town for a similar smell," Young recalled. "We investigated and found a huge cache of used medical waste from some health insurance scam, so we figured we were probably dealing with another one of those cases."

The detectives then saw the leaking can, however, making it clear that crime scene analysts were needed. CSIs Joe Matvay and Robbie Dahn arrived at Canyon Gate in about twenty minutes.

"When we got there, Joe looked at me and said, 'That smell is the unmistakable smell of death,'" Dahn said. "It was everywhere."

Matvay, forty-eight, is a legend in Las Vegas law enforcement circles, a walking encyclopedia of evidentiary expertise with thousands of crime scenes investigated and solved during his twenty-four-year career. The devout Catholic is tall and thin haired, a thick black beard accenting a face that shows no evidence of his being a crime scene investigator.

"I derive a lot of satisfaction from knowing I was the one who solved a case, whether it was fingerprints, hair, blood, fiber, tool marks, whatever," Matvay said.

Dahn is an attractive redhead who spent eighteen years as a manicurist in Las Vegas until deciding, at the age of forty, that it was time for a career change. She enrolled at the criminal justice program at the University of Nevada, Las Vegas, and now makes a living dusting for prints, scanning for fibers or tire tracks and gathering DNA to catch killers.

"I used to sit inside doing nails all day, and I wanted to be out there," Dahn said. "I was going nowhere fast, and I felt I had a lot more to offer."

"My friends say, 'Oh, crime scene investigation, that is

so cool,' and this and that," Dahn said. "They have no idea. There is no glamour."

The general assignment detectives and the CSIs gathered in front of the unit and started their investigation. The first step was seeking permission from the renter to enter the shed, and Unruh provided the cops with rental sheets identifying the renter as a Brookey Lee West, forty-seven. West, according to her rental agreement, started renting the shed on June 26, 1998. West wrote on the rental sheet that her mother, Christine M. Smith, was the only other person who was allowed access to the shed. West also listed her address as a post office box on Industrial Road in downtown Las Vegas, a seedy strip of earth where all-nude strip clubs and pornography shops sit next to plumbing stores and greasy auto repair shops. Unruh told the police West paid her monthly rental fee in cash. She usually paid ahead of time and the rent was current. There was a phone number for West on the rental sheet, but it was a bad number.

"Our manager had been calling numbers, and we never got anything," Unruh said. Rosenberg directed dispatchers to run West's name in a driver's license database, and it came up as an address listed in Santa Clara, California.

"We called the police out there and asked, 'Can you track this woman down? We need to have permission to go into her storage unit,'" Rosenberg said, "They came back and they said it wasn't a good address. The dispatch said the address doesn't even exist."

Immediately locating West and obtaining consent to search the shed looked unlikely, so Matvay and Dahn started a preliminary search of the premises. They had solid legal ground to do so, given their responsibility to try to pinpoint the source of the smell. Matvay crouched down and walked inside, waving his black flashlight back and forth in the light-starved shed. He noticed a potty chair and a shower chair built for senior citizens. Looking closer, he saw stacks and stacks of shoe boxes on the right interior of the storage shed. The boxes appeared to be wrapped with a green-tinted plastic wrap. A wooden cane was leaning up against some of the boxes, and a black trunk was visible under others.

Gradually, Matvay focused on the garbage can in a back corner as Dahn trailed behind, snapping photos with her department-issued camera.

"The trash can was a forty-five-gallon green Rubbermaid trash can on wheels," Dahn said. "The left side was buckled at the bottom. It appeared there must have been some crack or something, because there was fluid coming out."

The origin of the smell was unmistakable—it was coming from the trash can.

The can's lid was sealed tight with duct tape. A large amount of what appeared to be the light green plastic wrap on the shoe boxes was wrapped around the top of the can, and garbage bags were taped together and placed over the top of the plastic wrap.

"Big-time problem," Matvay said. "I know there is something dead in there. I just don't know what it is."

Matvay initiated a presumptive test for blood on the black, crusty fluid spilling from the can, and also on the wood floor underneath. It's a test he's done hundreds of times. He squeezed a drop of distilled water onto the tip of a cotton swab to moisten it. He applied a liquid chemical called phenolphthalein to the tip of the swab and rubbed it through the black fluid. Next, he dripped a droplet of hydrogen peroxide on the swab. If the swab turned purple, blood was likely present in the fluid.

"I repeated the process five times, and on one of the tests the swab turned purple," Matvay said. "At this point we're thinking there may be someone in this can and this could be a homicide. I told Rosenberg about the test results, that we had a marginally positive test for blood, and he proceeded to get a telephonic search warrant."

The ability to secure a search warrant over the phone is a godsend for Las Vegas police. Instead of having to leave the scene and drive back to the detective bureau to type up an affidavit detailing why police believe they have probable cause, detectives call a judge and tell them the facts of a case in a tape-recorded conversation.

Rosenberg called Las Vegas justice of the peace Deborah Lippis to request a warrant to search unit #317.

"I went back to the office at Canyon Gate to use the phone because the last thing you want to do is apply for a telephonic search warrant on a cell phone," Rosenberg said. "Number one, it could be intercepted, but more importantly, cell phones drop calls."

"You could be right in the middle of an application for a search warrant and the phone disconnects, and you've got to call back, then explain later to a defense attorney why the call disconnected," Rosenberg said.

Lippis approved the search warrant almost immediately. It was a logical move given the facts detailed for the judge.

"We had a storage shed that has been paid for several months in advance," Rosenberg said. "The information the renter has left with the storage business, her contact numbers and a contract address, were faulty. There's a terrible smell coming out of there; you can see some stuff leaking out of the plastic drum; and we have a positive presumptive test for blood, so any prudent person is going to think maybe someone's dead in there."

The search warrant cleared the way for Matvay to cut open the can, but he first had to figure out how to pry off the lid without destroying the wrappings. They might contain valuable evidence.

"The lid was secured all the way around the circumference of the lid with duct tape," Matvay said. "Then there were three large green plastic trash bags duct-taped together, and those were wrapped around the lid and upper portion of the can. And then there was this greenish-tinted plastic wrap, sort of like Saran Wrap, and it was wrapped all around the circumference of the lid and upper portion of the can," Matvay said. "A lot of thought went into this."

Matvay retrieved a box cutter and slowly started to cut through the wrappings.

"When I made the first incision on the plastic wrap, the plastic bag and duct tape, some liquid emanated from the can, as did dead maggots," Matvay said.

Matvay proceeded like a surgeon, slicing through the light green plastic wrap, preserving the evidence as much as possible. The three green trash bags were next, then the duct tape.

"Once I cut through the duct tape, I removed the lid," Matvay said.

Matvay looked inside and saw something so horrible, so gruesome, so frightening that it startled even the veteran crime scene investigator.

"There's a body in here," Matvay said. "Another homicide! It's a homicide."

In the bottom of the can was the badly decomposed body of what appeared to be an elderly woman. She was up to her shoulders in a thick, brown, soupy mix of human decomposition topped with a layer of insect larvae. A white plastic bag was tied tightly around the victim's face and a long stretch of gray and black hair descended into the pool of decomposition. The victim was leaning over in death; all that was left of her face was a partial, thin layer of skin on top of her skull, her head against a folded elbow as if resting her head for the last time.

"It appeared to be a woman from the hair," Young said. "The size was of a very small person. The thought had crossed our mind this could even be a child."

Young called Las Vegas police lieutenant Wayne Petersen on his cell phone so he could notify one of his sergeants, Kevin Manning, that homicide detectives were needed.

"It is clearly a homicide," Rosenberg said. "If you knew someone who died, you wouldn't say, 'Hmm, let's put her in a barrel in a storage shed.' It was bizarre."

Even more bizarre to the investigators was the bag tied over the woman's mouth.

"There was a portion of this white plastic bag knotted at the back of the head with the remainder of the bag going toward the front of the lower portion of the face," Matvay said.

Young wondered how someone could do something so heinous. Whoever the killer was, he or she stuffed a senior citizen in a garbage can like a piece of trash, then left her corpse to rot. It looked to the detectives as if the body had been there for years.

"It must take a pretty indifferent person to do something like that," Young said. "This person is out there, going to work, interacting with people, hanging with friends, and this garbage can is in there the whole time. This has to be someone who is pretty psychologically warped."

2

Dave Mesinar is a Vegas homicide cop who has spent the last three decades tracking down bad guys, leaving him no stranger to the brutality of Vegas' underbelly. Shootings, dismemberment, drug deals gone bad, domestic violence murders and deadly trick rolls are all on the homicide detective's resume of investigated murders.

"It's a noble profession," Mesinar said. "The victims can't tell you what happened, so you do right by them."

At six foot one and 220 pounds, he is a man who, like many cops, lives two lives. To his wife, Linda, and his two grown boys, he is a caring husband and father who worries about them constantly.

"It takes a special person to put up with someone who works homicide, with someone who does this for a living, and my family is very special to me," Mesinar said.

At work, he is far different: a human robot void of emotion, out of necessity. They say murder doesn't kill just one person—it kills everyone who knows the victim, too. Mesinar, fifty-eight, learned a long time ago you care about the deceased and their loved ones, but you don't get too close. It will destroy you.

"You get used to it after a while," Mesinar said. "I do it because someone has to speak for the victims."

He is an imposing, salt-and-pepper-haired figure with a stare capable of cutting straight through a suspect's bull-shit. It is a valuable skill that has served him well as lead detective on some of Vegas' most high-profile murders.

In June 1999, a man named Zane Floyd walked into an Albertsons grocery store on West Sahara Avenue in Las Vegas and, with a shotgun in hand, started blasting at everyone in sight, leaving a trail of blood up and down the store's aisles. Floyd's rampage was Las Vegas' most pro-lific spree killing. One victim, Albertsons employee Lu-cille Tarantino, sixty, was shot in the face as she begged for her life. Another store employee, Dennis Troy Sargent, was cut down in his prime. He left behind a seven-year-old son. Victim Thomas Darnell was shot in the back, and Floyd's fourth murder victim, Carlos Leos, forty-one, had just cel-ebrated his first wedding anniversary.

"This guy was just shooting throughout the store," Mesinar said. "The bread rack was full of shotgun pellets, and there was blood and dead bodies all over the place. It really enraged me to think one human being could do something like that."

The work of Mesinar and his now retired partner, Paul Bigham, yielded Floyd a spot on Nevada's death row.

In another case of Mesinar's that drew headlines, Mesinar was assigned in August 1998 to investigate the discovery of a body at a Las Vegas motel on the north end of Las Vegas Boulevard. The Del Mar XXX Motel is a sex addict's dream come true. Its rooms feature beds sur-rounded by mirrors and twenty-four-hour broadcasts of graphic sex flicks. Prostitutes regularly walk the surrounding streets, hoping to find work from the likes who frequent the Del Mar.

The body at the Del Mar was found by a guest who noticed a putrid smell in his room and called the police. Detectives snooped around to identify the source of the smell, and they found the body of Patricia Margello, forty-five, stuffed in an air-conditioning duct. The corpse had been in the duct for days.

Margello appeared at first to be just another dead hooker or drug user headed for a slab at the Clark County coroner's office. A blurb about the slaying in the city's largest newspaper, the *Las Vegas Review-Journal*, stretched a mere four paragraphs the next day. But within weeks, a trail of clues led Mesinar to the front door of one of America's richest families.

Mesinar learned that Margello's boyfriend was a man named Dean MacGuigan, the son of a woman named Lisa Dean Moseley. Moseley, in turn, is a direct descendant of the DuPont family, which founded the largest chemical company in America. MacGuigan told the detective that Moseley's husband, Christopher, hated Margello because he believed she was demeaning the family's prestigious name. Christopher Moseley was soon the prime suspect in Margello's slaying, prompting Mesinar to fly to the DuPont family estate in Delaware.

"Money," Mesinar said. "Their estate and the mansion they lived in were massive. The driveway leading to their home was at least a half mile long."

Christopher Moseley eventually confessed to carrying out a murder-for-hire plot culminating in Margello's body being stuffed in the air-conditioning duct. Moseley said he paid an over-the-hill porn star, Diana Hironaga, forty-one, and two other street thugs $15,000 to strangle Margello at the Del Mar.

"That was a crime that made no sense at all," Mesinar said. "These people were so rich they could buy anything they wanted in the world three or four times over. There was no need for it."

Mesinar was at home on the eve of February 5, 2001, getting ready to have dinner with his wife when his Homicide supervisor called.

"You are not going to believe this," Sergeant Kevin Manning said. "They found a body in a trash can."

Mesinar agreed to meet Manning and another Vegas police homicide detective, James Vaccaro, at Canyon Gate.

"Kevin said they found a body in a trash can, so I'm thinking, 'All right, it's a body in a Dumpster,'" Mesinar said. "Nothing unusual."

The idea of Mesinar, Manning and Vaccaro working together is a scary proposition for criminals. Combined, they've investigated nearly a thousand murders. Vaccaro, a cop with more than five hundred homicide investigations under his belt, is as good a detective as they come. He is best known in Las Vegas for his work in the "Black Widow" case of Margaret Rudin, who killed her millionaire husband, Ron, in 1994.

Manning is a crucial cog in the Las Vegas police Homicide Section and one of the most respected cops in the 2,500-member force of the Las Vegas Police Department. A former cop in Cape Cod, Massachusetts, he still has a slight New England accent. At about five feet seven inches tall, he supervises some fifty homicide investigations annually, monitoring teams of detectives like a father imparting wisdom to his sons.

"A lot of guys that I used to work with in narcotics ask me if it is fun to work homicide," Manning said. "I could never use that word to describe working homicide. It's one of two things—it's either very frustrating or extremely satisfying. It's very frustrating on the cases where you don't have cooperative witnesses, or caring families, or where you don't have much evidence at all."

Mesinar drove his police-issued Ford Expedition from his northwest Las Vegas home to Canyon Gate on West Sahara. He met with Manning and Vaccaro, and the three were escorted by patrol officers to an elevator. From there, the three were led to the front door of unit #317, where Matvay was waiting. Matvay sent Dahn home for the night because she was going to be needed the next morning at the autopsy.

"The odor of death and decomposition was overwhelming as soon as we arrived," Mesinar said. Matvay, Young and Rosenberg briefed the homicide detectives on what they knew so far. Brookey Lee West was the renter of the shed, but she couldn't be found. A corpse was in a can in the rear of the storage shed, and no one had an inkling as to who the victim was.

"I looked in there, and I saw a whole bunch of fluid in the can," Mesinar said. "There was this body in somewhat of a fetal position. There was some clothing on the body, there were insects on the victim and there was the back of a plastic bag sticking out from behind the head."

Mesinar has witnessed the result of hundreds of acts of violence in his career, but nothing as gruesome as this. His thoughts were racing.

Nobody deserves this. This woman should be buried.

Vaccaro was astonished at the contents of the makeshift tomb.

"In this business, you get to see a lot of people in pitiful positions," Vaccaro said. "But I was thinking, 'My God, I have never seen one like this, decomposition at that level, where all of the body fluids had stayed contained in a can like that with the victim.'"

Mesinar took special notice of the bag over the victim's face.

This lady was likely suffocated. This murder was pre-

meditated. We are dealing with something out of the ordinary, something personal.

Matvay walked the detectives through the crime scene, pointing out how the can was sealed with green wrapping, duct tape and plastic bags.

"It was like a cocoon wrapped in all this plastic wrap," Mesinar said. "It was taped real tightly. Whoever did it knew they were going to have an odor. They took a lot of time."

The first step, the four men decided, was to get the body to the Clark County coroner's office for autopsy, but this was not your typical crime scene. The body could not be lifted and placed in a body bag. There was a can full of decomposition fluid to deal with, and that fluid might contain clues like bullets, a broken knife or evidence of drugs.

"How do we move this package?" Manning asked. "We started to talk about it, and eventually we decided to give Vaccaro the police department–issued credit card, and we sent him to Home Depot to buy a huge roll of plastic."

The detectives decided they would wrap the garbage can in a plastic tarp and lift it onto a gurney, then roll it to an awaiting mortuary van for shipment to the coroner's office.

"We are going to wrap it up like you would a Christmas package," Manning said. "Wrap the plastic all the way around the can, tie it together with flex cuffs, and then actually put the toe tag on the package.

"It was a first for us," Manning said. "That's the creative part of the job."

Vaccaro made the five-minute drive to a Home Depot on West Charleston Boulevard to buy the tarp.

"I got this huge tarp. I went up to the counter and I presented the clerk with the credit card, and it actually says 'Homicide Section' on the credit card," Vaccaro said. "The clerk says, 'Plastic tarp? Homicide? Oh, I hope you are not buying this for some investigation.' I said, 'Lady, you don't even want to know what I'm going to do with this.' "

Vaccaro drove back to Canyon Gate, the 1,156-foot Stratosphere Tower rising into the skyline to the east, the glow of the Strip illuminating the clear winter night. He arrived at Canyon Gate, and the cops wrapped the huge tarp around the garbage can and tied it with plastic handcuffs.

"I thought it looked like an Easter basket," Mesinar said.

The can was heavy. The detectives, patrol officers and mortuary workers gradually got the can onto the gurney, and they wheeled it down to the coroner's van.

Whoever did this had to have help getting that body up here.

Manning, Matvay, Vaccaro and Mesinar started canvassing the contents of the storage shed for clues. There were at least two dozen boxes to search through, many containing shoes. There were enough shoes in here to last a woman a lifetime. Dress shoes, casual shoes, high heels, sneakers, loafers. Some looked like they were never worn or even taken out of the box.

"The green wrapping on many of the shoe boxes was the same width as the wrapping on the can—five inches," Matvay said. "It was the same color, same tinting, so whoever owns the shoes is the one who wrapped up the can."

The men opened each of the boxes and the black trunk. In the trunk, Matvay found a section of the *Las Vegas Review-Journal*, dated August 7, 1998. In a box that appeared to be a produce box from a grocery store, Matvay found a series of books, their covers worn thin: *The Satanic Bible*, *The Geography of Witchcraft*, *Necronomicon*, *Studies in Astrology*.

Manning, searching through a large box, found more books: *The Book of Black Magic*, *Amulets and Talismans*, *Jews for Jesus*.

"What is this stuff?" he said.

Mesinar found even more: *Satanic Rituals*, *Personal Aura*.

"Look at this," Mesinar said. "Here's a book on devil worship!"

This is unbelievable.

Vaccaro tried to comprehend the crime scene he was standing in the middle of. An elderly woman sealed in a garbage can, a bag over her face and books about Satanic worship and witchcraft near the body.

"How bizarre is that?" Vaccaro said.

Most homicide detectives will tell you they have a sixth sense about them, a feeling in the gut, so to speak, in assessing a crime scene. When the books were found, the instinct hit Vaccaro like a sledgehammer. He just knew there was a strong likelihood the perpetrator was a woman. "There's a female inside the can; there's all these women's shoes," Vaccaro said. "The whole thing had a female gender feel to it."

No one said a word about how strange this crime was. There was no need to—it was better left unsaid, because no one needed the distraction.

The men continued their search.

In one box, Manning and Mesinar found Social Security documents in the name of Christine M. Smith, date of birth February 15, 1932. She was a senior citizen, just like the woman in the garbage can appeared to be.

This may be our victim.

In a bag, Mesinar found a lady's wallet and a picture ID. It was a Citizens Area Transit bus pass for an elderly woman, Christine Smith. The picture on the bus pass showed a fragile, elderly woman. She was thin; her dark hair appeared to be long and bundled in back, just like the hair of the woman in the garbage can. She wore a wool knit cap on her head, and she was smiling. She looked happy.

3

Just one last chance before you go
You hold the secrets and I must know
Just one last chance to right the wrong
Before the clues are buried and gone

—"Speak for You," by Clark County deputy
medical examiner Gary Telgenhoff, aka Skinnerrat

In the early morning hours of February 6, 2001, a team of Las Vegas police and crime scene analysts gathered at the Clark County coroner's office on Shadow Lane in downtown Las Vegas. They were about to witness one of the most macabre autopsies in Southern Nevada history.

The victim in question was the nameless female found sealed in the garbage can at Canyon Gate Mini Storage. A toe tag was tied to the flex cuffs securing the tarp around the garbage can, and it read JANE "MINI STORAGE" DOE, a temporary label used to identify the woman until dental records and fingerprints could be secured.

Detective Mesinar arrived first. CSI Dahn arrived soon after, and she was joined by veteran Las Vegas police crime scene investigator Sheree Norman and coroner's office technician Damon O'Brien.

The job of determining the manner and cause of death for Jane "Mini Storage" Doe on this day would fall to veteran Clark County deputy medical examiner Dr. Gary Telgenhoff. He is stocky, mildly rotund, forty-six years old, with long gray hair and blue eyes that suggest he gets plenty of sleepless nights. He readily admits he is a man interested in death.

"I'm a dark person," Telgenhoff said. "A heavy thinker, and death fascinates me. It does everyone to a degree, but I think I was a little excessive with it."

By day, Telgenhoff makes a living dissecting dead bodies to determine the cause of their demise. He makes it clear he is not in law enforcement, but instead medicine.

"My job is not to convict anyone," Telgenhoff said. "It is not to set them free or anything else. I just want to make the best assessment I can. You learn right away, keep your mouth shut, observe, be methodical. I want all the information. I want to synthesize it and boil it out."

By night, Telgenhoff rocks. He has converted his garage into a soundproof music room. It is completely black inside, with a silver drum set in one corner and a keyboard with thousands of dollars of computerized recording equipment in the other. He retreats to his music room every night, writing dark, foreboding songs about murder and death.

"I compose on my keyboards, I record them on a computer, I lay down drum tracks, I play the bass and I sing," Telgenhoff said.

He calls his one-man band Skinnerrat, and it is music not for the faint of heart. It is heavy Alice Cooper–style rock-guitar riffs, drums, haunting synthesizers and grisly lyrics. In the background of one of Skinnerrat's songs is the sound of the whiz of a bone saw, which Telgenhoff uses at work to slice open human skulls like coconuts. It is as if all the ugliness he sees at work exits from his body and into his keyboard or drums. There, the ugliness is recast and reemerges via Skinnerrat.

I'll speak for you when your lips are cold and blue
Dead men do tell tales, and I'll speak for you
I know your soul is seeking some kind of rest
But you'll be unaware of my inquest
Our exchange will be somewhat extreme
But you won't feel my crude, cold sharpened steel

"The song is called 'Speak for You' because it's what I do," Telgenhoff said. "I speak for the dead."

Telgenhoff's song "Speak for You" was recently played on an episode of the national hit television show *CSI*. Telgenhoff has even served as an unpaid consultant for the show's producer.

"I like dark, and the lyrics are important to me," Telgenhoff said. "This is my real love."

The road to becoming a medical examiner was a long and difficult haul for Telgenhoff. As a boy raised in a strict Baptist home in Michigan, he was always interested in trying to figure out how things work. By the age of eight, he was taking apart toys or old appliances he found sitting around the home to see what made them tick.

"I like to tear things apart to see how they work, but I don't really care to put them back together," Telgenhoff said.

Telgenhoff snuck Beatles albums into his home during his teen years without his father knowing. His first love was music, and he pounded the drums throughout high school. He dreamed of rock superstardom and, after high school, played with famed guitarist Dick Wagner and his band Frost.

"One band led to another, and another, and another, and eventually I ended up in a traveling type of band, a small trio that ended up playing canned cover tunes," Telgenhoff said. "We ended up playing Holiday Inns and hotels and motel chains. It was a good living for me. I didn't have any bills, all the hotels were free and it was a nice, free lifestyle. All the money we made was just cigarette and beer money. I loved my life, but eventually I realized I'm going to get old, and I'm probably not going to be able to do this when I'm fifty. This was not going to work anymore, and I didn't want to end up a vagabond or street urchin."

Telgenhoff decided to pursue a career in medicine. He completed four years of undergraduate school, three years of graduate school, four years of medical school, a one-year internship and four more years in a pathology residency.

The worst time in those sixteen years, Telgenhoff said, was interning in a hospital during medical school.

"I hated my miserable life," Telgenhoff said. "You go in at five a.m. and leave at nine p.m. and the whole day is scorn, ridicule, abuse. Mental abuse and intimidation. It's like going to boot camp and having a sergeant in your face, but it continues for four or five years."

It was too late to quit, though, Telgenhoff said.

"Once you are there, you are so far in debt that there is no turning back," he said. "By the time I was done with everything, I had $100,000 in debt."

Telgenhoff ended up studying at the Cuyahoga County coroner's office in Cleveland, Ohio, where he started to entertain pathology as a possible career field.

"I didn't think some of the smells and stuff were tolerable," Telgenhoff said. "But then I got over that, and I thought, 'Hmm, I could probably do this.' I might have found something that is away from the hospitals, where they run around like Energizer bunnies on meth. Here, I can go home at four p.m., and it's still medicine."

He said the most important part of the job of medical examiner is pathology, because most of what Telgenhoff sees on the steel gurney at the coroner's office is natural death and disease.

"Any idiot can count bullet holes," Telgenhoff said. "It

is a special study to identify entries and exits. That's complicated, but most people can even figure that out with a little training. Where the doctor part comes in is diagnosing disease under the microscope. It is seeing a thousand livers and noticing that this one just isn't right," he said.

Telgenhoff landed his first job at the Clark County coroner's office in 1997. He performs about five hundred autopsies a year, and it is work that leaves him with a few dark stories to tell. One is of a woman who lost it mentally and locked herself in her Las Vegas home during the city's scorching-hot summer months. She took towels and stuffed them in the window cracks, and she barricaded the windows and doors like a horror-flick actress trying to fend off the bogeyman. She turned the heater and oven on full and lay down on the kitchen floor next to the open oven. The cops found her body a few days later.

"She was cooked like a Christmas ham," Telgenhoff said. "She had been there for two weeks like that. I went to move an arm, and it tore off like a drumstick. On the floor, there were drippings, just like in a broiler pan."

In another case, cops called Telgenhoff to the scene of a suicide on U.S. Highway 95 in northwest Las Vegas. A man took a steel cable and put it around his neck with a slipknot, then tied the other end to a freeway overpass and jumped.

"Pulled his head right off," Telgenhoff said. "The cops said, 'You've got to come out here and look at this.'"

Telgenhoff drove to the scene and saw a group of cops standing around in a circle.

"It looked like a coven or something, so I went over there and I couldn't believe what I saw," Telgenhoff said. "The guy's head was looking back at his ass."

Telgenhoff's dark sense of humor keeps him sane in an environment of horror and tragedy. Like Mesinar and the CSIs, he sees up close the murder, mayhem and grief of Las Vegas.

"I don't see any rhyme or reason to the daily tragedy I see except for stupidity," he said.

The garbage can containing the body of Jane "Mini Storage" Doe was rolled into the well of the coroner's office on a flat steel gurney at eight thirty a.m. Telgenhoff and Mesinar knew by the sight that this wasn't going to be a routine day at the office.

"The garbage can came in, the whole damned thing," Telgenhoff said. "I'm used to the odors, but this one was a little different. A little more intense. The average person wouldn't be hanging out. They'd be looking for the door, maybe on their hands and knees."

Dave Mesinar stood in the well of the coroner's office and ran the facts of the case through his head. A woman dead in a can. The identification next to the body was of Christine M. Smith. Her daughter, Brookey Lee West, was the renter of the storage shed.

We need an identification of the victim.

The can was in almost the exact same condition as it was when it was found. It was square and buckled at the bottom. It was covered with the green plastic wrap, duct tape and garbage bags.

Telgenhoff decided not to open the lid until after the fluid from inside the can was drained.

"Shit, how we are going to approach this?" Telgenhoff asked. "It's not something you get everyday, so you start thinking, 'What would be the best way to do this?'"

The challenge, Telgenhoff said, was to get the body out of the can without losing any potential evidence in the fluid. Coroner's office medical technician Damon O'Brien came up with a novel solution. Telgenhoff would use a drill to punch a hole in the bottom of the can, and then O'Brien would hold a strainer at the bottom and let the liquid strain through it into a sink. This way, if there was a bullet fragment or knife tip in the liquid, O'Brien would catch it before it entered the sink.

"Dr. Telgenhoff had a spaghetti strainer, but we knew that wasn't going to be big enough, so Sheree traveled back to the lab," Dahn said. "We do have a large sifter we use out at crime scenes in the desert, and she went and got that and came back with it."

O'Brien, Telgenhoff and the CSIs perched the can on the ledge of a deep, stainless steel sink and Telgenhoff used the drill to punch a four-inch hole in the bottom of the can. The can was stinking, and Jane "Mini Storage" Doe's body was sloshing about inside.

"I cut the hole in the can, and all of this spooge comes out," Telgenhoff said. "There is no way to describe it. Very thick fat mixed with fluids you've never seen."

The can kept tipping back and forth from one side to another, and Telgenhoff worried the can might fall over and spill its contents out onto the floor. Two medical students were in the building, so Telgenhoff asked one of them to help hold the can at the top so it wouldn't tip over.

"This one medical student was actually stabilizing the can from one side, and as we are working on it, his eyes are huge," Dahn said. "It was really smelly, and he is getting exposed to all this."

O'Brien was at the bottom of the sink with the strainer, sifting the soupy brown contents for any potential evidence.

"He got the good job," Telgenhoff said. "He will always remember that day. He still talks about it, because he had to shower twice and throw away his clothes."

After the initial rush of liquid and fat emanated from the bottom of the can, the flow of fluids slowed to barely a drip.

"It didn't really work because the body was blocking the hole," Mesinar said.

Telgenhoff gave the go-ahead for the group to crack the

lid and lift it up, then slowly pour the contents onto the
gurney in a slow, methodical fashion. Slowly, they gained
leverage on the can and angled it at forty-five degrees,
causing the plastic container to cast out the victim like a
cannonball. Jane "Mini Storage" Doe plopped down on the
gurney, and Telgenhoff witnessed something he had never
seen before. Jane "Mini Storage" Doe was almost completely skeletonized, and her corpse was morphed into a
large, round, gooey, smelly, Jell-O–like, half-oval ball.

"It looked like a white, waxy, smelly, cheese ball," Telgenhoff said. "You had to be there."

Telgenhoff's blood was flowing. This was something new.

"Sweet screaming Jesus!" he recalled thinking. "Wow,
this one is a top five. I've got to write this one down in the
journal."

Mesinar was shocked at the sight of a woman shaped
into a gelatinized ball of human decomposition. Some
bugs were on the outer layer of the body, too.

"They removed the body, and it came out in the shape of
the can," he said. "I remember thinking to myself, 'This is
amazing.'"

Dahn was snapping photos to document the bizarre
sight.

"It was kind of like a rubberized, solidified block,"
Dahn said. "Actually, when it came out of the can, it didn't
bounce, but it was like a blob and it just laid out. It was a
cubicle square of a person."

The woman had long gray hair, and she was clearly old.
Her hair was more than eighteen inches long, and it was
tied in the back with a pink scrunchie. She was curled up in
the fetal position with her hair draping backward into the
block. Her hands were gnarled, and her eyes and mouth
were wide open in an expression of horror.

Who could do something like this?

"The head was on its way to complete skeletization,"

Telgenhoff said. "Kind of like something you'd see in *Tales from the Crypt*."

There was one detail about the woman's body that immediately caught the medical examiner's eye. A common household trash bag covered the victim's face, and the bag was tied in a knot at the back of her head.

"It was white, and it was tied over the nose and mouth area," Telgenhoff said. "It wasn't real tight, but some of the hair in back was caught up in the knot."

Telgenhoff believed the bag may have been tied tighter when the body was originally placed in the can, but decomposition may have caused it to loosen slightly. Any doubt in Mesinar's mind that this was anything other than murder evaporated at the sight of the bag.

"The bag would cut off her air, especially with the assistance of a pillow or strangulation," Mesinar said.

It wouldn't have taken too much to kill a frail woman like this.

"When I saw the plastic bag, I said, 'I can't believe it,' " Dahn said. "I said, 'It's a homicide.' "

Telgenhoff and O'Brien worked the corpse by bending the arms and legs at an angle to flatten it out on the gurney. They had to repeatedly break the stiffness of the woman to get her supine on the gurney.

"We stretched it out, and it took more than one person," Telgenhoff said. "It tried to spring back."

Telgenhoff told his colleagues to collect samples of the insects.

"I suggested we collect all the maggots," Telgenhoff said. "Insects are very important. Only a couple of times in your career will they make a difference, but when they do, it is monumental."

Another fact that stood out to Telgenhoff from the gurney was a white, gooey substance adhering to much of the corpse. The material was adipocere—the first time Telgenhoff observed it during an autopsy. The gooey substance is the body's fat after it breaks down and is traditionally only found in bodies stored in moist environments.

"Usually, it's in cold waters, deep waters when the body has been there for a long time," Telgenhoff said. "They pull up a lot of bodies with adipocere in the Chesapeake Bay. I assumed I would never see it in the desert. One place where it also happens a lot is in the mausoleums," Telgenhoff said. "There have been people who go into a mausoleum and they've been in one hundred years and they pull them out. Their facial features, everything, is preserved in wax—a cheesy wax. It retains the shape of whatever it was."

A darkened, humid corner of a storage shed would provide the perfect moist climate for the phenomenon.

"It tells me the body has been there for quite some time," Telgenhoff said. "Most of the textbooks say it requires a good six months to form a layer of adipocere, but it is variable. This was the first time I had ever seen that," he said. "It took me a moment, looking, saying, 'What is that odd stuff?' This is different—a white, waxy, musty, earthy smell. 'Oh, yeah, this is what I read in the books.' It is exciting when your training clicks in."

The woman had on a pair of underwear, a bra, a thermal undershirt and a light-colored long-sleeved sweatshirt.

"When I saw the bikini underwear, I've got to admit, right away I thought that was strange," Dahn said, unable to envision an elderly woman wearing bikini underwear. "But maybe it's an elderly woman wearing bikini underwear all her life, and she just never switched," Dahn said. "To me, though, I found it odd that it wasn't high-topped underwear. Generally, they [older women] get a pooch on their belly, and they just—I don't know—go to the higher-topped underwear. As a woman, it is something I would think about."

Dahn said the victim was wearing was the type of clothing one would wear to bed.

"The first thing I thought was she was sleeping when she was killed," the CSI said. "They looked like sleep clothes. She had a long-underwear top on and a sweatshirt, then underwear. No pants or shoes."

Dahn photographed every inch of the body, the clothing and the bag. She and Norman also took DNA samples.

Upon closer inspection of the corpse, Telgenhoff concluded that determining a cause and manner of death was going to be a challenge. All of the internal organs were liquefied, including the brain. Telgenhoff had no gunshot or stab wounds to identify. Because of the decomposition of the throat, eyes and lungs, he could not tell if the woman was suffocated or drowned. The bag tied over the victim's face led him to believe the woman was suffocated, and he told Mesinar of his suspicions.

Telgenhoff was not ready, however, to issue a ruling on cause and manner of death. He needed to see the results of toxicology tests—if they were even possible—and he figured it was going to take several weeks to determine if there was evidence to prove murder.

"I couldn't be sure yet if this was just a bizarre way of disposing of somebody who had died naturally, or if a person was killed and then put in the can," Telgenhoff said.

But even though Telgenhoff stopped short of saying the case was definitely murder, the autopsy provided one instantaneous benefit to Mesinar. The lower mandible of the woman's jaw was still present, and when those teeth were compared with dental records of the woman whose identification was found next to the body, the coroner's office got a match.

The teeth from the woman in the can and the dental records from Christine Merle Smith, age sixty-five were iden-

tical. Mesinar's hunch at the storage shed was right—the
items of identification found next to the body belonged to
his victim, Christine Smith. The home address listed on her
bus pass and Social Security documents found at Canyon
Gate was the Orange Door apartments, 2829 West Sahara
Avenue, apartment #1.

Mesinar now had some solid leads to work on. He had
an official victim identification, he had her home address
and he knew from the Canyon Gate records that the victim
was the daughter of the shed's renter—Brookey Lee West.

"Based on Telgenhoff telling me he believed it was a
homicide, I made a decision it's definitely time to start
looking for Ms. West," Mesinar said. "Our whole focus
was going to be trying to find her, This was definitely
someone we wanted to talk to."

After the autopsy was over, Mesinar walked to his vehicle in the parking lot of the coroner's office. Even though
he didn't have a cause of death, in his heart he knew he was
on the hunt for a killer, whether it was West or someone
else. He also wondered who could take an elderly woman
like Christine Smith, put a bag over her face and store her
in a garbage can for what appeared to be an extended period of time. In Mesinar's mind, the age of the victim made
the killing particularly heinous.

*No one deserves this. She was probably a sweet little
old lady.*

4

A decomposing corpse in a garbage can is the perfect story for television news. It is bizarre, gruesome and shocking— a guaranteed ratings-booster that seizes on the morbid curiosity found in every one of us. The idea of someone melting away in a garbage can is unfathomable, an image of brutality beyond the everyday human experience, and when we see such horrors on the six p.m. news, we predictably react with disgust, condemnation and outrage. But deep down inside, we want more. We crave for the latest update like a crackhead searching for the next hit off that glass pipe.

A television news producer couldn't ask for more.

On the night Christine Smith's body was found, homicide sergeant Kevin Manning typed up a press release confirming the gory details of the discovery. He faxed it out to the three main Las Vegas television news stations, but he withheld the fact that books about Satanism and witchcraft were next to the body. Even without this salacious detail, the Vegas television media gobbled up the story like wolves sinking their teeth into an animal carcass. It was a damn good news story, and everyone knew it. Each Vegas news station ran sensational blurbs about Jane Doe in the garbage can on their morning, lunch and evening broadcasts, and in death Christine Smith was big news in Sin City.

Detective Mesinar usually pays little attention to the media coverage while carrying out a homicide investigation. He said the wave of stories rarely hurts an investigation, and in only a few cases does it help—namely, when a victim is unidentified or when a crazed killer is on the loose and the cops need the public's help tracking them down.

"I really don't think about the media a lot, because I don't have to deal with them," Mesinar said. "Either our lieutenant or sergeant deals with the press, and that allows us to focus on the job at hand. But in the same breath, I knew this case would be of interest because of the oddity."

In the case of Christine Smith, the media coverage was a mild concern for Mesinar during the first forty-eight hours of the investigation. The stories about the corpse in the can were flooding the television screens in the Las Vegas Valley, and the police hadn't found the renter of the shed yet. West was, at a minimum, a potential suspect in the eyes of police because, as the renter of the shed and the daughter of the victim, she had to have relevant information about her mother's death.

Mesinar was concerned West might see the news and flee before the cops could find her.

"I figured there is a good chance she was going to watch the news and see what was happening," Mesinar said. "She was either going to run or she was going to call us, and she never called us, so we started looking for her."

Mesinar said it was important to find West even if it turned out she wasn't the killer. If she was, by chance, simply a daughter whose dead mother was hidden in her storage shed without her knowledge, Mesinar wanted to tell

West about her mother's horrifying fate before she saw it on television.

"I knew it was important to try to find her," Mesinar said. "I know what happened to her mother, and in case she didn't know her mother was dead, I could give her the death notification."

Mesinar drove from the coroner's office to the Las Vegas police Homicide Section office on West Charleston Boulevard to begin the search for West. The Homicide Section is a nondescript, single-story office building offering no indication from the outside that it is home to some three dozen of the most veteran detectives in Las Vegas. The detectives work themselves to the point of exhaustion week after week in the never-ending pursuit of killers. Each detective is given a computer, a small work desk, a filing cabinet and a spot in the office not much bigger than your average walk-in shower. There aren't even any partitions to separate the detectives.

A detective who accepts the assignment to Homicide knows the investigation comes first and, on many occasions, his family comes second. The murder calls come in at all hours, and if a dead body is found sixty miles away in the desert outside Las Vegas at three a.m., the detective assigned to the case is expected to be at the crime scene as soon as possible. On some especially busy weeks at the Homicide Section, the sleep-deprived detectives look like walking zombies. If the trail for the killer is hot or the crime scene is especially complex, they may not see their wife and kids for days, but Homicide is still the most prized assignment in the Las Vegas Police Department because the detectives have, over the years, played a repeated role in history.

Perhaps the most well-known murder case involving Las Vegas police was the infamous 1959 murders of the

Clutter family in Holcomb, Kansas. The shootings of wealthy wheat farmer Herbert Clutter, his wife and two children inspired Truman Capote's classic true-crime book *In Cold Blood*. Kansas police successfully cracked the case with evidence linking career criminals Perry Smith and Dick Hickock to the shotgun slayings, but it was Vegas cops who helped collar the killers. The two thugs ended up swinging from the Kansas gallows for the heinous murders.

The cycle of high-profile homicides in Vegas is nonstop. In 1996, gangster-rapper Tupac Shakur was gunned down on the Strip in a case that remains unsolved to this day. In 1997, Las Vegas Homicide made news by solving the murder of seven-year-old Sherrice Iverson, an innocent little girl who was lured into a casino restroom, sexually assaulted and strangled to death by well-to-do Southern California teen Jeremy Strohmeyer. Strohmeyer is serving life in prison. And in 2002, Las Vegas Homicide carried out a massive investigation into a deadly riot between the Hells Angels and Mongols motorcycle gangs at a motorcycle run in Laughlin, Nevada. The two outlaw biker gangs clashed in a bloodbath inside the Harrah's Laughlin casino on the Colorado River. They shot, stabbed and bludgeoned one another in a chaotic melee captured on casino surveillance video, and when it was over two Hells Angels and a Mongol were dead. A two-year investigation by Vegas cops resulted in a 2004 indictment charging seven Hells Angels and five Mongols with murder.

Mesinar knew he had another high-profile case on his hands with Christine's death. It is not everyday you find an old lady melted in a garbage can. By midmorning on February 7, Mesinar arrived at the Homicide Section office and consulted briefly with his lieutenant, Wayne Petersen, and Sergeant Manning, about the results of the autopsy. He then started his search for West with a call to the Nevada Department of Motor Vehicles, and he learned West did have a driver's license in Nevada. A picture of West from the license showed an attractive, brown-haired, professional-looking forty-seven-year-old. The license, like the rental sheet at Canyon Gate, listed a post office box on Industrial Road as a home address for West. West was continually listing a post office box for a home address, and it left detectives wondering if she was trying to keep the location of her residence a secret.

Mesinar and Vaccaro drove to the address on Industrial and found it to be a traditional private mailbox business.

"The owner knew who Brooke West was, and she said West was living both here and in California, commuting back and forth between Las Vegas and San Jose," Mesinar said. "She said West was recently in to pick up her mail, and there was mail waiting for her. The employees of the business agreed to let us know when she came in again.

"We did have her driver's license picture, so we knew what she looked like," Mesinar said. "We decided to set up surveillance on the post office box, hoping she would come back, but she never showed up."

The next step was serving a subpoena in the name of Brookey Lee West with Nevada Power, which is the power company serving all of Southern Nevada. This time, Mesinar got a hit.

"I was able to locate power service in the name of Brookey West to an apartment complex located at 8000 West Spring Mountain Road in Las Vegas," Mesinar said.

"That was a big shot in the arm for us," Vaccaro said. "We've confirmed she's got a place here, and it gives us a chance to start looking into who this Brookey West really is."

The $1,200-a-month apartment West resided in was at the upscale San Croix condominiums in northwest Las Vegas. San Croix sits just a little more than two miles from the Canyon Gate Mini Storage where Christine's body was found, and most residents at San Croix can look out their window or back patio and immediately see the beautiful Sierra Nevadas to their west. To the east is the Las Vegas Strip and its magnificent lights, which radiate out of the sand like supernova emerging from the desert floor.

It appeared to the detectives Brookey West was living a comfortable life at San Croix with access to an elegant pool, fitness center and spa.

"The management said she still lived there, so we knew we had something to work with," Mesinar said. "We went ahead and got a search warrant for the apartment."

With the search warrant in hand, the detectives got a key for the apartment from San Croix management and entered apartment #2122. Vaccaro quickly noticed how nice the place was. Much of a homicide detective's work involves trolling through the gutters of humanity, and this was no gutter.

It appeared West was well-off financially.

"I was impressed with the apartment," Vaccaro said. "I thought it was a neat, well-kept place with nice stuff. It seemed like there was a little bit of money involved here."

There was a black couch and black love seat with a footrest in the living room. Long golden drapes lined the windows, and there was a television set, a boom box and a brand-new laptop computer in the central quarter of the apartment as well. The master bedroom was lived in, but the second bedroom was empty of furniture.

"The whole apartment had sort of a one-person-living-alone feel to it," Vaccaro said.

There was an easel with a half-finished pencil sketch on it in one corner of the apartment, leading Vaccaro to conclude West was a sophisticated woman and talented artist.

"This person was involved with doing sketches and art with pastels," Vaccaro said. "There were several works of art on the floor."

Mesinar sensed West was recently in the residence.

"There was food in the refrigerator, food in the cupboards," Mesinar said.

The two detectives proceeded to pore over the contents of the apartment like hunting dogs sniffing the trail of a wounded animal. In the spare bedroom, Mesinar found a garbage bag containing a crucial clue—bank statements from Nevada State Bank in the name of Christine Smith. The bank statements showed West's mother was receiving monthly Social Security deposits from the U.S. Department of Treasury, and the deposits were made within the last month.

How could this be? This woman has been dead for years.

More important, the records showed withdrawals were being made from Christine's account within the last few weeks.

Someone is stealing her money.

Some of the withdrawals from Christine's account were made at ATMs, and there were also point-of-sale purchases, known as debit card purchases, made within the last couple of weeks. Each of the purchases was made between Las Vegas and San Jose, California, each communities West had ties to. West resided in Las Vegas, and San Jose was in Santa Clara County, where a prior address for West had popped up when the cops at the storage shed ran her name through the police computer database.

The information in Christine's bank records immediately raised red flags in Mesinar's mind. Telgenhoff had been clear in his opinion that Christine Smith had been dead in that garbage can for at least six months, if not years, and the bank statements showed someone was spending Christine's Social Security money while she was rotting in the storage shed.

This lady is dead. She shouldn't be getting Social Security. All this stuff is in her daughter's apartment, and the money's being used.

"It really fueled our suspicions," Mesinar said. "Why is she getting Social Security when she is dead?"

West was now the number one suspect in her mother's murder.

This woman may have killed her mother for the Social Security money.

Mesinar and Vaccaro continued their search in West's kitchen, and while rummaging through the kitchen drawers Mesinar found a key and a roll of duct tape. The duct tape looked identical to the duct tape used to seal the garbage can containing Christine's corpse, and the key looked as if it would fit a lock that Unruh had pried off the door of the storage shed at Canyon Gate. Mesinar decided he would give the duct tape to the CSIs later to see if it matched the duct tape on the garbage can, but the detectives would not have to wait to see if the key could further link West to the shed.

"We still had the lock from the storage shed, so we put the key in the lock, and it worked," Mesinar said.

All of the facts were pointing to West as the killer of her mother. She was the renter of the shed, her mother's bank records were in her apartment and the records showed Christine was getting Social Security money long after her death. Someone was spending Christine's money in San Jose and Las Vegas, both communities where West listed an address. In the drawer in West's apartment was duct tape similar to duct tape at the crime scene, and the key in the drawer fit the lock to the storage shed.

"At this point, we're thinking Brooke is the suspect," Vaccaro said. "This lady has obviously got some explaining to do. I remember thinking, 'If this is the woman who did this, how bad is it to put your mom in a garbage can, store her away in a storage shed and not treat her remains with some decency and respect?' " Vaccaro said. "This is the person who brought you into the world? What do we owe our parents—storage in a storage shed?"

After concluding their search of West's apartment, the detectives started knocking on the doors of West's neighbors, and in minutes they came across a friendly, polite woman named Carole H. Wolf in a downstairs apartment at San Croix. Wolf said she'd known West for about a month, and she agreed to give detectives a taped statement.

"She was walking out front of my apartment, uh, hunched over with a bag, as if she was having problems . . . and I went out to help her," Wolf told the detectives. "And she brought me up the stairs to her apartment, and she invited me in for a cup of tea."

Wolf told the detectives West drove a small black pickup truck with gold trim and that West was probably still in the area. She knew West had an adult daughter who did not live in Las Vegas.

"She did say the other day she had four or five husbands," Wolf said.

Wolf told police West commuted back and forth to a second residence in the San Jose area of Silicon Valley, and West worked in the San Jose area as a technical writer before losing her job the week prior.

"A technical writer, writing books for computers, is what she explained to me," Wolf said.

Vaccaro's suspicion that West was a woman of financial means was correct. Technical writers prior to the dot-com bust in the Silicon Valley made good money, and it was clear their suspect was well-off compared to most of the dirtbags Vegas detectives deal with on a daily basis.

Wolf said she and West went to lunch together recently, and the two also went to a local oxygen bar called Breathe on Sahara Avenue at Decatur Boulevard in Las Vegas. Instead of bellying up to the bar to drink alcohol, Breathe patrons, known as clients, place a tube hooked to an oxygen tank over their noses and inhale oxygen in a Zenlike social setting symbolic of the West Coast's health-conscious populace.

On one of their trips to the Breathe oxygen bar, Wolf said West started reading peoples' psychic futures.

"She did a spiritual psychic reading for a client, and the owner at that time pulled her aside and said she was gonna give her free oxygen in lieu of her coming down to read for clients of Breathe," Wolf said. "God help us."

"So she does psychic readings?" Mesinar asked.

"Yes, she does," Wolf said. "And she does them correctly."

Wolf told the cops West used marbles to perform the psychic readings. She took the marbles and rolled them back and forth in her hands as if rubbing dice at the craps table for good luck. West said the caressing of the marbles magically transferred the psychic vibes from the universe into her body, mind and spirit.

"She reads what comes off the marbles," Wolf said. "However, she can also read anything you ask about her. She never did a reading for me here," Wolf said. "It's funny, because I never asked her to when she was in my house. But the first time we went into Breathe, she reads marbles—she carries marbles in her pocketbook, and she reads them."

"Does she charge for this service?" Mesinar asked.

"No," Wolf said. "She says . . . she does it for free as her gift."

Wolf said West talked to her about having some spiritual books in storage on Sahara Avenue, and West was apparently not shy about promoting her psychic talents—she was proud of it.

"She said she's seeing a doctor who was studying her because of her psychic abilities," Wolf said. "In fact, she even said, 'Oh, my doctor should come down and watch me when I give readings at Breathe. He'd be really impressed.' "

The detectives asked if West ever talked about her mother, and Wolf told police West repeatedly spoke negatively about her mother.

"Uh, [she] just said that she was a bad influence on her and she couldn't, [she] chose not to be around her," Wolf told the detectives.

"Did you get the impression that her mother was alive?" Mesinar asked.

"I didn't get the impression she was not alive, but I don't remember," Wolf said.

Wolf then remembered a specific conversation in which West had, in fact, indicated her mother was alive.

" 'When my mother calls, I'm just very aloof,' " Wolf quoted West as saying.

The idea of West claiming her mother was alive in a recent conversation with Wolf intrigued detectives because medical examiner Gary Telgenhoff had indicated Christine must have been in the can for several months, if not years. It was clear West was deceiving people about the well-being of her mother, and such a deception would be completely unnecessary if West wasn't involved in the killing. But Wolf had more. She said West told her a multitude of problems in her life were because of her mother. West said she suffered a nervous breakdown because of her mother, and that being around her mother caused her to be physically ill.

"The reason for her breakdown and the reason for her not being well was her mother," Wolf said. "All her friends told her this, and she now has gotten away from her mother. She doesn't see her mother, [and] she doesn't allow her mother in her life in any way."

West's dislike for her mother sounded to the veteran de-

tectives like a motive for murder. West's venomous criti-
cisms of her mother went beyond the tensions normally
found in a mother-daughter relationship. This sounded like
blood-boiling hatred.

"She just said, 'I don't let her into my life,'" Wolf told
police, quoting West. "[She] said, 'She's been a very dark
force, a very negative force in my life, and I no longer allow that in my life.'"

The case was quickly coming together like a jigsaw
puzzle. Mesinar had a dead elderly woman in a can in a
storage shed rented by the victim's daughter. The body was
surrounded by books about witchcraft, and West just happened to be a proclaimed psychic. West's apartment contained duct tape similar to duct tape found at the crime
scene, and a key in her drawer fit a lock to the shed. West
was telling at least one woman her mother was alive when
she was dead, and to top it off she was bad-mouthing her
mother as a "very dark force."

This is the strangest case I've ever had.

5

Joe Matvay may be the best crime scene analyst in the state of Nevada. He has, over the last quarter century, helped solve hundreds of criminal cases for Las Vegas police, putting dozens of killers in the Nevada state penitentiary. He is a tall, soft-spoken man, and one of his greatest skills as a CSA is an uncanny ability to lift fingerprints from evidence. In one criminal case, Matvay lifted a perpetrator's fingerprint off a brick. In another case, he retrieved a fingerprint from a tree branch, and he has even plucked a perpetrator's print off a piece of smooth leather at a crime scene.

"With today's technology, we can pretty much get fingerprints from anything except shag carpet and water," Matvay said.

The science of processing crime scenes for fingerprints has come a long way over the last century. The first person widely credited with recognizing the value of fingerprints to the criminal justice system was an Englishman named Sir Edward Henry, who in the 1890s oversaw the Bengali police in the East Indies. Henry was an acquaintance of a scientist named Francis Galton, and Galton had successfully documented how each human being has unique, identifiable patterns on the tips of his or her fingers. Henry was convinced fingerprints could offer a new way for Bengali officers to keep track of the people they took into custody, so he ordered his officers to start keeping records of prints gathered from suspects.

Henry then took the technology a step further by developing his own system of identifying and classifying fingerprints, and in 1901 he was named an administrator to Scotland Yard, where he ordered his investigators to begin collecting fingerprints, too. The program was an overwhelming success, and word of the new crime-solving technique quickly spread to police departments across the Atlantic.

In 1911, an American man named Thomas Jennings was arrested in Chicago for the fatal shooting of a homeowner during a residential burglary. Police found Jennings' fingerprints on a stairway railing in the victim's home, making Jennings the first person in the United States to be convicted of murder because of fingerprints left at a crime scene. Jennings appealed the conviction to the Illinois Supreme Court, and the court ruled fingerprints were credible evidence in a court of law in a ruling that cleared the way for fingerprint evidence to become a staple of the American criminal justice system.

For Matvay, fingerprint processing is part art, part science. The key, he said, is knowing what method will best highlight the presence of a print otherwise invisible to the naked eye. Some prints are best exposed when sprayed with chemicals. Others are revealed with powders, and some surface when exposed to alternate light sources. The temperature of the environment at a crime scene, the type of surface the print is on and the age of the print are variables the CSA needs to consider as well when determining what method to employ on a particular print.

"There are a lot of different techniques we can use," Matvay said. "It depends on the texture of the item, and it depends on how old we think the print may be, as to what techniques we'll use. So literally, we could use twenty or thirty different techniques on one item. It's called sequential processing, and with the advent of technology, there is more and more we can do everyday."

Matvay's intricate knowledge of the different methods of fingerprint processing has repeatedly produced results for Vegas homicide investigators. In 2002, Matvay's skills were crucial in solving the murder of a Cuban drug dealer named Enrique Caminero Jr., who was brutally strangled and shot in a drug robbery at the Capri Motel on Fremont Street in downtown Las Vegas. Caminero's killers carried out an extensive cleanup of the room after the slaying, but Matvay's persistence turned up a hidden bloody palm print on a bathroom countertop, and the print led to the arrest of three suspects. One, Sally Villaverde, was convicted of the crime and is now serving a life sentence. Two other suspects are awaiting trial.

The case Matvay is most proud of solving unfolded in 1986. Sylvia Pena, the operator of Richard's Produce, a small produce and nut shop in northeast Las Vegas, was butchered with a bread knife in her business during a robbery. It was a senseless, horrific crime.

"She wasn't well known, wasn't popular," Matvay said. "Just a hardworking woman. What the perpetrator did was take a bread knife, and he just slashed her face and her neck and chest. She was cut up badly—cut to shreds."

The brutality of the crime left Matvay with an extremely bloody crime scene. It took him hours to process the store for evidence, but while dusting the inside of a cabinet door in the rear of the business, Matvay found a single bloody fingerprint. He removed the cabinet door from its hinges, took it back to the police crime lab, photographed the print and preserved it. It was promising evidence that held the potential to identify the killer, but the print matched none of the hundreds of thousands of prints stored in Las Vegas police files.

Pena's murder went unsolved for the next seven years, until, in 1993, a woman in North Carolina went to police and said her boyfriend, Jeffrey Lark, told her he once carried out a robbery in Las Vegas in the mid-1980s.

"She said this guy was involved in some robberies in Las Vegas, specifically a robbery of a fruit and nut stand," Matvay said. "She knew he had done a robbery, but he never told her he committed a murder."

Police in North Carolina phoned Las Vegas authorities about the woman's information, and Las Vegas authorities started probing their old unsolved robberies. The murder of Pena was one of the old cases reviewed by detectives, and fingerprints from Lark were compared to the prints left behind by the killer at the fruit stand seven years earlier.

"I was on vacation at the time, and I was called in to do the fingerprint examination," Matvay said. "Lo and behold, seven years later, it was him."

On February 7, 2001, two days after the discovery of Christine Smith's corpse, Matvay and CSA Robbie Dahn met at the Las Vegas police crime lab on West Charleston Boulevard to process the evidence from the Canyon Gate storage shed for fingerprints. There were four items in particular from the crime scene the CSAs thought might yield fingerprints. The first was the bag tied tightly around Christine's decomposed face, but the bag was covered with human remains, and the thick, crusty material eliminated any chance of prints being retrieved from the bag.

"We are talking thick, caked, fatty tissue covering the bag," Dahn said. "It was like Crisco oil."

The other items from the crime scene, however, were ripe for processing. They were the 21 strips of duct tape used to seal the garbage can containing the body; the 151 feet of long green plastic wrap the killer wrapped around the can to contain the odor; and three green garbage bags placed on top of Christine's makeshift tomb.

"To do the plastic wrap, the plastic bags and the duct tape, it took about three days," Matvay said. "Some people may think that is tedious, and it is a little bit slow. But there are two keys I always say are necessary to be successful in crime scene investigations. Number one is thoroughness, and number two is paying attention to detail.

"You don't have to be a brain surgeon to do this job," Matvay said. "Of course, intelligence is important, but if you are thorough and pay attention to detail, you can be successful."

For the duct tape, Dahn took fingerprint powder known as sticky-side powder, and she mixed it with water and Ivory dish soap to produce a black, pancake-like batter. Dahn brushed the sticky-side powder mix on the adhesive side of the strips of duct tape, and an ultraviolet light was shone on the nonadhesive side of the tape. The processes turned up a single partial palm print, but the palm print was never identified.

Matvay now set his sights on the garbage bags and the plastic wrap, and he knew the best way to process the two was with a device known as a super glue chamber. The device is a three-foot-long glass container resembling a square fish tank. To use the chamber, the CSAs squeeze globs of clear super glue into a small cup inside the chamber. The glue is heated with an open flame until it melts, and vapors from the glue adhere to fingerprints, making them visible on the clear plastic.

"Most fingerprint experts would agree a good way to start with plastic wrap is to go ahead and super glue it," Matvay said.

Matvay is a master with the super glue chamber. He was the first in the state of Nevada to use the chamber to recover a print from plastic in a homicide case, and the print resulted in the arrest of a cold-blooded murderer.

"It was a case where this guy killed his girlfriend, and what he had done is he had gone into their kitchen and pulled off a bunch of plastic wrap, and he covered her face with it," Matvay said. "I made him on prints using super glue on the plastic wrap."

In the case of Christine Smith, Matvay placed the garbage bags from the top of Christine's garbage can in the super glue chamber, melted the glue and waited for a print to appear. None did.

The CSAs finally set their sights on the 151 feet of green plastic wrap. Because the wrap was so long and the super glue chamber so small, the CSAs had to cut the wrap into five-foot-long segments.

"We ended up with about twenty-four sections, and we did two sections at a time," Matvay said.

The first section of plastic wrap was placed in the chamber and produced no prints. On the second section of wrap, Matvay melted the glue, pulled the plastic out of the chamber and held it up to the light.

"After fuming it in the super glue chamber, we removed the plastic wrap, and, lo and behold, there it was—a beautiful print," Matvay said.

"I remember we were handing every sheet back and forth, and Joe was looking over this one piece and he said, 'Oh, my gosh, Robbie. Look at this!'" Dahn said.

The excitement from the discovery was palpable. Dahn and Matvay knew whoever left the left thumbprint on the wrap was either the unluckiest person in the world, or was involved in the disposal of Christine Smith's corpse.

"I was very thankful for finding the print, because a print like that is obviously a big part of the puzzle," Matvay said.

The print was photographed and preserved, and the CSAs proceeded with processing the rest of the plastic wrap. For the next two days, they meticulously fumigated the wrap with super glue fumes and found nothing. Their three days of work produced only one crystal clear print.

When Matvay and Dahn were finished with their work, the CSAs called Mesinar to inform him of the new evidence. The detective was ecstatic over the find, and he started searching to see whether the fingerprints of his prime suspect, Brookey Lee West, were on file. He learned West had a long criminal history in California, and police records showed she was once arrested in the shooting of a spouse in California. Mesinar had no details on that case yet, but he was able to get West's fingerprints from police records.

Matvay then compared the left thumbprint from the plastic wrap to West's prints on file.

They were a perfect match.

LOVED ONES

6

Tornadoes in North Central Texas usually crop up in the spring or summertime. They are the product of some of the most powerful and frightening forces in nature—extremely strong winds, thick black thunderstorm cells and updrafts of air combine to form a rotating mass of terror. The most powerful tornadoes rumble like freight trains, with wind speeds in excess of 250 miles an hour, and they kill at random, destroying communities and leaving behind a zigzagging path of chaos.

In February 1932, North Central Texas experienced the arrival of a rare winter tornado. Her name was Christine Merle Smith, and she was born February 14, 1932, to Clyde and Annie Sands in the city of Ennis. Ennis is located in Ellis County, in Texas's Blackland Prairie, where expansive flatlands serve as fertile ground for corn, soybeans, grain and hay. The origins of the small city date back to 1871, when the Houston and Texas Central Railroad made it a stop on a rail line connecting Houston to the heart of rural Texas. The railroad came through Ennis for one reason and one reason only—to get the cotton grown in Ennis' dark-soiled fields. Ennis produced some of the world's finest cotton crops, and Ennis soon became known as the city where the railroads and cotton fields meet.

One man who called Ennis home was Christine's father, Clyde Sands. He was a tall, slender man who spent years earning a living as a lineman in the depths of the Great Depression. One of Clyde Sands' six children—Christine's brother Billy Sands—said his daddy helped stretch power lines throughout the nation, and it was hard physical labor that required Clyde Sands to spend long stretches of time away from home.

"Work was a little tight," Billy Sands recalled. "So he had to leave home a lot in order to get work. It was a good job and it paid well, but he had to leave home an awful lot."

When Clyde Sands wasn't working as a lineman, he was driving a truck and hauling freight, and he worked for several years as a truck driver for Planters Cotton Oil Mill in Ennis, where he hauled cotton lint and seed to the plant so it could be crushed and refined into valuable products like cottonseed oil.

Clyde's wife, Annie, was a housekeeper and, by all accounts, a loving woman who gave birth to six healthy children. The Sands' first child was a beautiful little girl, Trudy, born in 1911. Their first boy, Woodrow, followed; then came Lawrence, Richard Bob, Billy and, finally, the baby of the family, Christine. She was a blond-haired child who was rambunctious from the start.

"I remember hearing my parents talk about how tight money was," Billy said. "When they done work for somebody, they did it in trade for garden vegetables, livestock, meat, something of that nature, because nobody had any money."

Billy Sands said Christine had a normal childhood growing up in Ennis. He and his sister successfully made it through Alamo Elementary School on the city's west side, and Sands said his parents were never abusive to him or his sister. It seemed like Christine was on the right track in life as a child.

"As far as I know, me and her both had a pretty good life," Billy said. "We had plenty of food, and our mother was home with us. Most of the time, we played in the neighborhood, things like that. . . . We went to movies a lot, normal things. To the best I remember, it was about eleven cents to get in the movie. Christine was happy, and she was mostly a good girl."

But while everything may have been perfect in Christine's early childhood, things started to go downhill in a hurry near the age of ten. Her daughter, Brookey Lee West, said her mother told her she was repeatedly molested by a family member when she was a young girl.

"He had been molesting her since she was eight," West said.

Billy Sands said he never heard about the molestation allegation involving his little sister and a family member. Molestation was something rarely talked about in Texas in the 1930s, but if Christine was molested, it would have been a terrible trauma for such a little girl—a trauma Christine would have carried with her for the rest of her life. Billy Sands said he and Christine both dropped out of the Ennis school system by the eighth grade. Looking back, their decision to drop out was likely a result of childhood rebellion and a lack of emphasis on the importance of schooling from Clyde and Annie Sands.

"There didn't seem to be enough pressure put on the kids to educate themselves," Billy said. "They could have put a little more pressure on us for that."

Christine's decision to drop out of school at the age of thirteen was just the beginning of a series of bad decisions that would end up scarring her for life. Within three years, Christine's wild side took off like a crop duster climbing into the rural Texas skyline.

"I think personally she was restless at home by herself," Billy said. "She was looking for anything that come along so she could grab a hold of it and get out of little old Ennis."

At the age of sixteen, Christine married Tommy Harris,* who was described by Billy Sands as a muscular, dark-haired, Ennis-area thug who was always up to no good. Against her parents' strenuous objections, Christine and Harris ran off to Houston and the big city.

"He was a bad character," Billy said. "I don't know what in the world she ever seen in him, because he was really something. . . . It was bad from the word go. Several people said he treated her like a dog."

"He abused her very badly," said Billy's wife, JoAnn Sands.

Within months, Christine's new husband forced her into prostitution on the streets of Houston, leaving Christine ashamed, degraded and angry. She knew she had to get away from Harris, so she called her daddy and asked Clyde Sands to come rescue her from Harris.

"She wanted somebody to get her," JoAnn Sands said. "So her daddy and [one of] her brothers went down and got her and brought her back to Ennis."

Christine was saved from her husband, but the damage was already done. A victim of childhood molestation and now a divorcée with a history of prostitution, Christine was already a young woman whose psyche had suffered some serious blows.

If life were a game of poker, then Brookey Lee West's father, Leroy Smith, was dealt a pair of twos as a kid. A child of Russian immigrants who emigrated to the United States when he was a baby, Leroy was just five when his father butchered his mother during a domestic dispute at the family home in the hills of Tennessee.

"He cut her head off with a machete in Tennessee," West said. "My dad said his father went to prison for about ten years."

Following his mother's murder, Leroy was left in the care of his three older sisters in Tennessee, and Leroy's siblings had little time to care for their brother. They put Leroy on a bus and attached a note to his jacket explaining the boy was orphaned by the murder of his mother. Leroy ended up on a street corner in Tennessee, where he was noticed by a caring stranger. The woman gave Leroy to another woman with the last name of Smith.

"My dad told me they took him to Arkansas, and they gave him the name of Leroy," West said.

Leroy's adoptive mother was an alcoholic woman unable to have children, but she and her husband took Leroy in because they worried how society would view a childless couple in the prime of their lives. Leroy later told his loved ones that he spent much of his early life living out of tents and shacks in Arkansas, and it was apparently not a good life. By the age of sixteen, Leroy was desperate to get away from his family, so he lied about his age and enlisted in the army. Leroy thrived on the structure and discipline of the military, and he also discovered a lifelong love—firearms. Leroy was an avid collector of guns, and he loved the power and control they offered. With a gun, Leroy Smith could instill fear.

"My dad liked shotguns, and he had some pistols, too, but my dad always had a big gun collection," West said.

The guns served to soothe a raging personality lurking deep inside Leroy. Leroy was an angry human being likely because of his troubled childhood, and anyone who came to know Leroy as an adult concluded he had a defensive, reclusive, antisocial personality. He was also extremely racist. He hated blacks, Mexicans and Jews, and racism flowed through Leroy Smith like rainwater rushing through a gutter in a summer downpour.

"My dad didn't like nothing that wasn't white," West
said. "That's just the way he was. I used to tell him, 'You
know what, Dad? If you tried to join the skinheads, you
would be president of them in six months.' He would be
like, 'Yeah, I would be.' He just felt that way."

Leroy Smith was stationed at Fort Bliss in El Paso, Texas,
when he met his bride to be, Christine Merle Sands, at a
skating rink in downtown El Paso in 1947. Leroy Smith, at
eighteen, was a blond-haired military man in a crisp U.S.
Army uniform, and he was quickly captivated by Christine.
Her long blond hair, blue eyes and shapely figure got the
army man's hormones flowing.

"Gee, I think you are beautiful," Leroy told Christine.

"I know it," Christine said.

"Oh, I've seen better," Leroy said.

"Well, not around here," Christine said.

There was an immediate animosity between Christine
and Leroy, and the tension left Leroy filled with lust. This
sexy little thing in a tight red dress had an attitude, and it
made him want her.

"The fight was on right away," West said of her parents'
first meeting.

It wouldn't take long for Leroy to have his way with the
infatuated teen. On weekends away from Fort Bliss, he
would take Christine to a picture show costing a couple of
dimes, they would spend a few hours at a soda joint and
then they'd set out for the local lover's lane. To Leroy,
Christine was likely just a tramp culled from the roller-
skating rink to screw. For Christine, however, Leroy was a
handsome, wavy-haired military man, and she wasn't
about to let this one get away. Within weeks of their meeting, Christine told Leroy she was pregnant even though she
wasn't.

"My dad said that's why he married her," West said. "He told me he wanted to divorce her after he was married to her for about three months. He said, 'I knew I'd been had.' "

Leroy Smith told his daughter he was also dismayed at Christine's level of intelligence.

"He said he went to some smoke shop with her, and she bought a book called *Nobody's Doll*," West said. "It was a second-grade book you would buy for a little kid, and that's when he realized my mother could barely read. My parents didn't know each other very well when they got married."

7

Within a year of his marriage to Christine Smith, Leroy's commitment to the army expired, and he promptly hired on as a patrol officer with the El Paso police department. The new job seemed a perfect fit for Leroy. The boy who came from modest, chaotic beginnings in life had seemingly gotten past his mother's murder and traded in his army uniform for a badge.

But according to Leroy's daughter and the woman who would become his second wife years later, Chloe Smith, Leroy's good intentions were quickly corrupted patrolling the streets of El Paso. El Paso in the late 1940s and 1950s may have been traditional Southern Americana, but like most cities of reasonable size, El Paso still had its fair share of pimping, prostitution and drugs, and Leroy indulged like a college boy in a whorehouse.

"This is when my father started using drugs, and this is also about the time my mom started using drugs, too," West said.

Leroy spent much of his time collaring drug dealers who were running drugs back and forth from Mexico through El Paso, and the busts provided him a prime opportunity to make a little extra cash to line his pockets.

"He'd take dope from some suspect and give it to some snitch to sell it to somebody," West said.

"He said it [police work] wasn't all organized like it is now," West said. "You just took care of whatever you wanted to take care of as a cop. There were a lot of drugs coming through El Paso, and he said he dealt with a lot of snitches."

Leroy's drug of choice was speed. He liked the energy it gave him on the night shift, and he was soon popping pills every day.

"He was a cop with a drug problem," West said.

"He used to tell me some awful things," said Chloe Smith. "He said they used to sit on the other side of the border, just on the other side of the river, and shoot the Mexicans' horses and donkeys. They did it for target practice. Not very nice things."

Leroy Smith told his daughter he patrolled the streets of El Paso with a heavy hand. The avowed racist had the ability to stop anyone he wanted in a city filled with Mexican Americans, and if you back-talked Leroy Smith, a beating or worse was likely.

"He said it was getting to the point where he was getting really violent," West said. "My dad wouldn't back down from anybody, and he had a real bad temper."

Christine, like Leroy, was doing drugs, and she was also starting to exhibit some very strange behavior. People who knew her noticed she was lying constantly, and one of her favorite lies was that she was a Native American. At times she claimed to be Apache. At other times she claimed a Cherokee heritage, and Christine's fascination with Native American culture did not go over well with her racist, hate-filled husband.

"He called them savages," Chloe Smith said.

"He told me he cheated on her all the time, and he made no bones about being a philanderer," Chloe said. "Leroy led me to believe Christine was crazy. So he cheated on her all the time, and he admitted to it. He said she had absolutely zero interest in sex, and he had lots of interest in sex. And he had a lot of availability for it as a cop."

When Leroy was away at work, Christine spent most of her time either in the downtown bars or at home in the couple's apartment, popping amphetamine pills, drinking liquor and smoking Camels as she waited for Leroy to get home. Slowly, the drugs and the alcohol started to wear on the couple, and by 1951 the two were fighting constantly. Following one of their episodes of domestic violence in their El Paso apartment, Christine sought out her husband's gun and, in a drunken stupor, crawled into bed next to her sleeping husband.

She put the gun to Leroy's head and pulled the trigger.

"He was a very light sleeper, and he heard her come into the room," West said. "She stuck the gun to my father's head and pulled the trigger. The gun was empty, so she just put the gun underneath his pillow and went to sleep.

"Who knows why?" West said. "But my mother didn't really need a reason to kill anybody. My mother was a very devious person. When you would get to know her, you would see that."

In 1952, Leroy decided to leave his wife once and for all and move on with his life. Problem was, Christine had bigger news.

She was pregnant.

"She never got pregnant, she never got pregnant, never got pregnant," Leroy told Chloe Smith years later. "Then, when the pressure was on, suddenly it happened."

Leroy was skeptical of the pregnancy. After all, he'd already bit once on Christine's pregnancy bait and got yanked into a miserable marriage, but any doubts about the pregnancy dissipated when Christine's belly started to bulge like a balloon.

"He always thought the baby may have been some other guy's," Chloe Smith said. "He always wondered about that."

Brookey Lee Smith, later to be known as Brookey Lee West, arrived in the maternity ward of an El Paso hospital on June 28, 1953. She was a beautiful, healthy baby with light brown hair and hazel eyes. West was, by all accounts, a sweet-natured child, and despite the differences between Christine and Leroy, both immediately fell in love with their little girl.

As a toddler, West was a bright child set on pleasing her mother and father. She loved her mommy and daddy, and when Christine wasn't partying, she took West to the park to play or to her aunt Trudy's house for dinner.

Any sense of normalcy in West's childhood, however, was short-lived because both her parents were raging alcoholics and drug addicts, and as a result West was frequently left home alone for hours on end.

"My parents both had their positives and negatives," West said. "The negatives were they drank and used dope."

In 1956, Christine got pregnant again.

"My dad was furious with her," West said. "My dad preached her up and down to no end, saying, 'You just did this to put another rope around my neck!' I heard that for years."

The couple's second baby, Travis Smith, arrived August 29, 1956, when West was three.

"My brother was a chubby, heavy baby," West said. "They put these striped shirts on him, and he looked like a wrestler."

But unlike West, Travis was a handful from the very beginning. He wore out three mattresses running in circles on

them as a young boy, and West believes her brother probably had attention deficit disorder long before the condition
was diagnosed.

"He would chew on Sheetrock," West said. "I'm serious. He was something else. He was like my mother in that
he did not have a good disposition. Him and my mother
adored each other."

Travis suffered from another pronounced medical problem as a child. His tongue was too long for his mouth. The
disability left him with a pronounced speech impediment
through much of his life.

"It made it hard for him to suck a bottle, and he couldn't
talk right, so he developed his own language," West said. "It
was like b'la ugh blabel ble. Instead of calling me Brookey,
he called me 'Kikey.' It was like speaking Chinese. He had
his vowels mixed up. People thought he was retarded, but he
really wasn't," West said. "He just had a speech impediment. He had to take speech classes throughout school."

As a toddler, Travis was also a biter. He regularly
chomped on the flesh of his sister or neighborhood kids
who got in his way.

"If anyone took something away from him, my mother
would say, 'Go bite them!'" West said. "So they used to
call my brother the snapping turtle. She couldn't take him
anywhere because he'd bite the hell out of you. My mother
would get invited to someone's house down the street, and
the neighbors would say, 'Don't bring him [Travis] over
here.' He'd draw blood."

Despite all the negatives in the Smith household, however, there were moments during West's childhood when
she and her brother were happy children. Family snapshots
show West dressed in an innocent cotton dress, her curly
brown hair combed until it looked just right. Christine
dressed Travis in fancy dark overalls over a white shirt,

and she would take the children outside and snap their photos in the hot Texas sunlight.

"My sweet little babies!" Christine wrote on the back of one black-and-white snapshot of the smiling children taken in the late 1950s.

The photos of smiling children masked the real truth. Mostly, the childhoods of West and her brother were of abandonment and loneliness. When West was left at home alone, she passed the time making paper dolls, dressing them like a princess or queen in a fantasy world far away from the solitude of her family's empty apartment. She had only one birthday party as a girl because her parents were too busy partying, and she remembers having to care for her brother for days while her parents were out barhopping.

"We had all kinds of medications in our cabinets," West said. "Speed, then tranquilizers to calm [my parents] down. My mother told me [years later] that they were both strung out, and they couldn't handle it [being parents]."

In the mid 1950s, Leroy bottomed out and was fired from his job as a police officer.

"My dad said he borrowed money from the police department, but if you borrowed money, you had to have people vouch for you that you would pay it back," West said. "If you didn't pay it back, they sort of blacklisted you, and blackballed you, is what he told me."

Leroy didn't pay the money back and he was booted off the force.

The story about failing to pay off a debt was the explanation Leroy gave his loved ones for losing the job he loved, but Leroy's family suspects it was only a partial explanation. Chloe Smith said years later, after she married Leroy that the firing from the El Paso police department remained a sore topic with her husband.

"My guess is he got in some trouble and he got kicked

out or pressured to leave," Chloe said. "That's my gut feeling. I don't think he ever wanted me to see him as a bad
guy, so he whitewashed it somewhat."

In an act of desperation, Leroy packed up his family and
headed to Bakersfield, California, for a fresh start.

8

Leroy Smith realized it was time to get out of El Paso for good. His prized job as a city cop had blown away with the Texas winds, so in 1959 Leroy, his wife, Christine, and their two children, Brookey and Travis, packed up their belongings and headed west. They stopped briefly at low-rent motels in New Mexico and Ventura, California, before finally settling in Bakersfield.

The municipality of 234,000 sits at the southern tip of California's four hundred-mile-long Central Valley, where thousands of acres of flat farmlands produce oranges, grapefruit and almonds in abundance. The picturesque Central Valley is responsible for more than 60 percent of the state's agricultural production, and its farms contribute to roughly a quarter of the nation's food supply, making California one of the most prolific farming states in the country.

Bakersfield, however, is largely a city still dependent on what the locals call "black gold." Derricks on the outskirts of the city pump for oil, producing some 570,000 barrels of oil a year, and some of the nation's largest oil companies, including Chevron-Texaco and Shell, carry out huge extraction and refining operations in Bakersfield.

In 1959, Leroy and Christine were a perfect fit for Bakersfield. The city was home to thousands of Oklahomans and Texans who fled their native states during the Great Depression of the 1930s. Bakersfield was also in the midst of a honky-tonk heyday fueled by the Oklahoma and Texas transplants. The city's nightclubs were overflowing with couples yearning for the twangy, unique brand of Bakersfield country music, and Christine and Leroy spent plenty of nights drinking and dancing at downtown bars like the Cellar and the Blackboard, where Buck Owens and Merle Haggard made history developing the sounds of the legendary Bakersfield musical scene.

Leroy found work in Bakersfield laying carpet in homes. The job didn't pay a lot, but it was a steady income, and it allowed the Smiths to rent a house in a lower-income section of the city.

"Bakersfield is where it got interesting and sort of strange for my family, because we had a lot of neighbors who were Oklahomans, and if you've never been around Okies, they are a real experience," West said.

"Most of them are just like my parents," West said. "Alcoholics, drinkers, partiers, sitting out in front of their homes drinking and working on some old wrecked-out car, saying, 'Go in the house there, baby, and get daddy a beer! Go in there and get me my shotgun!' They'd all be out there shouting at each other in the yard with their rifles pointed at each other," West said. "That's what I'm talking about when I say, 'If you've never been around Okies, it's a real experience.' "

Leroy and Christine tramped through the Bakersfield bar scene night after night, and the nonstop partying made for a volatile home life for West and her brother. At seven, West said she was pretty much solely responsible for taking care of four-year-old Travis while her parents were hitting the bars.

"We had periods where we were left home alone for two to three days," West said. "I always took care of my brother."

When Leroy was at work laying carpet, Christine usually spent her days in bed recovering from self-inflicted headaches and a bloodstream filled with liquor.

"My mother was always in bed sick, and she had turned this really dark gray—weird looking," West said. "She was always, 'This hurts, that hurts.' Then my dad would come home after work and say, 'You want to go out tonight?' And all of the sudden, my mother would pop right out of bed and say, 'Let's go.'"

Leroy chugged wine like water, and his kitchen cabinet was filled with a large stash of amphetamines and tranquilizers. Leroy was driving himself into the ground with drugs and alcohol, and he didn't seem to care.

"That's about the time when my parents started going to doctors to get more and more pills," West said. "They were writing prescriptions for my parents for painkillers, and then my parents would sell them. Sell them to their friends or whoever wanted them. A buck for this, a buck for that, and that's how they made their money.

"I took care of them and all their problems," West said. "If I could hide something for them, I did. If they told me to lie, I lied. Someone would call up and say, 'Can I speak to your dad?' And I'd say, 'Well, he's not here. He went to a doctor.' Meanwhile, my dad was right there smashed out of his mind."

Leroy could be frightening during his drunken rages. On more than one occasion, his anger was unleashed on the children in the form of violent spankings that left bruises in the shape of handprints on their bottoms.

"One time, my dad came home from work with a box

of chocolates for my mother on her birthday, and I said, 'Oh, can I have some?' " West recalled. "My dad just lost it, and he spanked me so hard I had his whole handprint on my butt.

"There were times that he would spank us with a two-by-four," West said. "I'd go to school with bruises all over, but no one ever said anything."

Guns were everywhere in the house—handguns, shotguns, rifles. The firearms were tucked underneath couch cushions or hidden beneath the bed. Leroy regularly carried a gun on him, and it was well known in Bakersfield that Leroy was an individual to be feared.

"My dad didn't back down from anybody," West said.

West remembers witnessing her father chase down a man he noticed driving too fast through his Bakersfield neighborhood.

"My dad actually went out and physically pulled this guy out of his car," West recalled. "He said. 'You see all these kids around here? If you want to run over somebody's kid, make sure you run over somebody else's, because if you run over one of my kids, I'm going to twist your head off your shoulders and use it as a doorknob.'

"If my mother was angry, you couldn't talk to her," West said. "She wasn't bad about hitting, but she was a screamer, saying things like, 'Shut up! Turn that damned television down!'

"I was frightened of both of them," West said. "I had to be careful because they both had their idiosyncrasies about things. My parents were not educated people, and they didn't know anything about encouragement and praise. They basically treated me how they were treated when they were children. They saw you as an object. 'What do you know? You are only seven.' "

The home life of violence, alcohol, drugs and arguments left West and Travis emotionally damaged inside.

Especially hurtful for the children was the fact that their parents were continually separating and getting back together. Christine would run off for days, and when she came back, Leroy would disappear. There were continual threats of divorce between the husband and wife, and West and her brother wondered whether they were the problem.

The stormy relationship between Leroy and Christine seemed to come to a boiling point in 1961 when Leroy left his wife for a cocktail waitress named Faye. Leroy took his daughter and son with him, and they moved into Faye's home in Bakersfield, where the waitress was already living with her six children. West and Travis were suddenly living in a large family with a new mother figure.

Christine, meanwhile, replaced her missing husband with a married man. David Gilmore* was a mason by trade, and for a few months Gilmore and Christine burned up the Bakersfield nights together in a steamy hot romance. They dreamed of running off together and leaving their spouses behind for a new life someplace else.

"He was married and I was married, and we snuck around," Christine would later tell Bakersfield police in a taped statement.

The affair between Christine and Gilmore was so torrid, Christine even alleged that she and Gilmore once plotted to kill his wife, Susan.*

"He wanted me to kill her, and I thought, 'You son of a bitch, if I killed her, where would I be with you?' " Christine said in the taped statement. "Who would he get to kill me? That's the way I felt about it."

She said the plot to murder Susan Gilmore involved "sleeping medicine, a lot of sleeping stuff."

But before any plot to kill his wife was carried out, David Gilmore had a change of heart. He decided he was going back to his wife, and he told Christine of his decision in the first few weeks of 1961.

Christine was enraged.

"I said, 'Well, you know, you can take me to the water, you son of a bitch, but ain't going to drown me because I'll kill your ass,' " Christine told the police.

David Gilmore was about to learn a very valuable lesson: No one fucks with Christine Merle Smith.

9

In 1961, Christine Merle Smith was the meanest, angriest bitch in all of Bakersfield, California. Her secret lover, David Gilmore, had promised to leave his wife for her, then dumped her, so on January 24, Christine called Gilmore and asked if he would meet with her one last time at the Cellar bar in downtown Bakersfield.

At about seven thirty p.m., the five-foot-four-inch Christine walked into the lounge at 1918½ Eye Street with a loaded shotgun tucked underneath her jacket.

"I had the gun under there," Christine told police. "It was a sawed-off shotgun. [Had] it over my shoulder. I had a shoulder strap."

Christine sat down at a table in the bar and rested the 16-gauge shotgun on her lap underneath the table. The bar was nearly empty, and the few who were there didn't notice Christine covering the weapon with a sweater and her jacket.

Gilmore showed up at the bar with his wife, Susan, just after seven thirty p.m., and the couple sat down across from Christine.

Christine grasped the shotgun, leveled it at Gilmore and pulled the trigger.

"I reached under the table, I had the gun under there . . . and I shot him!" Christine said.

The blast ripped into David Gilmore, who was sitting just two feet from the end of the barrel of the gun. Shotgun pellets shattered his right arm and tore a sizeable chunk of flesh from his torso. He slumped to the floor of the bar in a pool of blood, his horrified wife looking on in shock.

Gilmore, thirty, was rushed to Bakersfield's Mercy Hospital where he underwent surgery. His life was saved, but his arm would never be same. He was maimed for life.

"It hurt him bad," West said. "He was in a cast for months, and he was a brick mason, so I'm sure it took a toll."

City police had no problems apprehending Christine, who was hauled away from the scene in handcuffs to the Kern County jail. She was fingerprinted, photographed and booked on a felony charge of assault with a deadly weapon with intent to commit murder, according to police records.

"I didn't have the least feeling of sympathy," Christine told the cops. "Hell, no."

When asked by a California homicide detective what she'd intended to do to Gilmore that day, Christine said simply, "Kill him."

The shooting was big news in Bakersfield, and the city's newspaper, the *Bakersfield Californian*, ran a front-page account of the crime the next day.

Woman Held in Shooting at Downtown Café
Wednesday, January 25, 1961

Police today were holding Mrs. Christine M. Smith, 28, of 1019 Casa Loma Dr., mother of two small children, for investigation in the shooting of David Gilmore, 30, of 1013 Sandra Drive. Gilmore was reported in "good" condition in Mercy Hospital with shotgun pellet wounds in the side and the right arm. Police said they were told the arm may have to be amputated.

Mrs. Smith is in Kern County jail on suspicion of assault with a deadly weapon with intent to commit murder. Police said she fired a single blast from a 16-gauge sawed off shotgun at Gilmore in The Cellar, 1918½ Eye St. The incident occurred about 7:30 p.m. Tuesday.

Lt. Richard Mason said Mrs. Smith told him she carried the shotgun into the cafe under a coat draped over her arm. She waited nearly half an hour to meet Gilmore and his wife, Susan.

Mrs. Smith, separated from her husband, told Mason she had been dating Gilmore during his separation from his wife. Earlier Gilmore had told her he was reconciling with his wife. At Mrs. Smith's request, the Gilmores were to discuss with her how she might win back her husband, Leroy.

Mrs. Smith told officers she did not know where Leroy Smith and the children, ages 7 and 4, were living.

Investigators said she was seated at a table with the gun under the coat and a sweater when Gilmore sat down next to her, his wife across the table. Officers said he was about two feet away when Mrs. Smith, without warning, pulled the trigger of the gun in her lap.

Asked if she would deny the shooting, Mrs. Smith said she would not. Asked the reason for it, she was reported to have said "that will come out later."

Christine went to trial in downtown Bakersfield in March 1961. The mother of two was convicted by a jury of assault with intent to commit murder and sentenced to fourteen years in prison.

Years later, Christine the ex-convict bragged about the shooting to dozens of people, saying it was the greatest accomplishment of her life.

"My mother talked about that shooting like she was some sort of movie star," West said. "The first thing out of her mouth about it was, 'Well, you know, I went to prison because I shot that son of a bitch. He deserved it. Every pellet he got.'"

10

One would think Leroy Smith would have completely disowned his wife, Christine, when he learned of the shooting of David Gilmore, but he did the exact opposite. His relationship with Faye the cocktail waitress crumbled, and he went running back to Christine with his daughter and son in tow.

"It was traumatic," West said of her mother's arrest. "It was on TV and everything. A lot of people knew about it."

At the age of eight, West was deeply ashamed of her mother. She remembers going with her father to visit her mother at the Kern County jail in downtown Bakersfield following her arrest, and she also remembers going to see her mother during Christine's trial at the Kern County courthouse.

"My dad took a dress down to her, and it was a honky-tonk dress with no back, so her lawyers put a sweater around her because they didn't want her in court in that thing," West said. "They wrote in the paper that she was a Lolita."

Christine was convicted and sent to the California Institution for Women (CIW). The prison is a cold, hard expanse of concrete and prison bars built in 1952 on 120 acres in Riverside County, just outside of Los Angeles. CIW was originally called "Frontera," which the California Department of Corrections says is a reference to the inmates' hope for a new beginning. But to this day, there are plenty of inmates at CIW who have no hope of ever being released. CIW is home to some of the state's most notorious female killers and thieves, and perhaps the most famous resident of CIW is Leslie Van Houten, who participated in the 1969 stabbing murders of Rosemary and Leno LaBianca with the followers of Charles Manson.

Christine fit in well at CIW.

"My mom somehow had a thing with these people," West said. "She understood them. It was some sort of unspoken communication."

Christine worked in the prison kitchen serving food. She would sneak some inmates pies or sweets, and she became so popular in the cafeteria that the inmates were furious when she was moved to another job in the prison.

"So when they took my mother off that detail, and another inmate tried to serve them, they threw hot coffee all over this new server," West said. "My mother had that in her. I don't know what it is, but she had that thing where she could connect with people, and she manipulated them."

West said losing her mother to CIW as a little girl was a life-changing event, and there was no escaping it no matter how hard she tried.

"I knew exactly what was going on," West said. "I failed the second grade, and they couldn't understand why. But it was because my mother was in prison, and I couldn't think. I couldn't learn.

"I didn't talk to anybody about my mother being in prison," West said. "I didn't tell the teachers, I didn't talk to my friends and I didn't tell anyone about it because people would make fun of you and be rude about it, so I just grinned and bore it."

Travis was crushed as well, and his emotional trauma was exacerbated by Leroy's method of dealing with Christine's imprisonment. Instead of telling now five-year-old Travis his mother was going to be gone for fourteen years, Leroy instructed West to tell Travis his mother was dead and buried.

" 'You just tell your little brother your mom died,' " West quoted her father as saying.

"My dad felt he wouldn't understand it. My brother cried and cried when I told him our mother was dead," West said. "I felt bad about lying to him, but I didn't know how else to handle it, you know? It was the wrong way to do it."

Having his eight-year-old daughter tell her little brother their mother was buried and gone was perfectly acceptable in Leroy's mind. It was a way of making sure West was developing from child to woman.

"I was supposed to understand everything," West said. "I was to take care of my brother, and my dad was like, 'If you want to be treated like an adult, then act like an adult.' "

It was a terribly turbulent time for West and her brother, but it was about to get worse. Within a year of Christine's incarceration, Leroy took his children to Fresno for a few months. Then they moved to Oregon, where they stayed for five months, and then it was to San Luis Obispo, California, and finally back to Bakersfield.

"We were always going through something, or we were always worried about something, and we were always moving," West said of her childhood. "There was always some trauma in our lives all the time.

"Drink all day and half the night," West said of her father. "It was getting to where he couldn't even work anymore. We were living in another run-down motel, and he was feeding us crackers for dinner. Pillar to post and motel to motel. If you didn't have something to eat that day, you asked the neighbors for something."

In 1962, Leroy decided the children would be better off without him, so he took his son and daughter to a local orphanage in Bakersfield. West was eight and Travis five when they were dropped off at the Baptist Sunnycrest home for youths.

"My dad told us he was going to have to put us there, and I just started screaming," West said. "I thought it was something I did, and that he was going to have to put me there because I did something wrong. I said, 'I'll be good, I'll do what you tell me,' but it wasn't that," West said. "He just couldn't take care of his kids."

The abandonment of the children was now complete. Christine was serving hard time at CIW, and West and her brother had not heard from their mother in nearly two years. To make matters worse, their drunken father felt his drinking was more important than his kids.

But in the months that followed, West and Travis quickly came to love their new home at the orphanage. The orphanage housed about twenty children in two single-story buildings adjacent to a large playground, and the facility was run by an older husband and wife who took the time to show each child the love they were starving for.

"We started going to school regularly at the orphanage, and everything got a little better for me," West said. "My grades were good, I had clothes to wear, and they fed me right."

Travis immediately warmed up to the orphanage as well, and the five-year-old gravitated to the husband and wife who ran Sunnycrest.

"My brother became attached to both of them," West said. "The woman, she was sort of a big, buxom type, very motherly, and she would hold him a lot. He became very attached to her."

For the first time in their lives, West and Travis were in a nurturing environment that allowed them to blossom. The orphanage's managers may not have been the children's parents, but they treated West and her brother like kids are supposed to be treated. They fed and looked after the children, and when West or her brother were sad, they showed them unbridled love. West realized she really didn't miss her mother and father at all, and as far as she and Travis were concerned, they were content staying at Sunnycrest for as long as the church would have them.

And then, Leroy came back.

West's father drove into the driveway of the orphanage with a woman in the front seat of his car. The woman was thin, blond haired, with tight black pants and an even tighter black sweater. A pair of dark sunglasses covered her eyes, and as she got out of the car, West recognized who it was: Christine.

"My parents show up—both of them," West said. "I didn't want to leave the orphanage, but we had to. My brother's screaming and crying, and he didn't want to leave, either. My mother actually wanted to leave my brother there and let him adjust, but my dad wouldn't have it."

Christine was fresh out of prison just two years into her fourteen-year sentence. The parole board released her on her first appearance, and her chance at freedom mandated she complete only a five-year parole.

"I think [my parents] sought each other out after my mom got out of prison because it was one of those types of relationships, like when an abused woman keeps going back to her husband," West said. "They didn't want each other, but then, when they were apart, they really did. And then, they didn't want each other again. That's the way their relationship was. On and off all the time."

The stability West longed for in her childhood was gone again. She and her brother were whisked out of the orphanage by their parents, and the family moved north to San Jose. It was the city where West grew into a woman, and it was the city where West's father dedicated himself to the Prince of Darkness.

DEVIL WORSHIP

11

Sitting forty-five minutes south of San Francisco in the center of the Santa Clara Valley is the city of San Jose, a municipality that gets little attention when compared to the other major cities of California. There are no golden beaches like the ones found in San Diego. There is no Golden Gate Bridge, no Hollywood and no massive state government center like in nearby Sacramento. But San Jose may still be the most pleasant place to live in all of California.

The city's diverse population is extremely congenial, and anyone who visits immediately recognizes San Jose has struck a perfect balance between country living and big city. On the outskirts of the city, one is greeted with a charming view of green pastures and farmlands leading to lush, even greener hillsides. In the interior of the city, downtown is a wonderful mix of modern office complexes, shops and restaurants offering exotic cuisine from around the world. San Jose's residents and tourists seem to act as if they are in paradise as they walk through the city's downtown Center Plaza, where commuter trolleys whisk by every few minutes.

Founded in 1777, San Jose is one of the oldest communities in the western United States, and much of San Jose's cultural and religious history can be traced to the Spanish missions, which spread across California like wildfire to teach the Catholic faith to the Native Americans. Today, the city's economic power can be traced to its massive technology industry, which has earned San Jose the internationally recognized nickname "Silicon Valley." Hewlett-Packard was started here in the 1930s, and some of the brightest computer programmers on the planet come to San Jose and surrounding areas from India, China and other countries to work at companies like HP, Sun, Cisco and Apple, where monitors, hard drives and programs are churned out like nowhere else in the world.

In 1965, Leroy Smith and his family were attracted to San Jose by its beauty and economic opportunities. Leroy quickly found another job laying carpet, and the Smith clan eventually settled into a single-story rental home on Lafayette Street, near Santa Clara University, in a mostly Hispanic neighborhood.

West said she always felt like she never quite fit in her neighborhood as one of the few white kids in the entire community. She ended up spending much of her grade school years playing alone or with her little brother in a grassy field of a Catholic church near her family's house.

"The kids weren't very friendly to me," West said. "I was always big for my age, and by the time I was twelve, I was tall. I didn't look twelve, and I didn't look like everyone else."

West's little brother didn't fit in, either. By the age of nine, Travis was acting out, fighting with neighborhood boys and engaging in self-destructive behavior uncommon for a child so young.

"My brother started using drugs when he was nine," West said. "Pills right out of the cabinet. The bathroom cabinet couldn't hold all these pills. Any color you wanted."

One of the Smiths' family friends in San Jose was a buxom woman West knew only as "Mrs. Beauford." She lived in a Victorian house about six blocks away from the Smiths, and she was especially close to Leroy. According to West, Beauford was a practicing witch, and West's father was captivated by Beauford's proclaimed ability to cast spells on others.

"She was from Kentucky," West said. "Her husband and two of her sons had been murdered, and they had run her out of Kentucky."

West said she was thirteen when her mother asked her to go to Mrs. Beauford's home to return a dish Christine had borrowed.

"I knocked on her door, the door sort of came open and I said hello, and nobody answered," West said. "I stood there for a second, and I hear this moaning, groaning, kind of like screaming. It's coming from the basement," she said. "You had to go to the back of the house, so I walked in, went down the stairs, looked around the corner, and they have all these black candles. This son of hers, who was going to Santa Clara University, was doing some sort of spell or something."

Spells and witchcraft quickly became Leroy's passion, according to West. He was consumed by the premise that, with a spell, he could make his enemies suffer. By the late 1960s, Leroy was meeting regularly with Mrs. Beauford and a network of San Jose occultists. They gathered to carry out secret, candle-lit ceremonies in which they wore dark robes, practiced spells, recited chants and worshipped the devil.

"He'd go to these meetings, and he got to where he was crazier, meaner, doing more dope, drinking heavier," West said. "A lot of people that are alcoholics and dopers, especially mixers of the two, have tendencies to get into weird things like that."

Covens of Satanic worshippers were not necessarily unusual in Northern California in the late 1960s and 1970s. In fact, the region was a hotbed for the movement. The modern day Church of Satan was founded in nearby San Francisco in 1966 by a man named Anton LaVey. LaVey, an ominous-looking creature with shaved head and goatee, played the part perfectly, wearing black robes, wielding long swords and giving countless media interviews promoting the worship of Satan. The sins of the flesh were to be indulged in, LaVey said, in a message that shocked mainstream Christian America.

But LaVey's words struck a chord with thousands in the late 1960s. One estimate put LaVey's followers at 25,000, and the movement even attracted some Hollywood elite.

LaVey's book, *The Satanic Bible*, is widely regarded as the religion's gospel. It is an intensely dark and frightening mantra outlining the tenets of the religion and its ceremonies.

Leroy read every word.

Of Christ, Leroy said, "I don't believe it. I think he was just a man, nothing more than a rabble-rousing troublemaker, and that's why they crucified him."

Leroy started calling himself a "warlock," and he saw himself as a high-ranking male witch in Satan's legion.

"He had books, knives and other stuff," West said. "They wore their robes, almost like the Ku Klux Klan, and it was a secretive organization. You had to be taken in by someone who was already in.

"It was about worshipping Satan and being as faithful to him as Christians are to the Lord," West said of her father's beliefs. "Like it says in the Scripture, when he [Satan] had Jesus on the mountain, Satan tells Jesus, 'I'll give you all the world, bow down and worship me. The power was given to me, and I can give it to anyone I wish.' My dad identified with that stuff. He didn't go around killing people, but he believed Satan was the ruler of this world, and he could give you anything you wanted. You just have to know how to get in touch.

"He never took me to any of these meetings," West said. "My father was the type of person who believed you should just find your own road. He wasn't forceful like, 'I like baseball, so you'll like baseball.'

"I understand all of it," West said. "I know what their belief systems are. I know how they meet. I know what they do. Is there any validity to it? Yes, there is. There are people who are true Satanists, who are faithful to him. Can they cast a spell? Can they wreak havoc in your life? Absolutely. It's real. Their spirits are real. But not your average person or everyday Joe, some guy who buys some book, is going to be able to do that.

"But, I have to tell you, it works just like any other faith," West said. "If you are a Christian and you have the faith, the Bible speaks of the faith and you must have faith. Well, its the same way with the other side. You have to be given to that. You have to belong to it, or it won't work for you.

"Have I practiced it?" West said. "No. But I've read about it, and I've done a lot of in-depth study on all of it. I can't go that way, because it is just not my path. I know it is a reality, and I know that it works for them. I know people that are in it, people in very high positions."

12

A witch is one who worketh by the Devil or by some curious art either healing or revealing things secret, or foretelling things to come which the Devil hath devised to ensnare men's souls withal unto damnation. The conjurer, the enchanter, the sorcerer, the diviner, and whatever other sort there is encompassed within this circle.

—George Gifford, a British clergyman in the sixteenth century

In Salem, Massachusetts, in 1692, two little girls decided they were going to dabble in the occult. One of the children was Betty Parris, the nine-year-old daughter of Salem village reverend Samuel Parris, and the second was Elizabeth's eleven-year-old cousin, Abigail Williams.

The two children loved to listen to stories told to them by the Parris' Caribbean family slave, Tituba, who weaved for the little girls wild tales of sorcery. The children were captivated by Tituba's stories, prompting them one day to try their own brand of sorcery. In a haphazard experiment, the girls dropped hot wax into a glass of water, and Betty then peered into the water with the hope of seeing what the future held for her and Abigail. But instead, Betty saw the image of death, frightening the two children out of their wits.

Soon, Betty and Abigail's behavior was out of control.

They were observed going into convulsions and wildly thrashing back and forth. The village doctors were summoned and provided a disturbing diagnosis for Reverend Parris and his loved ones—the children were suffering from a witch's spell.

Within days of the diagnosis, other children in Salem started to suffer as well. The children talked gibberish or blasphemy, and their bodies contorted at all angles. The leaders of Salem quickly realized something had to be done.

Carrying torches to illuminate the pitch-black night, they searched through the village and the dense New England woods for those responsible. The first to be charged with crimes of witchcraft were Salem residents Sarah Good, Sarah Osborn and Tituba. Tituba confessed to consorting with the devil under questioning from religious leaders, and her life was spared. The others were taken to trial, convicted and hanged in front of angry mobs on Witch's Hill in Salem.

"I am no more a witch than you are a wizard," Good said prior to her hanging. "If you take my life away, God will give you blood to drink."

When the mayhem was finally over, nineteen suspected witches were hanged, and a man was pressed to death. It was the deadliest witch hunt in American history.

Sonny Armas is a pack rat. In the garage of his single-story home in rural Central California, Armas keeps boxes and boxes of stuff stacked on top of one another like cord wood. Most of the boxes are filled with tapes, CDs, books, tools, hardware and various other knickknacks he's collected over the years.

Armas, thirty-nine also collects furniture at his Los Banos, California, home. The admitted clutterbug said most of the items he's gathered were given to him by family and acquaintances.

"I'm always helping someone move, so I get a lot of the stuff that way," Armas said. "I guess I keep stuff because, once I get rid of something, I usually find out about a week later that I needed it."

In 1994, Armas and his wife, Genia, bought their Los Banos home from its original owner—Brookey Lee West. When West moved out of the residence, she left behind stacks and stacks of boxes in the garage. In one box, Sonny Armas found a book titled *The Truth About Witchcraft Today*. The cover of the book consists of a glossy photo of an attractive female model in a business suit, and she is holding a briefcase in her hand. The message from the cover of the book makes clear that witchcraft, in the author's opinion, is an acceptable religion practiced by modern professionals.

The Truth About Witchcraft Today was written by the late Wiccan author Scott Cunningham, who spent much of his literary career trying to dispel the premise that witchcraft is a form of devil worship. Instead, he worked to promote the idea of witchcraft as a respected religion that honors the natural universe. Tragically, he died young at the age of thirty-seven.

But *The Truth About Witchcraft Today* wasn't the only odd item Sonny Armas found in his garage. In a toolbox, Armas found a handful of items belonging to West's father, Leroy Smith. In the box was a black knit ski cap, commonly referred to as a burglar's cap, and an electronic listening device capable of picking up the conversations of unsuspecting people from hundreds of feet away. It was as if Leroy was equipped to be a professional burglar.

There were weapons in the garage, too. They consisted of a series of long, steel, curved knives with gothic handles, and next to the knives was a brown leather pouch with a drawstring. When the drawstring was loosened, the pouch produced a macabre, miniature white skull with long, protruding fangs. The skull looked like something a Satanist might wear around his neck during a ritual.

"I thought, 'Wow, this is some really weird stuff,'" Sonny Armas said. "It totally tripped me out."

And finally, Armas found a black leather notepad in Leroy's belongings. The notepad, containing about eighty sheets of paper, was the type of tablet a cop might fit in a shirt or pants pocket.

One entry in Leroy's notepad listed the address for a gun parts store in Glendale, California. The entry is followed by a drawn red cross, and there are then a series of writings on the final three pages of the pad. The writings can only be described as a succession of sinister-looking symbols and letters that come together to craft a secret code.

The code is written in black ink on stained, faded white paper, and a close inspection of the letters show them to be of the ancient Theban alphabet, which is commonly referred to as the "witch's alphabet."

"I thought maybe it was a foreign language when I first saw it," Sonny Armas said.

The Theban alphabet first surfaced during the medieval period, and today it is an alphabet claimed by witches and Wiccans. The alphabet, according to myth, adds a powerful, mystic quality to a witch's spell.

"It is an old, hieroglyphic-type writing put together by witches in this country when they first came here in Salem," West said. "It's like a secret language. My dad always used it, and he had a special book to translate it."

The writings in Leroy's notepad, when translated from the witch's alphabet, are a series of prayers. Like the image Betty Parris observed in the water glass, the contents of the prayers are an ominous foretelling of the future, because they show that Leroy knew one day his wife, Christine, and his daughter were going to desperately need the favors of his God.

The prayers read:

Please, oh God, take care of my loved ones.
Dear God, please take care of Brooke
and her mother Chris, Christine.

13

At age fourteen, Brookey Lee West enrolled in Santa Clara High School in San Jose, and she was no longer the awkward-looking girl of a few years ago. Puberty had morphed her into an attractive, well-built young girl on the verge of womanhood.

"I was a dancer when I was a teenager," she said. "Ballet, and I was really built because of it. I had gorgeous legs."

With her curly brown hair, beautiful hazel eyes and shapely figure, West was starting to attract the attention of several boys at Santa Clara High. What really made her attractive to the opposite sex was the way she dressed—she donned tight-fitting sweaters and short skirts, just like the outfits her mother wore in the Bakersfield honky-tonks nearly a decade earlier.

"I dressed very sexy," West said. "I was a looker. The boys all wanted a date with me, but I didn't want to go. I was very standoffish about men. Probably because of the way my home life was, I couldn't invite anybody home. I couldn't have a normal life. I didn't really do well in school, too, because I had so much stress."

West got less than average grades throughout high school, and she was pretty much an aimless teen without a plan for the future. Her underachieving was probably attributable to the tumult in her home, which came to a head when she was in high school. In the late 1960s, her parents' marriage hit the rocks for good when Christine caught Leroy in a series of affairs he wasn't even trying to hide.

"My mom moved out," West said. "My dad was running around with other women, and he was drinking heavily, and my mother was always trying to change him, and she never could."

The couple divorced in yet another emotional trauma for West and her brother. The divorce was especially hard on Travis, who dropped out of high school to pursue a life of doing drugs.

"My brother loved speed," West said.

Leroy tried to convince his son to work with him laying carpet, but Travis had little interest in working for a living. Travis was constantly lying and stealing to get drugs—mostly methamphetamine—and he ended up repeatedly in trouble with the San Jose police department and the Santa Clara County sheriff's office.

There were, however, positive developments stemming from Christine and Leroy's divorce. Christine, tired of feeling poorly from drinking and drugging seven days a week, swore off all drugs and alcohol. She started attending Alcoholics Anonymous, was gradually successful in giving up her bad habits, West said.

"My mother cleaned herself up, and she got off the dope," West said.

Christine, now sober, decided she was going to come to terms with her sinful past by attending a little Episcopalian church called Faith Temple in San Jose with her daughter.

For Christine, religion was a chance to try to find answers to some of the most perplexing traumas in her life. Why was she molested as a child? Why had she, at age sixteen, married a wife beater, Tommy Harris, who forced her into prostitution? Why, when she finally escaped that abusive relationship, had she hooked up with Leroy, an avowed womanizer and Satanist? And why, with two small children, did she shoot a man in Bakersfield and go to prison?

In short, it was time for Christine to find God. Christine was soon talking regularly about the word of God and the power of Jesus. But according to West, Christine was still far from a perfect Christian. She wanted to be forgiven, but she didn't want to put in the work. She paid attention to the teachings of the Gospel, yet she was still a bitter woman filled with spite and anger for anyone who crossed her.

"My mom started going to church with me when I was in my teens, but she still viewed religion as a matter of convenience," West said. "She wasn't book smart enough to learn the Bible, or even read it, and she didn't apply herself."

By the late 1960s, Christine was also on the verge of another personal revelation—she was mentally ill. While at a local doctor's office for one of a dozen or so mysterious ailments she complained about constantly, a doctor referred her to a mental health professional.

"My mother was always going to doctors because she always had something wrong with her," West said. "Her back hurt. 'My foot hurts, my earlobe hurts.' She was always in bed, always had some sort of chronic cough, and doctors would always tell us, 'I've given her enough medicine to cure a horse.'

"It was finally determined all her ailments were psychosomatic," West said. "There wasn't really anything wrong with her."

Christine was sent to a mental health clinic in San Jose,

and during a screening interview with a psychologist, she attacked her doctor with her boot.

"She took her boot heel, and she beat him over the head with it," West said. "He had this big old gash in his head, and he's running around, screaming in the hallway."

The attack led authorities to send Christine to a state psychiatrist, Sidney Goldstein, who concluded Christine was mentally unstable. Christine visited Goldstein for the next ten years, and during one visit to Goldstein's office, West realized just how seriously ill her mother was during a conversation with Goldstein's secretary.

"She said, 'Oh, um, well, anyone who sees Dr. Goldstein has got a real screw loose,'" West said. "'He only takes the sickest patients.'"

Moments later, the secretary left her mother's psychiatric case file open in front of West, and West scanned her mother's diagnosis.

"Sociopath with psychopathic tendencies," West said. "That was my mother's diagnosis . . . someone who cares for nobody but themselves. They see the world as a place to be manipulated for their own comforts and use.

"She was a total sociopath," West said.

14

I was about thirty and I was going to work. I got out of my car, and I felt this wind. I stood there for a moment, and it was like I was watching a movie. I could see this man, and there was a little girl behind a green sofa. She was five years old, and she was watching this guy in a Halloween costume kill her pregnant mother. I see this guy cutting her open and taking the baby out. This is not my imagination— I knew I was having a premonition. The next day, the whole thing is on the news. It happened on Halloween night.

—Brookey Lee West

The premonitions usually come without warning to Brookey Lee West. Her mind flashes like a time machine, and a whirling sensation takes her into the future, allowing her to witness events yet to occur. When TWA Flight 800 plunged into the Atlantic Ocean in 1996, killing all 230 passengers, West knew the tragedy was going to happen before it actually unfolded. In San Jose, West said she witnessed the murder of a pregnant woman in her mind the day before news of the slaying showed up on her television screen.

"It's like I'm watching a movie," West said. "It's not something I acquired. I was born this way."

West said she's had the premonitions since she was a little girl growing up in San Jose. The phenomenon can likely be traced to West's father, who actually encouraged his child to explore the occult and different methods of predicting the future. When West was eleven, Leroy Smith bought his little girl two gifts used to tell the future—a crystal ball and some tarot cards. The tarot cards were West's favorite, and they remained a fascination for her throughout her adult life.

"I know all about those cards, and I have studied them for years," West said. "They are valid. The only issue I see about those cards is that what the books say they mean, and what they really mean is much more vast."

Tarot cards are twenty-two pictorial playing cards dating back to fifteenth-century Europe. The cards feature elaborate picture designs of several symbols, including the Moon, Justice, Hanged Man and the Devil card. The most ominous card in the deck is the Death card, which is adorned with a skeleton riding a horse.

"An amateur person does not really understand the depth of the cards," West said. "They can be helpful, and they can also be very dangerous. I take the deck, cut the cards, and I just lay them out in a certain format," West said. "Each position of the card means a certain thing, and each card means a certain thing. The cards are all interlinked."

West does not call herself a psychic. She prefers the term "empathic," meaning she draws upon the feelings of other people to see what the future holds.

"If I meet someone, or if I'm in the presence of someone for a long time, I take on how they feel," West said. "If they are angry, I feel their anger. Or if they are upset, I feel that."

And in Las Vegas in the late 1990s at the oxygen bar Breathe, she used marbles to predict futures.

"I'll usually do one marble at a time," West said. "I have the person hold it, then they lay it down, and I pick it up.

It's like a camera, and I see things. But I could pretty much use anything to do it. I can do the same thing with straws. I just use marbles because they are easy to carry around.

"I do run into skeptics, but after they get to know me for a while, they know I'm for real," West said.

"I always wanted to try and help the police, because I know about all kinds of stuff before it happens," West said. "Murders, bank robberies, plane crashes, assassinations. TWA 800?" West said. "I knew about that one. The plane that crashed into the Potomac River? I knew about that. The assassination of that guy over in Israel a number of years ago? All of it, I know. I know it is going to happen.

"This thing that happened in New York, September eleventh? I knew that," she said.

"But the problem is, you can't help the police with this stuff, because you can never trust the police."

15

In 1971, Brookey Lee West graduated from Santa Clara High School in San Jose and decided it was finally time to get away from her nutty mother, her devil-worshipping father and her high school dropout brother. But with less than average grades in high school and no plans for college, West had few career options in front of her, so she joined the army.

"I signed up for military intelligence," West said. "I wanted to be a spy. I thought I'd make a good spy, and what got me on that track was my dad. He loved war stuff and cop stuff on television, and basically to have any kind of relationship with him, I'd watch these shows with him. So I would watch combat shows, shows like *Secret Agent Man*, with my dad. I had all these visions of glory in the army, and I was going to do all this interesting stuff."

West enlisted in San Jose, was shipped out to basic training and then was stationed at the now closed Fort McClellan in Alabama. It didn't take long for West to realize that military life was not the glamorous existence depicted in the television shows. "All the restrictions were stupid to me," West said. "It didn't have the sophistication I thought it would, and I like to do my own thinking. I was like, 'Why do I need to follow what everybody else thinks?' But that is the way they do it, the military, the government, the FBI, the CIA," West said. "So when I really found out the way it was, I said, 'I'm not doing this.' "

West was begging for a discharge from the army within nine months of her enlistment, and remarkably, the military agreed to cut West loose with an honorable discharge even though her only reason for wanting out was disillusionment. Broke, disappointed and without any post–high school education, West returned home to San Jose to live with her mother.

It was a depressing time for West. She took odd jobs as a waitress and a legal secretary, and at just twenty years old West was paying all the bills and taking care of all her unemployed mother's needs. Deep down inside, West was desperate to get away from Christine.

In 1973, West thought she found the perfect chance to escape in the form of a man named Ray Alcantar.* Alcantar was a parishioner at the Faith Temple church attended by West and her mother, and West soon came to believe Alcantar was the love of her life. "One night, I came home from church, and Ray asked me, 'Do you want to go out and have something to eat?' " West recalled. "So we went out, and we had something to eat, and we started going out."

Alcantar was a handsome, smooth-talking man who was three years older than West. He had dark skin, deep brown eyes and dark hair parted down the middle.

"He was good-looking, he was charming, so we dated for a while," West said. "We dated maybe six or seven months, and I was wild about him. I was in love with him. Completely gone."

Alcantar, however, didn't see the relationship that way. In a statement later given to California detectives investigating West, Alcantar said of the relationship, "I visited with her a few times, not a whole lot of times. Maybe seven times total, visiting and talking."

In 1973, West and Alcantar went on a weekend trip to Los Angeles and it was there, in the City of Angels, that the couple first made love. Within a few months of returning from Los Angeles, West started feeling ill, and a doctor confirmed she was pregnant.

Alcantar, according to West, wasn't excited about the news, and his disappointment crushed West's dreams of a storybook relationship with Alcantar.

"I just told him I was pregnant, straight up, and it was over the phone, because he called me to see how I was feeling," West said. "That's when he gave me this snotty-assed remark, saying, 'How do you know it's mine?' I'm naïve up to this point. I think I knew in my heart he was already out seeing other women on the side, but I really couldn't face that.

"As soon as I told him I was pregnant, he was gone," West said.

Abortion was not an option for West, and she knew she was going to have to tell Christine and Leroy she was pregnant. As expected, they were furious.

"My parents crucified me," West said. "They called me all kinds of names. Bitch, whore, slut, a tramp. 'Why don't you have an abortion?'" West quoted her father as saying. "'You don't need that baby. He doesn't love you.'"

West gave birth to a beautiful baby girl at O'Connor Catholic hospital in San Jose in 1974, and she named her blue-eyed daughter Susie Alcantar.* West loved her child, but when her daughter was born, she was not ready to be a mother. She was immature, emotionally unstable and suffering from extreme mood swings.

"I was having a nervous breakdown," West said. "I got to where I was having [mental] episodes, and I couldn't stand being around people. I couldn't do my job. I made a bunch of mistakes, I couldn't remember things and I was highly temperamental . . . it was getting to where I was out of control. I knew I was spinning down. I felt like I was going to crash."

West worked long hours as a legal secretary in a law office to support her daughter and her mother, and all the while West was struggling with the pressures of being a single mom. She worried about leaving her daughter alone at her apartment with Christine for hours on end. By the time Susie was four, West had had enough of motherhood, so she sent her little girl off to a boarding school in Arizona.

"To protect her, I sent her to school really so I could have someone take care of her," West said. "I was working two and three jobs, and I wanted her to have a good environment. The teachers at this school took good care of her. It cost me a lot of money to put her in private school. It was a hard decision, but I was never emotional like a lot of people are over their kids," West said. "I look at things over the long range."

With West's decision to send Susie off to private school out of state, history was repeating itself. Nearly two decades earlier, Leroy had dropped West and her brother off at an orphanage in Bakersfield. Now the same thing was happening to West's daughter.

"I went down for her communion, but I didn't have a lot of time or money," West said. "She would come home on holidays. I'd make airline reservations, and she'd fly by herself. She was in school about five years."

By the time Susie was nine, West had no plans to bring her daughter home from private school. Instead, she decided she was going to give Susie to her teachers at the private school. Suffering from increased mood swings and mental instability at the time, West said she did not think she would be a good parent for Susie.

"They [Susie's teachers] were good people," West said. "They had two teenage children, they had a younger daughter and they wanted her. It was the best thing for my daughter because it was a stable environment. She was not used to living with me, and my environment was not stable."

There was one problem, though, with West's plan to give Susie away. Susie's father, Ray Alcantar, still had parental rights to the child, so West approached Alcantar and asked him to relinquish his parental rights.

He refused.

"I asked him to sign the papers, and he goes, 'No, I won't sign that,'" West said. "And I thought, 'Well, okay, don't sign it.' He didn't understand I didn't need his signature. I got this lawyer who knew the law about adoptions."

West initiated legal proceedings in the San Jose courts to terminate Alcantar's parental rights to Susie.

Alcantar, meanwhile, offered a different account of his confrontation with West over Susie's fate. He said in a statement to police that he was mortified at the idea of Susie being sent away to a private school in Arizona, and he was even more shocked at West's intentions to give away their daughter. He told West he would never sign any papers relinquishing his parental rights to Susie.

"She was wanting me to sign over legal guardianship papers to her, [so] that she would be able to put her up for adoption," Alcantar said. "She wanted me to be in agreement with it. I didn't agree with it . . . I said I would adopt her."

It was a decision that infuriated West, and it enraged West's father, too. No Mexican was going to tell Leroy Smith's daughter what she could or couldn't do.

"I wanted to have custody of my daughter, full custody," Alcantar said. "It was not up for conversation with them. It wasn't in their heads."

16

Ray Alcantar's decision to maintain parental rights to his daughter, Susie, infuriated Brookey Lee West and her father in 1984. Weeks later, on the night of January 14, 1985, a man paid a visit to the home of Alcantar's eighty-six-year-old grandmother, Juanita Alcantar, in Sunnyvale, California. The man knocked on the door of Juanita's residence, and when the elderly woman emerged onto her front porch, she was confronted by a man dressed completely in black.

"Is Ray here?" the man asked.

"No," Juanita Alcantar responded.

The man lifted his arm, pointed a handgun at Juanita Alcantar's chest and pulled the trigger at point-blank range. A bullet from a .22-caliber handgun pierced the elderly woman's torso, knocking her backward. She regained her footing and stumbled inside the home to a nearby bed, where she collapsed in a pool of blood. Juanita Alcantar's daughter happened to be inside the house and called 911 while comforting her gravely wounded mother. Juanita Alcantar was rushed by ambulance to nearby

Kaiser Hospital in Sunnyvale, and remarkably, her life was saved during surgery.

Sunnyvale police immediately kicked off an extensive investigation to identify the gunman, but from the beginning of the case, police had little evidence to work with. According to police reports, a witness got a brief glimpse of the gunman fleeing in a light-colored foreign car. A forensic examination of the crime scene turned up no fingerprints on the front door of Juanita Alcantar's residence, and one of the few physical clues available was a faint tire impression left on the side of the road by the gunman's vehicle.

There was not even a shell casing at the scene. It was as if the gunman knew to retrieve the shell casing in order to eliminate any evidence.

The gunman was described as a thin, white male, possibly in his thirties, and he may have had a mustache. One account given to the police indicated the gunman may have been wearing a Halloween mask. He spoke in Spanish, but it was clear that Spanish was not his native language.

Juanita Alcantar, described as senile by one family member, wasn't much help to detectives, either. She could never identify her attacker, and her version of the shooting changed over time.

Ray Alcantar was devastated by his grandmother's shooting, and his pain was only exacerbated a month later when he received a letter in the mail that scared the living hell right out of him. The letter arrived in the mail at his home on the 100 block of Browning Way in Vallejo, California, on February 13. The letter was in an envelope with no return address, and it was postmarked the day before in Vallejo.

The letter consisted of a single piece of paper adorned with a handwritten pentagram and a series of Satanic chants predicting the murder of his entire family.

"Satanic chants and curses . . . the letter was a threat,

[a] threat, you know, to kill me and my family," Ray Alcantar told the police.

You pray to your God, I'll pray to mine. We'll see whose God is stronger.

There was little doubt in Ray Alcantar's mind as to who sent the letter. Ray Alcantar told police when he dated West briefly in the 1970s, West talked as if she had intimate knowledge of the occult.

"She would speak of different demons, that they would attack people and afflict them physically," Ray Alcantar said. "She had a knowledge of that kind of thing, you know, things I've never heard anybody else talk about."

Ray Alcantar also told police West's father was a follower of Satan, and Leroy Smith was the only person he knew who was capable of sending such a letter.

"She had said that her father was a warlock, or you know, something like that, in the religion," Ray Alcantar said. "I didn't feel like they were the kind of gang that I wanted to hang out with." Ray Alcantar and his wife turned the letter over to authorities investigating his grandmother's shooting. The letter was processed for fingerprints, according to police reports, but produced no results.

After the shooting of his grandmother and his receiving the letter, Ray Alcantar was shaken to the core with fear. He abandoned his attempts to keep his daughter, and the little girl was adopted by her teachers in Arizona within the year.

"After that, I never tried to get in touch with them. Never," Alcantar said.

The shooting of Juanita Alcantar remains unsolved to this day.

17

By the early 1980s, Christine Smith was a lonely, fifty-year-old woman hungry for a man's tender touch. Leroy was no longer in the picture following the couple's divorce, and for Christine, having a big, strong man around to satisfy her physical needs was an absolute necessity.

Christine's loneliness caused her to make several romantic overtures to strange men. One man who came over to fix an appliance at the house that Christine shared with her daughter was suddenly subjected to not-so-subtle hints that Christine was yearning for a man's company.

"I came home from work, and my mom said, 'There was a real good-looking man who came out here today,' so she started in on him," West said, quoting her mother. " 'You know, if you are not married . . .' "

But time and again, Christine's efforts were rebuffed by members of the opposite sex, who saw her as strange and, sometimes, downright creepy. Christine eventually started to focus on her chiropractor, David Hobson.* Hobson was a divorced professional with children, and Christine regularly visited his office for what she said were numerous back ailments. After a few visits, Christine was enamored with her chiropractor, and she made it clear to Hobson that he could have her if he wanted.

"He was not interested in my mother, but in my mother's mind he was," West said. "She wanted him because he was successful, and he had money."

Hobson's lack of a romantic interest in Christine didn't deter Christine, and she literally believed she could make Hobson love her. She started going to the chiropractor's office more and more often, and Christine was interpreting every hello and good-bye from Hobson as covert overtures that he wanted to have sex with her.

" 'I know he loves me, and pretty soon he's going to ask me to marry him,' " West said, quoting her mother.

Christine was so hot for Hobson, she decided to make a pornographic audio cassette tape of herself masturbating, and she planned to give the tape to the doctor. On the tape, Christine can be heard moaning and groaning as she fondles herself, and in between her sounds of orgasmic ecstasy Christine narrates her love for Hobson in a slow, sultry Texas drawl.

You [Hobson] are probably gone to your son's [house] by now. I hope you enjoyed yourself. I hope you caught lots of fish. You sounded quite tired, Doc, on the phone. I know you really needed to get away, and to be more rested when you come back.

Oh! Doc! Ohhh. God. Come on. Fuck me. I love the way you make love to me. Oh! Baby! Oh! Oh, God. Oh! Ohhh! Come on. [Panting] Ohh! Ohhh! Ohhhhhh! Oh! Oh! Oh! Oh! Oh, God! Ohhhh! [Heavy breathing]

Oh! [Heavy breathing] Oh, God! Ohhh! Call me a bitch! Ohhh! [Heavy breathing]

Christine's sex tape seems to offer a rare insight into her twisted mind. Hobson has no interest in her, yet Christine talks as if they are in a consensual, passionate relationship. She actually sounds like she is fucking the doctor on the tape.

Baby, I'm laying here just thinking about you. You know you just drive me crazy. Had breakfast with you. Then you took us over to the office. Ohhh, God. I wanted you so bad! I don't think you realize how much I love you. I want your body. Do you know, Doc, that's a form of love, too, when a woman wants you, and desires you that much?

I've never felt this way toward no man in all my life until I met you. You kind of rubbed my ass in there, and then you come up. Ohh, God. Oh, my God, Doc. I wanted you!

I wanted to rub your legs. Oh, Doc, it's different with you and I. You know that. You know you want me. You know you want me. It is not a friendship with you and I. You don't [touch] your friend's ass. You don't accept porno tapes from them. Don't tell me you don't want to fuck me. You do. Ohhh, Doc. Don't wait. Don't let this fire inside of my belly die!

Christine, it seems, is in a delusional state. She is overcome by sexual fantasy and desire for a man who, in real life, has no interest in her.

Oh, I want you, oh, God, how I want you! I can hardly stand it. I'll get on you so bad. Oh, Doc, there's so many men who wish they could have a woman who wanted to love them like I want to love you. I desire you sexually. I love you as a person, as a man, as a doctor. I love you, period. I wish I could just say, 'Okay, I'll be your friend,' and just treat you like you do a friend, and walk away. Hello, every now and again, but, oh, Doc, I can't treat you like a friend. No, it has gone too far between you and I. I don't want to be treated like a friend. I want you to love me.

I want our love to be kept a secret, because I know it may touch your life. It would never be told. I would never tell. I would never cause you trouble.

A promise of secrecy. A sexual relationship that will never be revealed. Christine's lust for Hobson and her promise that no one will ever know sound familiar, of course, when compared to the tryst Christine had with her married lover, David Gilmore, in Bakersfield. Christine will do whatever it takes to get her man, even if it means blasting him with a shotgun and then going to prison.

Oh, I just want you to put your cock in my belly! I want you to fuck me! I want you to make me feel good! I want you to make me holler. I'm fixin' to do it in a few minutes. I start thinking of you, and I rub my ass . . . and I just climaxed all over the place. Don't take much from you to pop my nuts. Ohhh, my baby! Ohhh, Doc! Don't give up a wonderful love because of some man-written ideal, that if you are a doctor, you can't touch your patient. They do all the time. [Heavy breathing] So what. I want to love you, and that's all I want.

I don't want your money, I don't want nothing else. Just to love you, and have you fuck the hell out of me. Oh, God, Doc. You just have the wildest imagination. Oh, I want to get all over you, and just suck you good. You know, you need to be sucked. Fucked and sucked. Oh, baby. Oh, damn, when you get around me, I just can't take it. I get so hot. Just pretend that you're not a doctor and I'm not your patient. I'll love the hell out of you.

Did you know there was a man who wanted to climb Mount Kilimanjaro? He saved his money all his life, and by the time he got to the mountain, the guy there told him he couldn't because he was too old. Well, Doc, don't wait until you are too old to love me. Don't wait until you don't have a home run left in your lovely legs down there. There has to be a place you would meet me. A place where we could be together. Oh, Doc, don't take this away from me. I've never wanted a man like I wanted you. I've never been loved by no one in my whole life. Oh, Doc. Please, love me. I beg you to love me. I'm so hot, and there is so much desire and passion for a man.

Ohhh. Ohhh. [Heavy breathing] Ohhh. Ohhh. Ohhh. Ohhh. Ohhh. Ohhh. Love you. Fuck me. Oh, God Ohhhh. [Heavy breathing] Ohhhh! Ohhhh! Ohhhh! Baby! [Heavy breathing] Baby. Oh.

What can be heard next on the tape is truly bizarre. On the tape, Christine interrupts her orgasmic sex sessions to record a twenty-minute television sermon proffered by an unidentified televangelist. The televangelist is an African American man, and he was apparently recorded off Christine's television set. The unidentified preacher is heard screaming at the top of his lungs as he praises God during a Fourth of July celebration.

For 210 years, we have been led by the inspiration of the Constitution of the United States. It is the only document existing in the world today that has gone 210 years that a revolution has not substituted. We have amended it, but we have not destroyed it, because God started it, and God's going to end it.

We've got our share of sinners, but we've even got them under God. We have our agnostics, but we are working on them. They are beginning to believe. For no man can look at a black cow who eats green grass and gives white milk and churns yellow butter, and not know, there is a God somewhere. [Crowd applauds, yells Amen]

Christine's taping of the preacher's religious rantings in the middle of her sexual fantasy tape is, by all accounts, strange. But those who knew Christine—including her own daughter—could hardly have been surprised she mixed sex with God in her private life.

Christine, West said, was a woman obsessed with religious imagery, and even though she was a sinner, she talked about Jesus regularly. Taping herself masturbating, then splicing it with a preacher's sermon, seems to offer prolific insight into the twisted workings of Christine's mind and her maddening, grandiose obsessions in life.

We've made progress. We have a nation. We've got Chicago. We've got New York. We have Miami. We've got Los Angeles. We've got San Francisco. We've got Orange County. We are a nation. We have an army, we have a navy, we have all kinds of military preparedness. But thank God, we have steeples on almost every block, calling on the name of the Lord, Jesus Christ.

God bless you, America. You are just a little baby. I'm going to give you time to grow up. I may not be here, but when you get a little bit older, you will perfect your vision. One nation, under God, indivisible, with liberty and justice for all. You are going to do it! You are going to do it! You are going to do it! And I'm going to help you do it! I'm going to pray for you. And I'm going to ask God, God bless America! [Crowd cheers]

Christine's voice then returns to the tape, and she begins to talk to her doctor again as if he was with her. She explains to Hobson how the preacher is a favorite of hers, and she resumes her sex-crazed fantasy for the doctor.

Hello there. It's me again. I hope you enjoyed what he had to say. I like his teaching, I like his preaching. I hear him every once in a while on TV. He speaks a lot of truth. He don't butter everything up. He puts it out like it really is. That's why I like to hear him. He's a great big, heavyset, fat black man. He's really a minister, and one of the few that don't beat around the bush. He tells it like it is. Well, baby, it's getting late. I'll sign you off. I'll talk to you, maybe about three o'clock in the morning. I really feel that way.

Christine wants to fuck this man, and she wants to fuck him hard—even if it is all in her mind.

Ohhh, I sure do. I'll get you at about three o'clock in the morning. I'll just come right into your bed, and you won't even know it. Just start loving you. Ohhh, I'll just get all over you. It's so much fun, because you can't stop me in my mind. Ohhh, sweet thing. I could just stick my tongue in your mouth and suck your tongue. Oh, God. Just suck your cock. Oh, you are so sweet. You are sweet all over. I'll just kiss you, love the hell out of you. You are so sweet, so wonderful. I just want to feel that hair on your chest, stick my tongue in your little navel hole. Suck your little balls. Just tongue and love the hell out of you.

Oh, please don't keep turning away from me. Don't cheat yourself. All you have to say is, 'I'm going to make love to you.' Do it! You don't have to make it so damned complicated. We'll do it however you want to do it, wherever you want to do it. I know, you probably think I'm being pushy again. I don't mean to be pushy, I just want you so bad. I've never had a burning desire to want anybody in my whole life like I've wanted you. I want to start munching on you. Kiss those sweet ears. You have the sweetest little mouth. I just want to search down in there and find that tongue. We can get away, and you can take me somewhere.

Oh, Doc. Think about it. Just think about it. I just want

you so bad. You think about it. Oh, my baby, sleep tight. I want you so bad.

End of tape.

Christine never gave the tape to Hobson. Before she could, her dreams of a romance with the chiropractor were crushed when his secretary informed Christine that Hobson was in love with another woman.

Christine was fuming over the slight, even though her relationship with Hobson had been a figment of her imagination.

"My mother came out of his office and she was as white as a ghost," West said. "She was shaking, and she said, 'Take me home.' We get home and I said, 'What happened? Did they hurt you?' She goes, 'No, that son of a bitch is leading me on. That damned doctor, he loves me, and he's been advancing toward me, putting his arm around me, and I know he loves me, and that son of a bitch has another woman.' "

West was stunned.

"I was looking at her, like, 'Mom!' " West said. "It was in her mind, but she believed it. She said, 'I'm going to get me a gun, and I'm going to shoot that son of a bitch, just like I shot that other one.' "

But unlike the revenge Christine exacted on David Gilmore, Christine never followed through on her promise to shoot her chiropractor.

That's because West wouldn't let her.

"She wanted me to get her a gun, and I said no," West recalled. "I never would have no guns around her, because she meant it. I said, 'No, I won't let you do that. If I know about it, it's not going to happen. He didn't do anything to you.' "

18

In late 1975, Chloe Smith was a woman in desperate need of money. The twice-divorced thirty-four-year-old was working as an accounts payable clerk in San Jose, and the few hundred dollars a month she was making was hardly enough to support herself. As a result, Chloe started looking for a second job, and she found one slinging beers at a hole-in-the-wall tavern near Santa Clara University.

"I had a friend who was a bartender, and she knew somebody who had just taken over a little beer bar down by the San Jose bus depot," Chloe Smith said. "This guy needed a barmaid part-time, and I was like, what the hell? It's money. I can do that."

At first glance, Chloe Smith doesn't seem the type to sling beers at a juke joint. A soft-spoken woman with a diminutive figure and short, grayish hair cut at the neckline, she is quiet and extremely polite, making her seem more like a librarian, than a cocktail waitress.

But Chloe Smith needed the money, so she took the job, and it was a decision that changed her life forever. Within a few weeks of starting work a patron of the bar, Leroy

Smith, was courting her, and within two years Chloe and Leroy married.

"It was not love at first sight," Chloe Smith said. "I was very much not interested in getting involved again at all."

Despite Chloe Smith's resistance to Leroy's advances, he was persistent in his attempts to get to know Chloe, and over time, she recognized there was something about Leroy that made him different from the rest of the men in her life. He glowed with affection for her, and his fondness made Chloe Smith feel special. She realized Leroy genuinely cared for her, and during a slow-moving two-year courtship, Leroy convinced Chloe Smith to believe in his love.

"He was wonderful," Chloe Smith said. "He was very loving to me. In fact, that is what finally attracted me to him. Very affectionate, very protective. Just a feeling he gave me."

Leroy's affection was a much-needed boost for Chloe Smith given her prior struggles in life. Chloe was born in Massachusetts to an alcoholic father who moved Chloe and her three siblings to rural, middle-of-nowhere Arizona when she was a little girl, in the 1940s.

"We lived in a place called Apache Junction when there was nobody there but the Apaches, the junction and me," Chloe said. "It was pretty desolate and pretty awful. The nearest neighbor was several miles away, and my dad was somewhat reclusive. My sister and two brothers and I had to take the bus into school, and it was like an hour ride to Mesa, and an hour back," she said. "We were the last ones on and the last ones off the bus. It was not fun, and I hated it.

"We had no television and no telephone in the house," she said. "Once school let out for summer, I never saw my friends until the fall. To this day, if you say 'Arizona' or 'cactus' to me, I shudder. I would never live there again, and I would never wish it on anybody."

Chloe Smith escaped Apache Junction by marrying her

high school sweetheart when she was just sixteen. She and her husband, a military man, jumped from state to state, and the marriage produced two beautiful children. But the relationship soon soured, and Chloe found herself a single woman. A second marriage followed on the rebound, and after that relationship failed as well, her children, ages thirteen and fourteen went to live with Chloe's first husband in Texas.

With Leroy, Chloe Smith was holding out hope that things would be different. The two married in 1977, and the couple rented a small house on Lawrence Street in San Jose. Chloe called Leroy by his last name, Smith, and he in turn called her by her middle name, Jean. Leroy, the mustachioed, sturdy-framed carpet layer with a turbulent history, seemed to thrive on Chloe's stability, and Chloe grasped on to Leroy's unconditional love. But, without question, Leroy brought a great deal of baggage into the relationship. Chloe Smith knew Leroy had a history with women and that he had been a womanizer throughout much of his life.

"He had a way of lighting up when a woman would walk in the room, and he was very attractive to women," Chloe said. "A woman would come up to him, and he'd just sparkle. I thought it was amusing. It didn't bother me, because I felt very secure about how he felt about me. But he just had a way of twinkling around the opposite sex."

Leroy was socially dysfunctional to an extreme. He was defensive in public, and he was rarely interested in talking to other people.

"He was very defensive, very hostile to guys probably," Chloe said. "It depended on the circumstances. If he were meeting you, and you were a friend of somebody, he would be polite, but he didn't have any friends. He could only be outgoing for very short periods. A very short attention span for being social. He didn't trust people."

During one particularly heated argument with Chloe, Leroy made mention of his mother's murder in Tennessee.

"We were arguing and he said, 'You are going to make me so mad that I'm going to do what my dad did. I'm going to chop your head off,'" Chloe said. "I was like, 'Okay.' It was something he never wanted to talk about."

There were other faults, too, such as his avowed racism and hatred of minorities.

"There was no one more racist than Smith," Chloe said.

And he was a recovering alcoholic who was routinely falling off the wagon.

"He was an alcoholic, and he had to fight it a lot," Chloe said. "He would fall off the wagon once in a while, but then he would fall off the wagon and he was like off for two weeks. But then he was back on the wagon, and he got it back together."

Leroy also kept a large stash of firearms in their residence. At any given time, there were usually about twenty guns in the house. Some guns were stored under the cushions of their couch. Others were stashed in the bedroom, and there was always one handgun on the nightstand. Leroy kept a firearm in the kitchen "just in case," she said.

"He certainly had plenty of guns, and he could be a hostile person . . . [and] I don't think he would have a fear of shooting people," she said.

When asked whether her husband was ever a follower of Satan, Chloe said her husband dabbled with multiple religions throughout their twenty-year marriage. She never saw Leroy involved in devil worship, but in retrospect she can remember two instances that hinted at the possibility her husband was once involved in Satanism. The first incident, in the 1980s, involved a Mexican couple who lived on Lawrence Street, just a few houses down from them. The neighbors had spent thousands of dollars landscaping their front yard, and after they were done they started parking their cars in front of Leroy's house so everyone on the street could have a full view of their prized new yard.

Leroy was pissed.

"He wrote them this awful, devil-threatening letter," Chloe Smith said. "They turned it over to the police, and the police came to the house."

Like the letter sent to Ray Alcantar, it threatened the neighbors and mentioned the powers of Satan. Chloe didn't learn of the letter until the Santa Clara deputies came knocking on her door. Dismayed and shocked, she confronted her husband after the officers left.

"What are you thinking? Are you insane? This is so stupid," she said to her husband.

Leroy's response was somewhat cavalier.

"He said they were Mexicans, and he figured they were real religious and just talking about the devil would scare them," she recalled. "That's what he told me."

The second incident unfolded when Leroy was given some furniture by his ex-wife, Christine, and his daughter, Brookey West. Chloe said Leroy was moving the furniture into his garage when she noticed Leroy placing a large, "grotesque" Halloween mask into a secret compartment he had built into a cabinet in his garage.

"It [the secret compartment] was open, and he was putting a mask of some sort in it," Chloe recalled. "All I know is, it was ugly. It was very dark. A very dark and grotesque face. I said, 'What in the world?' And he says, 'This isn't mine. This is Brooke's and her mother's. You never saw this. It has got to do with devil worship, and you don't want to get involved. I'm just sealing it up in this wall.' I was like, okay, and that's the only time I ever saw anything."

Chloe Smith didn't pursue the matter further, and despite these strange events, she loved Leroy, and he loved her. Leroy certainly had his faults, but he was still a good husband.

"He always made me feel loved," Chloe said.

Chloe said the best example of Leroy's love was demonstrated when she decided she needed to get a college education. Chloe is an especially intelligent woman and was tired of working dead-end jobs in the 1980s, so she headed back to school. Leroy offered his full support for her decision to get a degree in business.

"He was very supportive when I decided I needed to go back to school because I only had a high school education and I knew I wasn't going to get anywhere," Chloe said.

"He encouraged me to go to school, and I ended up actually getting a four-year college degree. He took over everything in the house while I was at school. I would come home [from school] and say, 'I'm tired. I can't take it anymore,' and he would say, 'The longer you put this off, the worse it is going to be. You're never going to go back,'" she recalled.

Leroy's treatment of Chloe Smith was the exact opposite of the way he treated his first wife. It was as if she had married a man far removed from the Leroy Smith of the 1960s in Bakersfield and the early 1970s in San Jose. If he was still active in the Satanic church, it was on a much more covert level. He was not drinking all the time, and to Chloe Smith, at least, he was a kind, considerate and compassionate man.

"He didn't like to talk about his prior life," Chloe said. "It was like it was another time, another place, another world."

But deep down inside, the old Leroy was really still around. It would take two decades of marriage for Chloe Smith to come to the conclusion that she never really knew her husband and that, in fact, Leroy Smith had a frightening side to him.

"I think he was two different people," Chloe said. "That wasn't the guy I knew."

* * *

Throughout Chloe Smith's marriage to Leroy, he always made sure his wife followed one very simple rule—under no circumstances was Chloe to associate with his ex-wife, Christine.

"They had been apart a lot of years and divorced a long time before I met him," Chloe said. "He told me she was crazy and that I didn't want to be around her."

Leroy also instilled in his wife the belief that his daughter, Brookey Lee West, was to be kept at a distance.

"I always thought it would have been very nice if we all could have gotten together. . . . I asked him, 'Why can't we get together on the holidays?' " Chloe recalled. "He would say, 'Nope. No, no. You are not going to get involved with them. They are crazy. You are not going to get involved with them . . . they are not very nice people.' "

In fact, Chloe didn't even meet West until approximately three years after she married Leroy.

"He knew she was coming over to the house, and he answered the door, and they just let it be known that I wasn't needed," Chloe said. "It didn't necessarily strike me as anything strange, because he had already told me he didn't want me around his family."

West visited her father's house from time to time, but she rarely spoke to his wife. When West would show up at the house, she went directly into her father's office and they closed the door to talk.

It was as if Chloe Smith wasn't even there.

"He didn't think it would be good for our relationship," Chloe said. "He just kind of explained that it would cause all kinds of problems for us."

There was one person in Leroy's family, however, with whom Chloe did have some contact during her marriage, and that person was Leroy's son, Travis. A towering figure with long, bushy, black hair, Travis was hopelessly addicted to drugs, unable to hold a job and often homeless.

"I don' think he even graduated from the seventh grade," Chloe Smith said. "He started using drugs very young, and I think he burned himself out. He did poorly in school, and I just don't think he was very smart. He didn't get it."

When Travis would show up at the Smith household, like his sister, he would go into Leroy's office, where his father would shut the door behind them. At first, Chloe Smith had only minimal interaction with Travis, but she did see a noticeable difference in the way Leroy treated his son compared to the way he treated his daughter. West, Leroy believed, could take care of herself, but Travis was in constant need of his help, prompting Leroy to do whatever he could to make his son's life easier. He bought Travis a truck, got him several jobs in the flooring industry and set up his son in one apartment after another. But Travis was too busy partying to maintain any semblance of a normal life, and Leroy was in misery as he watched his son's slow decline.

"He despaired for his son," Chloe Smith said. "He tried so hard to make things easier for his son, and he ended up only making things worse. Buying cars, giving him cars. An enabler. He didn't give to Brooke like he gave to his son. He made excuses for his son. He didn't for Brooke. My view is, he absolutely favored his son."

Out of concern for his son's future, Leroy even started his own flooring business in San Jose. He called the business Smith's Floor Covering, and he hoped to give the business to Travis one day. But just like all the other dreams Leroy had for his son's future, the idea of leaving a legacy for his son quickly evaporated.

"He hoped to start something for his son," Chloe said. "And his son told him, 'Dad, I have no interest in this at all.'"

Leroy disbanded the business within a few months of starting it.

"He was doing it for his son, and after six months it was real clear that his son didn't want any part of it," Chloe said. "He told his dad, 'I don't want to do this. It's too hard.' So Leroy said, 'Why am I doing this? Why am I killing myself?' So he just gave the business up, and he started doing security work."

Travis hit rock bottom by the early 1980s, when he was in his late twenties and early thirties. Completely overcome by drugs and alcohol, he lived on the streets. Any money he had he spent on drugs, and he survived by eating a meal a day at the local missions. It was a sad existence, likely due to a childhood of undisputed emotional pain. His mother was not affectionate and was in prison during his developmental years, and Travis likely questioned his own self-worth. To kill the pain and self-doubt, Travis turned to methamphetamines and the streets.

Police records show Travis was arrested at least ten times in seven years by the San Jose police and the Santa Clara County sheriff's office. Many of the offenses were drug related. Others consisted of arrest for public intoxication and for loitering by a homeless drug addict.

But two of Travis' arrests were particularly serious. In one instance, Travis was found incoherent and rambling in front of a low-rent motel. Delirious on drugs, he had taken a chair from his hotel room and set it on fire in front of the motel, prompting police to take him into custody on an arson charge.

In another instance, Travis attacked an ex-girlfriend in a methamphetamine-induced rage.

"My brother liked speed, meth, and he had some guns," West said. "He and a friend went over to this gal's house, and they broke in, and she was in bed with this other guy. So my brother strips them all down naked, and he goes in another room, and he gets this woman's little boy, and he brings him back in, and he says, 'Now you see what a whore your mother is?' "

A neighbor heard the commotion and called 911, and Travis was arrested at the scene by Santa Clara County authorities.

"The cops tracked him down, but it took six cops to take him down," West said. "By the time he calms down in jail, his hand is broke, his nose is broke, and they were like, what do you expect? So he was going to go to prison for a long time."

But Travis's arrest record was so long and these two crimes so bizarre, he was examined by a state psychiatrist and diagnosed as being schizophrenic. A Santa Clara County judge deemed him criminally insane, and Travis was committed to the Atascadero State Hospital for the criminally insane in San Luis Obispo County. The hospital houses some of the craziest, most dangerous people in the California criminal justice system, and a third of Atascadero's patients are some of California's most violent sexual predators.

Chloe Smith said Travis rarely received visitors at Atascadero. Leroy went to visit his son about once a month at the hospital, and at first Leroy wouldn't let Chloe go with him. But shortly before Christmas, she baked a huge batch of Christmas cookies for Leroy to take to Travis, and on this occasion Leroy invited her to go along with him.

"I went in, and I saw him, and he was this big huge guy," Chloe said. "He came across as a big guy with all this hair, but to me he just seemed like this big, harmless woolly bear."

Touched by Travis' fate, Chloe walked across the room, gave him the cookies and then gave him a big hug.

The response she got from Travis startled her.

"Do you know what he did?" Chloe Smith said. "He cried. It was like nobody had hugged him in God knows when. It was the saddest thing. It was just an automatic thing for me, and I was like, 'My God.' It was like I was the first person who had done anything nice for him."

The tears streaming down Travis's face were likely the result of a lifetime of emotional emptiness. His mother was a crazy bitch who had no need for him, yet his father's second wife—a woman who had no investment in Travis— took the time to bake him cookies and give him a hug.

"Maybe he never remembered even having a hug," Chloe said.

Travis was eventually released from the state mental health system, and he immediately went back to the streets. Every now and then, Travis would come by his father's house with a little gift for Chloe Smith.

"He brought me little presents, probably stolen from somewhere, but whatever," she said. "He knew I collected little [figurine] elephants, so he'd find elephants, and he'd bring me ones he found around in different places. I don't think he had a mean bone in his body. In fact, I think that is part of why his dad despaired so much. He didn't protect himself. He was just there. He was out on the streets, and people could take his money, people could take his drugs. He wasn't a hurting kind of person."

Leroy continued to try to help Travis after his release from Atascadero. But Travis had used so many drugs that he developed severe swelling in one of his legs and there was little hope he would ever work again, because of the condition. He was eventually deemed disabled by the state of California, and he started receiving monthly disability checks from the Social Security Administration. Leroy made sure his son had access to the money by getting the checks automatically deposited for Travis in an account at the Bank of Santa Clara in San Jose.

In the early 1990s, Leroy tried to help his son one last time. He sought his son out on the streets of downtown San

Jose, trying to see if he could convince Travis to come home. It ended up being an encounter that crushed any hope Leroy held of rescuing his boy. "[Leroy] told me the last time he saw his son, his son said, 'Dad, I don't want you coming down here anymore,'" Chloe Smith said, quoting Travis. "'I like living on the street. I've got lots of friends. When you come down here, you just bother me, you disturb me. I don't want you coming down here anymore. I want you to leave me alone.'"

Leroy's encounter with his homeless son may have been the last time anyone saw Travis Lee Smith alive.

19

They will steal anything, and call it [a] purchase.

—William Shakespeare, *Henry V*

On July 21, 1985, Brookey Lee West walked into the Nordstrom department store on Rio Vista Avenue in San Jose, and almost immediately store security took notice.

Security employee Ann Vallier watched as West picked up three black blouses and two gold ones from two circular clothes displays. West walked with the clothes into a fitting room, where she remained for a few minutes. When West emerged, she was carrying more clothing—one black blouse, one gold blouse, two plaid skirts, a vest and a pair of pants.

Vallier was at first confused, but she soon became convinced West was engaged in some sort of ruse. West was leaving the fitting room with items she didn't go in with, and two of the blouses she was originally carrying were missing.

Vallier stopped West with a security officer as West left the store, and Vallier suspected they were about to catch West with a blouse stashed underneath her clothing.

"She came back to the security office willfully, and in the security office I asked West if she would like to give back [the] Nordstrom merchandise, and she said yes," Vallier wrote in a statement for San Mateo police.

To Vallier's surprise, however, West didn't just have a blouse.

"In her purse, she had four blouses—two black, one rust colored, and one gold," Vallier wrote. "She also had in her possession one scarf and six necklaces. West [also] pulled two blouses out of her pants that she was wearing."

When asked by police why she took the items, West responded, "They were my size."

West was booked at the Santa Clara County detention center on two counts of felony grand theft. Court records show one charge was dismissed, and West pleaded guilty to a misdemeanor theft charge. She was ordered to pay a fine.

Three months later, West was at it again, and this time she was with her mother, Christine.

The mother and daughter strolled into the Emporium department store in a Palo Alto shopping mall on November 20, 1985. The two women started rummaging through a display of high-priced sweaters, causing store employee Jane Casas to take notice. Casas saw the two take four expensive sweaters into a fitting room, and when they exited, it appeared Christine was wearing one of the sweaters. Casas quickly checked the fitting room, and the three other sweaters she saw the women with were not there.

Casas called Emporium security, but officers were busy at the time responding to another theft incident. When the officers finally did meet with Casas, Smith and West were long gone, and the Emporium figured it had been swindled.

But the very next day, the thieves returned. Casas saw West and Christine walk through the front door of the store, and she called security immediately. She and officers watched from a distance as West grabbed a white-and-tan wool Evan-Picone sports coat off a hanger. Two security officers also saw West pick up two identical pairs of tan pants and a gray shirt from a nearby hanger. They watched West go into a fitting room, then emerge with only one pair of tan pants.

West browsed through the store some more, picked up a white sweater and returned to the fitting room again. She walked out of the fitting room carrying the sweater, and now she had a black purse and a red-handled shopping bag. The purse and the bag, officers believed, were smuggled into the store under West's clothing so she could then use them to carry the stolen items.

West found her mother inside the store, and they exchanged words before separating again. The security officers watched Christine go into a restroom and walk out; West then approached her mother again and handed her a purse. Christine then left the store.

It appeared to the officers the women were trying to carry out an elaborate game of deception in case anyone from the store was watching.

One security officer trailed Smith out of the Emporium to a nearby Macy's store, while another officer trailed West as she walked through the Emporium. Gradually, West made her way out of the store to Macy's, and she met up with her mother in the women's shoe department. Christine and West were on their way out of Macy's when the Emporium security officers stopped them and identified themselves.

"Go ahead, call the police!" West said loudly. "I have a receipt for everything in that bag!"

West was being difficult. She asked to use the restroom, but the security officers told her she would have to wait until police arrived. West started screaming and making a commotion so nearby customers would take notice.

"Do you want me to pee my pants! I have to use the restroom!"

West was allowed to use the restroom, and the two women were then escorted to the Emporium's security office. Inside West's bag, officers found the blazer, a skirt, two hangers and a used pair of pants.

"We then noticed that [Christine] was wearing a pair of pants that looked like the pants I had seen West with," security officer Joshua Cohen wrote in a report for Palo Alto police.

A search of West's purse revealed a pair of heavy-duty scissors with marks on them suggesting they had cut the metal fasteners off sensor tags from the store. Those sensor tags were subsequently found in a fitting room. Also in West's possession were a series of return-exchange receipts from various stores dated over the previous five days, but they had nothing to do with the clothes West and Christine were caught with at the Emporium.

A Palo Alto police officer arrived at the scene and separated the two women. He interviewed both, and each denied any wrongdoing. Christine and West each told identical stories—they were doing Christmas shopping. Yet the officers took notice of the fact that both were unemployed at the time but carried $500 in cash each.

The officer wrote in a report that West had a prior arrest history for theft. Christine's criminal history came up empty, but she was quick to correct any notion that she had no arrest record.

In fact, she started bragging to the officer about having once shot a man.

"She stated she had been arrested for attempted murder a long time ago," the officer wrote in his report.

Both women were transported to the Santa Clara County detention center and booked on charges of burglary and conspiracy. The mother-and-daughter theft team pleaded guilty to felony burglary charges, and each received thirty days in jail followed by two years of probation.

Brookey Lee West poses for a snapshot during interviews with the author at the Southern Nevada Women's Correctional Center in North Las Vegas. West is serving life in prison without the possibility of parole for the murder of her mother. *Photo by Ralph Fountain. Legal rights to photo owned by the author.*

Brookey Lee West talks with the author about the murder of her mother, Christine Smith. West claims her mother died a natural death, and was not murdered—a claim authorities say is implausible given the evidence in the case. *Photo by Ralph Fountain. Legal rights to photo owned by the author.*

LEFT: Brookey Lee West's husband, Howard Simon St. John, is pictured in this vacation snapshot. Weeks after marrying West, St. John was found shot to death and his corpse was dumped in rural Tulare County, California. *Photo courtesy of Wayne Ike.*

RIGHT: Daniel Haynes, formerly a homicide detective with the Tulare County Sheriff's Office, stands at the crime scene where Howard Simon St. John's body was found in the Sequoia National Forest. St. John, the husband of Brookey Lee West, was found murdered in Tulare County just weeks after surviving a domestic dispute with West in which he was shot in the neck. *Photo by the author.*

Brookey Lee West's brother, Travis Smith, is pictured in this Wanted poster issued by Las Vegas police. *Photo courtesy of the Las Vegas Police Department.*

Christine Smith is pictured as a young woman in Texas. *Photo courtesy of Billy Sands.*

Christine Smith was sixty-four when this photo was taken for a bus pass in Las Vegas. She was later found sealed in a garbage can in her daughter's storage shed. *Photo courtesy of the Clark County District Attorney's Office.*

The trash can containing Christine Smith's corpse is pictured at the Canyon Gate Mini-Storage shed, where Brookey Lee West stashed her mother's body in 1998. *Photo taken by Las Vegas police; courtesy of the Clark County District Attorney's Office.*

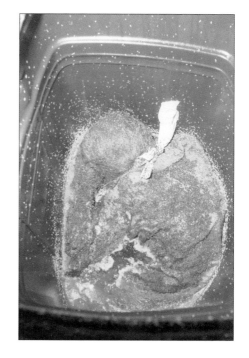

Christine Smith is pictured in death at the bottom of a trash can. On her body are insects that forensic scientists later used to show that Smith's murder was likely premeditated. *Photo courtesy of the Clark County District Attorney's Office.*

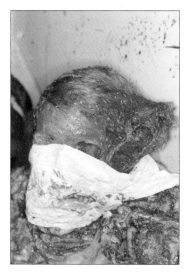

LEFT: Christine Smith's decomposed body had a plastic bag tied tightly over her face. Authorities believe the bag was likely a device used to hasten Smith's death after she was sealed in a garbage can. *Photo courtesy of the Clark County District Attorney's Office.*

RIGHT: Books found next to Christine Smith's remains in a storage shed are displayed in a Las Vegas police crime scene photo. The books include *The Satanic Bible* and *The Geography of Witchcraft*. *Photo courtesy of the Clark County District Attorney's Office.*

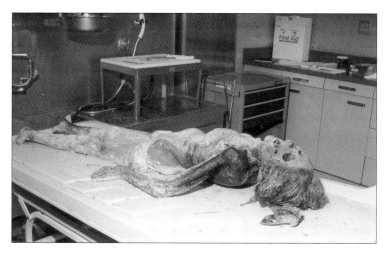

Christine Smith's decomposed body is displayed on a gurney at the Clark County coroner's office after the bag covering her face was removed. *Photo courtesy of the Clark County District Attorney's Office.*

Brookey Lee West's father, Leroy Smith, is pictured in this driver's license photo. *Photo obtained via an open records request.*

A skull that Brookey Lee West's father, Leroy Smith, likely wore around his neck during Satanic ceremonies is pictured along with its carrying pouch. *Photo by the author.*

Las Vegas homicide detective Dave Mesinar was the lead detective in the case against Brookey Lee West. Much of the evidence he gathered earned West a life sentence in prison. *Photo by the author.*

Clark County prosecutor Frank Coumou is pictured in his office. Coumou, along with prosecutor Scott Mitchell, secured Brookey Lee West's murder conviction. *Photo by the author.*

Clark County Deputy Public Defender Scott Coffee, who was Brookey Lee West's lead defense attorney. *Photo by the author.*

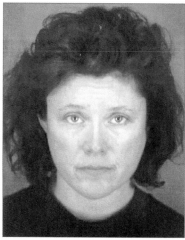

LEFT: Brookey Lee West is pictured in this grade school photo. *Photo courtesy of Billy Sands.*

RIGHT: Brookey Lee West is pictured in a Los Banos, California, mug shot. The photo was taken shortly after West shot her husband, Howard Simon St. John, in the neck. He survived the shooting, only to be found murdered weeks later. *Photo courtesy of the Los Banos Police Department.*

Brookey Lee West, a talented artist, stands next to a sketch she drew of Mona Lisa while incarcerated at the Southern Nevada Women's Correctional Center in North Las Vegas. *Photo by Ralph Fountain.*

HOWARD

20

Sequoia National Park and Forest is a magical stretch of wilderness located just west of the California-Nevada border. The 866,000-acre park features some of the state's most beautiful natural wonders, including the Kaweah and Tule Rivers, which bubble over rocky terrain and through thick woodlands as they flow south into Central California. There are dozens of rugged trails featuring spectacular, breathtaking views of the park's immense forest and snow-capped Mount Whitney, which, at 14,494 feet, is the tallest mountain in the lower forty-eight states.

But without question, the most amazing feature of Sequoia National Park is its grandiose sequoia trees. The sequoias are the largest living trees on the planet, and they grow only on the western slope of the park's forest. Many of the trees grow up to forty feet in diameter at their base, and one particular giant sequoia in the park, the General Sherman Tree, has an astonishing circumference of 103 feet at its base, making it the largest tree on the planet.

The beauty of the trees, the mountains, the rivers and forest-lined canyons draw visitors from around the world to a place that defines God's grace—a place of peace and serenity.

It is not the type of place you would expect to find a dead body.

On the morning of June 6, 1994, California outdoorsman Jerry Doyle was scouting out a potential fishing hole with his wife, Doris, when he pulled his three-quarter-ton 1975 Chevy pickup into the Lower Coffee Camp recreational area in Sequoia National Forest. It was 9:25 a.m., and it looked like a beautiful morning to try to land a rainbow or brown trout in a nearby fork of the Tule River.

Doyle got out of his truck, and within a few steps, he noticed what appeared to be a corpse stretched out on a sloping bank leading to the river.

"Immediately, upon spotting the body, Jerry turned to his wife and told her to get back in the vehicle, but he did not tell her why," an officer wrote in a Tulare County sheriff's office report. "Doris assumed that Jerry had possibly seen a rattlesnake."

Jerry Doyle rushed to a nearby park attendant, Michael McTighe, and told McTighe of the grisly discovery. McTighe then flagged down a passing California Department of Forestry van loaded with prison inmates, and a supervisor in the van called the authorities.

As they waited for the police to arrive, the Department of Forestry supervisor, Kevin Martin, and an inmate retrieved a blanket from the bus and covered the corpse.

The body was clearly that of a long-haired man, and his pants were halfway down his legs. A plastic bag partially covered the victim's face.

*   *   *

The investigation of the dead body at the Lower Coffee Camp recreational area was assigned to Detective Daniel Haynes of the Tulare County sheriff's office's violent crimes unit in Visalia, California.

"We were still in the office, drinking our first cup of coffee, when the call came in," Haynes said.

Haynes, forty-five, is a bulldog of a detective. A short, thin-framed man with brown hair and mustache, he is a native of Tulare County who was born in the nearby city of Exeter. His father supported the family with a job as a mechanic; his mom was a housewife.

Haynes said he never figured he would end up spending his entire professional life as a police officer, but as a young man working construction in Tulare County, he stumbled across a career in law enforcement. A friend convinced him he should take a law enforcement class at the community college in Visalia, and within weeks of starting the class, Haynes was hooked. He joined the police reserves in the small city of Wooklake, doing volunteer work to help the local cops while still keeping his forty-hour-a-week construction job to support his wife and two children.

"I never had any intentions whatsoever of being a full-time police officer," Haynes said. "But one night, I came home [the police department] called and they asked me to go talk to the chief. I did, and he offered me a job.

"The job provided benefits when I was raising my children," Haynes said. "That's not something you can usually get working in construction. Hindsight is 20/20, but thank God I did it."

Haynes was quickly promoted to sergeant, and when a coveted spot in the Tulare County sheriff's office opened up, he jumped at the chance. The sheriff's office is based in Visalia, a city of 92,000 that serves as the central hub of Tulare County. The county itself is home to some of the state's most productive farmlands and borders the Sequoia National Forest on three sides.

"It's just a nice, slower pace of life," Haynes said of life there. "It's an agricultural area that is not nearly as populated as other areas of the state."

Haynes was promoted to detective by the county in 1991, and in 1994 he was assigned to the violent crimes unit of the sheriff's office, the unit responsible for investigating all homicides in the county. On June 6, 1994, the dead body at Lower Coffee Camp officially became Haynes's case.

On that morning, Haynes and his fellow detectives in the violent crimes unit—Detective Greg Hilger and Sergeant John Zapalac—headed out to the Sequoia National Forest to begin their investigation. They drove west from Visalia in their Chevrolet Luminas, speeding down state Route 190 for a little more than an hour, passing through the tiny community of Springville before arriving at Lower Coffee Camp.

"Coffee Camp is a day-use recreational area, almost like a rest area," Haynes said. "It's on a two-lane, real winding, narrow road, with water on one side and mountains on the other. There are picnic tables on the edge of the water, there are restrooms, and that's about it."

Haynes is limited on what he can say about specific evidence he observed at the crime scene, but in a sheriff's office police report, Tulare County deputy Joe Teller memorialized his observations of the victim and his surroundings.

I observed the adult male victim to be lying on his back approximately 20 feet below the asphalt parking area. Victim was wearing a light green T-shirt and black jeans. Victim's pants were down almost to his knees, and his belt was still buckled. The pants appeared to be still zipped up and buttoned. Victim's underpants were pulled slightly down, but

not as far down as his pants. Victim had no shoes or socks.
Victim had a plastic bag covering his face.

To Haynes, it clearly looked like Coffee Camp was not the site of the murder.

"It wasn't a crime scene as much as it was a dump site," Haynes said. "It wasn't like we had extensive evidence lying around. It looked like someone had backed up [a vehicle] to the edge, and the body was pulled from a vehicle."

The detectives interviewed Jerry Doyle, his wife and any park workers familiar with the operations of the campsite. Witness statements were taken, and one witness, Michael Seymour, said he had helped pick up trash from the camp at five p.m. the prior day. He told the Tulare County investigators the body was not at the site at that time.

This information led Haynes and his fellow detectives to suspect the body was dumped by the killer or killers sometime overnight. It seemed plausible the killer or killers may have also been to the area before, because Coffee Camp is a remote place and is sparsely traveled at night.

"It's not a road that you would go up unless you had a reason to be up there," Haynes said. "It's very steep, very crooked. It is a highway, state Route 190, and it does lead into the park, but unless you were specifically going there as a tourist, you wouldn't be going up there."

While Detective Hilger and Sergeant Zapalac helped crime scene analysts process the crime scene, Haynes drove to a nearby trash collection area and started poking through the bags of trash collection at Lower Coffee Camp during the previous twenty-four hours. It was a smelly, stinky job, but it needed to be done in case the killer or killers carelessly discarded evidence in a public trash bin.

"I thought it sucked," Haynes said of the task. "But as they say, no job is perfect."

Haynes found nothing of value in the trash. Upon returning to the location of the body, Haynes, Hilger, Zapalac and crime scene analysts meticulously scrutinized every potential piece of evidence. They collected beer cans, paper debris and various pieces of clothing from the ground surrounding the corpse. It appeared the victim had been shot, but the detectives would rely on an autopsy for a formal cause of death.

"You don't take anything for granted," Haynes said. "I'm big on believing you don't take anything at face value. Wait until you get the big picture."

Of interest to the detectives was the plastic bag, according to police reports. The bag was partially on the victim's face, and detectives hoped the bag might have fingerprints on it. It was collected and processed for prints, but it turned up nothing, according to police documents.

Haynes said detectives had very little to work with at the crime scene. Their victim had no identification on him, and there were no obvious clues to immediately lead them to any suspects.

"We didn't know who he was and how he got there, but obviously the body didn't fall out of a plane," Haynes said. "He had to be hauled there in a vehicle, and that was really about all we had to go on."

But within a few hours, the detectives got a big boost. Zapalac rolled the victim's fingerprints at the crime scene, then returned to the sheriff's office in Visalia to enter the prints into California's computerized fingerprint identification system. Within hours, the victim's prints were matched to a Native American man named Howard Simon St. John.

St. John was from San Jose, which is about a five-hour drive northwest of the Sequoia National Forest and Tulare County. The detectives wondered what St. John was doing so far away from home.

The fact that their victim was a Native American, however, did offer one possible explanation. Just a few miles away from Lower Coffee Camp is the Tule Indian Reservation, and the detectives speculated St. John might have some connection to the reservation.

"We have an Indian male, and a reservation is on the other side of the ridge, so obviously it's something to think about," Haynes said.

Over the course of the next day, Haynes gathered more details about St. John. He was thirty-five years old, five feet ten inches tall and weighed 230 pounds. He had brown eyes and black hair, and an autopsy showed he had been shot in the back with a .38-caliber handgun.

Curiously, St. John also had a .32-caliber bullet in his neck, and the autopsy indicated the .32-caliber bullet was from a shooting prior to the one that killed him.

Haynes learned through background checks that St. John was a former parolee whose arrest record showed apprehensions for approximately fifteen misdemeanor arrests. The crimes included drunken driving, public drunkenness and drugs. St. John had only one felony—a drug charge. The background checks showed St. John had eight different aliases.

Haynes contacted St. John's parole officer, Richard Toledo, in San Jose, and the detective learned St. John was not a native of the Tule Indian Reservation. In fact, St. John was a Sioux Indian who hailed from South Dakota. As far as the parole officer knew, St. John's father, Sylvester, still lived on the reservation in South Dakota.

"We contacted the sheriff in South Dakota where he lived, and they tracked down the father on the reservation, and they got a number for me," Haynes said.

Haynes called Sylvester St. John to find out as much as he could about his victim. Haynes said it was immediately apparent Sylvester St. John had a distant relationship with his son. Sylvester St. John told Haynes that Howard had struggled with alcohol and had at times lived in a rehabilitation center for alcoholics in San Jose.

Sylvester St. John also told the detective that his son was married to a woman who lived in Los Banos, and the couple had an apparent history of domestic violence.

Howard's wife was Brookey Lee West.

21

No power on earth or above the bottomless pit has such influence to terrorize and make cowards of men as the liquor power. Satan could not have fallen on a more potent instrument with which to thrall the world.

—Eliza Stewart, temperance advocate, 1888

Tyla Knotchapone attended Alcoholics Anonymous meetings at the Native American Indian Center in downtown San Jose in 1992 because they allowed her to enjoy life again. No more partying in Knotchapone's life—just clean, day-to-day living that allowed Knotchapone to cherish the clarity that comes with being clean and sober.

At the meetings, Knotchapone made several friends. One was a man named Howard Simon St. John, a full-blooded Sioux Indian from South Dakota. Quiet and shy, he was also a man whose noble heritage had been ravaged by substance abuse. St. John had a huge beer belly, at times looked dirty and had rotted teeth. But Knotchapone said she could see behind St. John's weathered exterior, and to her there was a kindhearted, soft-spoken man inside who needed a little sobriety to shine.

"I was close with Howard," Knotchapone said. "I used to laugh with Howard. I used to cry with Howard, and we enjoyed our friendship."

Knotchapone, a Zuni Pueblo from New Mexico, said
she bonded with St. John immediately. They enjoyed discussing their heritage and often attended powwows together throughout the Northern California region.

Knotchapone and St. John also had another thing in
common—they were both recovering alcoholics, and
throughout their relationship St. John sought out
Knotchapone for advice and counseling. But St. John was
consumed by the bottle, and despite repeated attempts to
quit, booze had ruined him by early 1992.

"He was very honest about it," Knotchapone said. "He
would say, 'I have no excuse for drinking, for doing this to
myself, but yet I find myself doing it.' He was the kind of
guy who was very honest about his faults."

St. John was born in Redwood City, California, on May
15, 1958, to Sylvester and Katherine St. John. The second
oldest of seven children, Howard was born into one of the
most prestigious Native American tribes, the South Dakota
Sioux. The Sioux ruled the plains of North America for
hundreds of years, and their most famous leaders, Crazy
Horse and Sitting Bull, were known for their courage,
bravery and fighting skills.

After Howard's birth in California, the St. John family
moved back to an Indian reservation in South Dakota, and
Howard spent much of his early life growing up on the
reservation. It was there, in the 1970s, that tragedy struck
the St. John family when one of his brothers, Michael, was
killed in a car accident. His cousin Elmer "Sonny" St. John
told police Michael was killed when he slipped and fell underneath his friend's car in the driveway of his home following a night of drinking.

"He was drinking with them, I guess, and they took him
home to drop him off, and he didn't want to stay there,"
Sonny St. John said in a taped statement. "So when they

went to drive off, he [Michael] was arguing with them, I guess, and he hung on to the car. He slipped under the car."

Michael St. John was crushed by the weight of the vehicle, and his death was devastating for Howard. But the loss of his brother wasn't the only event that left him scarred emotionally.

Friends said he had a disastrous relationship with his own father, Sylvester. When Howard was a young man, he badly beat his father during a domestic dispute. Such violence and disrespect to the family's paternal figure was not tolerated on the reservation, and Howard was ostracized from the family.

"He beat up his dad pretty bad, and he sent him to the hospital," Sonny St. John said. "I guess it was the drinking and stuff like that. He didn't get along with my cousins back there [in South Dakota] and they told me they didn't get along with him, so I didn't have much to do with him, either."

By the 1970s, St. John's family left the reservation and moved back to California. They settled in the tree-lined, lower-middle-class neighborhood of Northwood Park in San Jose. One of their neighbors, Thomas Gutierrez, who is now a forty-two-year-old cement mason and father of three in San Jose, said he became close childhood friends with St. John while growing up in the neighborhood.

"I used to play with my cousins, and Howard lived next door," Gutierrez said. "We all played baseball, football in the street, what have you. Howard loved playing sports and stuff. He was a nice, average kid, and he was a good person."

Gutierrez said the St. Johns were nice people as well, but Howard and his brothers had a reputation for partying in their neighborhood. By the age of sixteen, Howard was drinking regularly.

"He started [partying] young, and it got out of control," Gutierrez said. "I don't think he had a proper upbringing to where he was told, 'Hey, these are the things you do, these are the things you don't.'"

St. John dropped out of Piedmont High School in San Jose during his sophomore year, and when his family decided to move back to South Dakota, Howard stayed behind.

"There was [another] incident with his parents," Gutierrez said. "They threw him out. They didn't want him back, and he sort of got abandoned. He just started living on his own."

With his family now thousands of miles away in South Dakota, St. John lived with neighbors and family friends as a teenager.

"He was sleeping in his car, sleeping at friends' houses and partying," Gutierrez said. "That was his lifestyle from that point on. He would wait for his friends to come out of school, and when they did, he'd say, 'Lets go get some beer now.'"

St. John did, however, have one true passion in life. He was fascinated by cars. He spent countless hours working on vehicles, tweaking them to run as fast as possible, and some of his best times in life were spent running his souped-up cars through the rural countryside of Northern and Central California with another friend, Tony Mercado.

"One time, Howard and I went to a powwow in Sacramento right after high school," Mercado said. "He had an old Dodge, a former police car, and he had this car all pumped up. It usually takes an hour and a half to get from Sacramento to San Jose, and we made it in like forty minutes. We were going like a hundred something miles per hour."

Mercado, an expert mechanic, said he and St. John worked on vehicles in front of Mercado's home on Postwood Avenue in San Jose almost every day. Mercado imparted his wisdom about cars to his friend, and the two gained a reputation in the neighborhood as quality mechanics.

The experience led St. John to dream of a career as a mechanic.

"He was a good mechanic, a good helper and a good handyman when we worked on cars," Mercado said. "He never said no when I would tell him to go get parts. We were partners, and we were making good money at the time."

But slowly, St. John's boozing became more important than work. His alcohol consumption was completely reckless, and St. John was starting to experiment with cocaine as well. By his mid-twenties. St. John drank himself into unconsciousness almost daily, and those who saw him drink were amazed at the amount of alcohol he consumed during his binge drinking.

"He would take a bottle of tequila, and he would down it," Gutierrez said.

"He could hold a lot of liquor," said Gutierrez's wife, Dana. "It was unbelievable."

St. John was living on the streets by his late twenties because of his alcohol abuse. His teeth were rotted, and his beer belly protruded more than a foot over his waistline. He was often unkempt, and friends said he was at the bottom of the human barrel when he turned thirty, in 1988. His drunkenness resulted in multiple arrests for public intoxication, robbery, assault and battery, and drunk driving, and a felony conviction resulted in a sentence of probation. In a report crafted by his probation officer, St. John confided in the officer his grave concerns over his drinking.

"[Howard] believes [his drinking] is a problem," the officer wrote. "[He] consumes three to four bottles of hard liquor per week; five cases of beer per week. Drug usage includes peyote during Indian ceremonies only. Cocaine began in 1983. Occasional use. No marks on arms."

During some of St. John's binges, he would walk the streets of San Jose for hours on end or hang out in city parks to pass the time while the alcohol wore off.

"I think in his early twenties it was more beer and drugs, and by his late twenties and early thirties he started drinking more and more liquor," Thomas Gutierrez said. "Alcohol was his problem. It was eating up his liver, and he'd get in fights, he'd get beat up, or he used to get rolled. He would get rolled a lot on the streets. He would pass right out, and people would take his money. He'd be walking downtown, and he would just pass out against a building or something."

Watching St. John's decline was an extremely sad affair for Gutierrez and his wife, Dana. The couple liked St. John, and they allowed him to visit their home regularly despite his troubles, because they recognized St. John was a decent man suffering from a terrible disease.

"He was never violent," Dana Gutierrez said. "He was actually a very good guy. I would never have someone around my children who I felt fear from. He liked our kids, and if you needed something, he'd do it for you. He helped work on our car, and he'd do whatever you asked him to do. Never, at any given time, would you feel fear from him."

By the mid-1980s, St. John's life was in shambles, and he recognized he needed help to overcome his addiction. He started frequenting the Native American Indian Center on Rhodes Court in San Jose, and he enrolled in an alcohol rehabilitation program at the center called the Four Winds program, which specifically helped Native Americans recover from substance abuse. As part of the program, St. John moved into a house adjacent to the center, at 109 Rhodes Court in San Jose, where he lived with eight other recovering alcoholics. The home was the end of the line for the men—it was either quit drinking and stay at the house, or go back to the bottle and live life on the streets.

"He cleaned himself up, so he was trying," Thomas Gutierrez said. "He was saying, 'Okay, I'm on the right path now.'"

Part of his enrollment in the Four Winds program required St. John to attend the AA meetings, and while attending them, he met Knotchapone. Knotchapone said that during their first meeting, St. John volunteered to fix her car for free.

"I had this little old sports car, and sometimes I needed a tune-up, a tire change or an oil change," Knotchapone said. "Howard always had himself under a hood, and he was a good mechanic. He was always working on my car, and he never, ever asked me to pay him a penny."

Knotchapone and St. John became close friends, and he was always asking her to cook up his favorite food, her deep-fried bread.

"Howard would always tell me, 'Tyla, I want you to make a dozen of that fry bread for us,'" Knotchapone said. "'We are going to have it for dinner. We don't want no white bread slices, and we don't want no regular bread. We want some of that fry bread.' I would never turn him down," Knotchapone said. "I would say, 'Howard, here I come with my one dozen fry bread,' and he would really appreciate that."

To Knotchapone, St. John was a good spirit trying to cure himself of his alcoholism, but in the end, Howard couldn't stop drinking. He was constantly falling off the wagon, and Thomas Gutierrez said he knew of at least seven occasions in which St. John quit drinking for a few weeks, only to go back to the bottle.

"He was a depressed person," Thomas Gutierrez said. "He was a sad person because of his life. He would break down and cry when he got real drunk, and he would talk about his dad, and his family, that they don't love him, and how come."

To those who knew him, St. John was a desperate man. He was desperate for sobriety, he was desperate for hope and he was especially desperate for genuine, unconditional love.

Brookey Lee West met the first of her four husbands through a classified ad in the *San Jose Mercury News*. The advertisement sought a female vocalist for a country-western band, and at twenty-four-years old, West's curiosity was piqued.

"I thought, 'Well, I'll make some extra money or something'—that's the way I was thinking about it," West said. "I wasn't really interested, because it was country music, and I loathe country music."

But West responded to the advertisement anyway, and the decision kicked off a brief, ill-fated romance with a man nearly three decades older than West. The person who placed the ad was country music promoter David,* a fifty-eight-year-old native Oklahoman with a shock of red hair. David was infatuated with West, and in David's mind, West's sex appeal might make her America's next big country music star.

The two married within a few months of meeting.

"He was real good to me at first," West said. "The one thing I always thought was real good about him was he never tried to hit me, never tried to raise his hand toward me, even though we had some nasty arguments. That's the good thing I can say about him. But he had drinking issues, dope issues, same thing all my husbands had. I guess it was the caretaker syndrome."

West sang lead vocals in David's country band, and she sang songs about heartache, broken love and drinking at a handful of redneck bars in Central and Northern California.

"You have to be drunk to sing that trash, it is just so depressing," West said. "My wife left me, etc."

But after a few weeks on the country music circuit, it quickly became apparent to West that country music stardom was little more than a pipe dream. The same could also be said for her marriage to David, and West divorced her husband within three months of their wedding.

"I married him, and then I divorced him," West said. "I sang in his band, but my heart wasn't in it, and I guess it wasn't what I really wanted. After about six weeks, I looked at him and I said, 'Who the hell are you? What do I want with you? This is just not working.' I'm the kind of person that when I make up my mind it's done. I'm done."

In retrospect, West said her decision to marry David was a rash impulse caused by mental illness. She said she is a bipolar manic-depressive who, without medication, has trouble resisting impulsive decisions like a quickie marriage.

"He seemed like a nice enough guy, but what was really going on was this disorder I have," West said. "When you have this disorder, you do all kinds of strange things. You get married, you get divorced. You buy stuff, and then you go, 'What did I buy that for?'

"I have a disorder in my brain," she said. "People will equate that with you being incapacitated, being stupid or being crazy, but it isn't that at all. It's really a disorder in the brain where the chemicals are not balanced."

After her divorce from David West took a job as a security guard at a Palo Alto computer company called National Advanced Systems. West was quickly promoted from security guard to secretary, and while working at the company West met her second husband, West.* West was an administrator at National Advanced Systems, and like David he was an older man infatuated with Brookey West.

"He was tall, slender, very Norwegian, with sharp features," Brookey said. "Good-looking, blond haired. I was about twenty-eight, and he was twenty-one years my senior."

Like her marriage to David, the courtship with West was extremely quick.

"I was working in a different area of the company, and I took some papers to his office," Brookey said. "That was the first time I ever met him, and when he looked up at me, he was just staring at me, and he goes, 'Would you like to go out for a drink?'"

Brookey accepted the invitation, and the two left work for a bar in downtown San Jose.

"We are having a drink, and he looks at me and goes, 'Will you marry me?'" Brookey recalled. "And I looked at him, and I said, 'Are you serious?' And he goes, 'Yeah, I'm serious.' So I said, 'Yeah, sure.'

"It was our first date, and we got engaged," Brookey said.

The two were married in five months, and at first West was happy with her marriage to West, but her mother did not approve of the relationship with such an older man. West, in turn, couldn't stand Christine, whom he viewed as a mean-spirited, wacko bitch. The two fought constantly, and West found himself having to bring Christine along on any social outing with his wife.

"Mom was always hanging around," Brookey said. "She didn't live with us, but she was always there, and we would all go out to functions together. He was, quite frankly, irritated with her, and they did not like each other. My mom did not like to share me, and she was a man-hater to start with. She used to tell me, 'I don't care if he's next door to Jesus. I don't like him.'"

The dispute between West and Christine came to a head during a dinner outing just a few months after the marriage. Brookey, West and Christine were having dinner at a San Jose restaurant when a waitress approached the trio's table and mistakenly addressed the older West as if he were Christine's husband—not Brookey's.

"I looked at the waitress and I said, 'Well, I'm his wife,'" Brookey recalled.

"And my mother goes, 'Well, that's what you get for marrying some old man,'" Brookey recalled. "He was sitting there, and she says to him, 'And that's what you get for robbing the cradle, for trying to marry some young woman when you are old enough to be her father. You look ridiculous, and the waitress thinks you look ridiculous.' I was red in the face, and he was upset," Brookey said.

Christine wanted to know if West was going to leave her daughter any money in his will.

"She started ragging on him," Brookey said. "'Aren't you going to leave my daughter any money?' Blah, blah, blah."

Within months, the marriage was over. Once again, Brookey's pursuit of an older man ended in divorce, and once again, Brookey said her decision to marry West was due to her manic-depressive condition.

"I wasn't stable back then," she said.

But unlike David, to this day, West speaks with great disdain for her second husband. She said after the marriage was over, she heard rumors West molested her daughter while Susie was visiting during a weekend visit from the Arizona boarding school.

"I was told about the molestation allegations years later," Brookey said. "If the allegations were true, I think I might have killed him. I think I might have."

Nothing was ever substantiated or even reported to the police.

"If I would have had a reason to kill somebody, it would have probably been him," Brookey said. "If I wanted to kill him for money, it would have been ideal, because he had $250,000 in life insurance."

Brookey said that before he changed his wills, West's estate was designed to be given to her if he died.

"He signed everything over to me in case of his death, so if I had a reason to kill somebody, it would have been him," she said.

Brookey Lee West's decision to take a job at National Advanced Systems was an extremely beneficial career move over the long run. West was quickly promoted from security guard to secretary, and then to the company's hardware and mainframes division, even though she had never even gone to college to study computers. West's increasing work responsibilities convinced her to pursue a career in the computer industry, and she started studying computers extensively on her own time. She checked out books on computer programming and engineering from the Stanford University library, and she read them tirelessly to prepare herself to work in the Silicon Valley's bustling computer industry.

"Computer engineering, I don't know why, but it was just in my head," West said. "I can read that stuff, I understand all the logic, how to troubleshoot computers, how they work, everything."

West gravitated to the field of technical writing. She enrolled in a series of classes to learn the job, which involves writing complex instructional manuals for purchasers of computer software. By the late 1980s and early 1990s, West was landing technical writing jobs for San Jose's most renowned computer companies, and by all accounts West was a whiz at the job.

"She was very good at her job, and she was very talented," said Natalie Hanke, who was one of West's technical writing supervisors. "One of the best I've ever worked with."

West, Hanke said, understood computers, and she had a knack for using the printed word to explain in simple terms the intricacies of computer software.

"My resume is about eight pages," West said. "I worked for all of the best. I worked for Sun, Intel, and I did a lot of stuff for Cisco. I'm a contractor, and they hired me for short periods of time. Sometimes, the contract would be for a few weeks, and sometimes it would be six months."

The jobs brought in a lot of cash for West—she was making $65 to $100 an hour—and the money offered her a chance at a lifestyle she previously never dreamed of. She bought a Jaguar; she owned expensive clothing; she bought a house on Fir Street in Los Banos, California, which allowed her to make the one-hour commute to San Jose.

But despite all the success, there was still one big problem in West's life:

Her mother.

Christine was living with West, and West was paying all her mother's bills, buying her clothes, groceries and anything else Christine needed. The relationship was often strained, and West spent much of her time trying to make sure her mother didn't do anything crazy. The need to monitor her mother was evidenced by Christine's actions while the two shared a home in downtown San Jose in the early 1990s, just before West bought her home in Los Banos.

At that time, Christine, West said, was obsessed with a neighbor's dog who kept walking through the yard of their rental home. As a result, Christine bought a huge bag of cayenne pepper and spread it all over the neighbor's yard.

"She sprinkled it all over their lawn so this dog would get a snootful of cayenne pepper," West said. "The guy is right next door, working in his driveway, and he's out there wiping his eyes. My mother said, 'I told that son of a bitch last week, keep that dog off my lawn.'"

The pepper didn't solve the problem, and the German shepherd continued to annoy Christine by prancing through the yard and barking late at night. Christine decided she would fix the problem for good with gopher poison stuffed in raw hamburger meat.

"The guy's German shepherd ate it," West said. "The next day, the guy's pissed off because he finds his dog with his teeth through a wooden board. I guess it was from the spasms. So I went to my mother, and I said, 'Did you feed that dog that?' and she said, 'Yeah, I did. I hate that son of a bitch.'" I told her, 'If they ever found out you poisoned that dog, they'll put you in prison for that,'" West said. "She said she hated the guy, and she didn't like other people's dogs."

But while West and her mother were often at odds, they also loved each other. It was a complex mother-daughter relationship, and West said she was always looking out for her mother. There were plenty of times when they enjoyed each other's company, and one of their favorite hobbies involved frequenting Native American jewelry stores in the San Jose area, where they bought art, jewelry and other Native American artifacts for West's Los Banos home.

The mother and daughter became obsessed with Indian culture, and Christine claimed she was half Apache Indian. West claimed the Apache heritage as well, and the two women even started frequenting the Native American Indian Center in San Jose.

22

Tyla Knotchapone will never forget the day Brookey Lee West and her mother, Christine Smith, walked into her Alcoholics Anonymous meeting at the Native American Indian Center in late 1993. Knotchapone could tell the two women were bad news.

"The energy was real strong," Knotchapone said. "We could see it, and we could all feel it."

The bad vibes were particularly strong for West, who wore skintight clothing in a room full of Indian men, and she was strutting around like a hooker trolling for a date.

"She had jet-black hair and red fingernail polish, and her dress was very inappropriate," Knotchapone said. "Her cleavage was exposed, and her makeup was like Elvira's. She had her eyeliner way up, and she wore all black clothes.

"I could tell Brooke wasn't there for herself, her soul or her sobriety," Knotchapone said. "She was there to cause trouble. It was like she was a demon."

Another attendee of the meeting, Henry Murillo, took notice of West, too.

"She was, like, dressed in all black, she had bright red lipstick, bright red fingernails, bright red shoes," Murillo said in a statement to police. "I was, like, trying to avoid her, because I just got an eerie feeling."

"She was just like staring at me, checking me out, like she wanted to be picked up," Murillo said.

Virtually everyone who was present at the meeting wondered what the two white women were doing in a meeting designated for Native Americans. The mother and daughter said they were Apache Indian, but no one was buying it because their skin was white as snow.

"Who let these two in?" Knotchapone said.

"I pretty much knew something was up with this woman," Murillo said of West. "She was kinda just using the place as a pickup joint . . . she was fishing for someone."

After West and Christine made their entry, the twenty or so people in attendance gathered in a circle and, in a ritual dating back nearly seventy years, started to share with one another their troubles with alcohol. Christine was one of the first people to stand up, and she recounted for the group her years of substance abuse in Texas and California.

"The mom shared with us about being in prison, that she did time in the joint," Knotchapone said. "A real Bible-thumper. I told her that our purpose here was to share about alcohol, and we needed to limit it to that."

West sat quietly in the circle of recovering addicts, listening to their confessions. Everyone started to assume West was going to remain silent, but just when the meeting was about to conclude, West stood up and went off on a venomous tirade about her ex-husband.

She said he was a no-good bastard who deserved to be dead.

"She was talking about spitting on this guy's grave," Murillo said. "She went off for quite a while. I thought, jeez, she's kinda flipped out."

When the meeting was over, Knotchapone huddled with some of her Native American friends, and they all agreed West had frightened them. She was mean-spirited, she dressed like a whore, and no one could figure out what she was doing there.

"I went and huddled with some of my sisters, and I asked them, 'Are you experiencing what I'm experiencing?'" Knotchapone said. "One of my sister—her name was Linda—said, 'They are really strange, both of them. Don't talk to them.' They gave me the creeps, and we all agreed there was something wrong with these two."

Murillo discussed the women with his friends as well, and they made the same observations.

"Somebody mentioned she was the black widow," Murillo said.

23

The first month of sobriety is a miserable experience for most addicts. The party is over, the body is adjusting to a chemical-free existence and most find themselves grieving the loss of their best friend—drugs or alcohol.

Wayne Ike was going through such torture while living at the rehabilitation home for alcoholics on Rhodes Court in San Jose in 1993. The Shoshone Indian from Elko, Nevada, was at the Native American Indian Center because of extensive alcohol abuse, but despite his anxiety, he found some comfort in the camaraderie he shared with the eight other Indian men who were in rehab with him.

"It was really a nice house, and we all pretty much got along," Ike said. "All the food was paid for."

Ike was at the house for a little more than a month when something very strange happened. He was cleaning the kitchen of the residence in late 1993 when a fine-looking young woman in tight clothes strutted in. She walked up to Ike, introduced herself as Brookey Lee West, unbuttoned her blouse and showed Ike her breasts.

"She sees me, she walks up, she pops open her blouse,

and I'm looking right down at her titties," Ike recalled. "She said, 'I like a man who cleans house, and I'm horny as hell.' I was asked out for dinner," Ike said. "She was good-looking. She had nice, big green eyes and big red lips. She was well dressed. She had nice clothes and a nice car."

Ike went out on a series of dinner dates with West, and West always paid for their dinner and drinks. Within a few weeks, Ike was fucking West hard during overnight stays at San Jose area hotels, and sometimes they fucked in West's Toyota MR2 two-seater.

"She was wild in bed," Ike said. "We'd even do it while we were driving down the road, in a parking lot, wherever. She was just easy to latch on to," Ike said. "You just got to get to know her . . . and then just grab her, and you have her in your arms and stuff. That was no problem. She was really crazy about me. She was crazy about Indians. She wanted to marry an Indian guy."

But while the sex was good, Ike recognized there was something wrong with West. Something just wasn't right with this person. For example, he couldn't understand why West, an apparently well-off technical writer, was frequenting the rehabilitation home on Rhodes Court and looking for a companion in a home filled with recovering addicts.

"I really don't know what in the heck she was doing there for an intelligent woman," Ike said. "She needed a man or something. [It was a place] where nobody would . . . look, you know. Drunken Indians. She was a smart lady, she was good-looking . . . and I smelled a rat," Ike said.

Ike was bothered by West's comments about children. She said she wanted nothing to do with children, and the remarks turned Ike off. He had two kids and loved them both.

"She didn't like children," Ike said. "She [said she] gave her daughter away."

"She always talked about money, and it would get on your nerves," he said. "She always had money."

The monthlong relationship came to an end when, while sitting in West's car in front of the rehab home, West told Ike no man was ever going to cheat on her and get away with it. West reached into her purse, pulled out a .38-caliber revolver and pointed it at Ike.

" 'If I ever catch you messing around, I'll use this on you,' " he recalled West telling him. " 'If I catch you fucking around, I'll shoot your ass.' "

Having a firearm pointed at him was the final straw. Ike realized West was crazy, and he started hiding from West whenever she showed up at the rehab center. Slowly, West gave up on Ike, and she focused on another resident of the rehabilitation home—Howard Simon St. John.

"It was crazy," Ike said. "My friends were telling me to get away from her. To me, [the relationship] was kind of spooky. She was like a black widow type. She was like a lady who knows how to suck a man dry. She loved being in power."

Brookey Lee West had everything going for her in 1994. She had a lucrative job, a nice house in the rural community of Los Banos, California, and a Jaguar parked in her driveway. She seemed an unlikely match for Howard Simon St. John—a penniless, homeless drunk with rotting teeth.

But after her relationship with Wayne Ike faltered, West set her sights on St. John, and she asked him out to dinner despite their starkly different positions in life.

"When I first met Howard, he looked kind of bad," West said. "He was real overweight, and his hair was sort of long. Yet I could see that if he lost some weight, and if he got his hair cut, he would be really good-looking. He had a gentleman quality about him, and that part of him was un-believable. I view life this way—people can be down. They can be sick, and they can have a lot of bad things happen, and they can pull themselves back up. That's the way I saw it."

St. John's friends, however, were at a loss to explain West's interest in him. West was an attractive, professional businesswoman, and she was hooking up with an obese, convicted felon in rehab.

"I was shocked," Thomas Gutierrez said. "I was like, what is this good-looking woman doing with Howard?"

Thomas and his wife, Dana, remember meeting West for the first time. She showed up with St. John at Dana's mother's house in 1994, and Thomas noticed St. John was no longer in his street clothes. He was well dressed, his hair was cut and he was groomed.

"When he came to the house, and brought her over for the first time, I said, 'Holy mackerel,'" Thomas Gutierrez said. "She looked like she was well put together, and she had her stuff together. Real responsible, and she was pretty."

Dana Gutierrez found the relationship extremely strange as well.

"The first time I ever saw her, I definitely got a bad feeling," she said. "I thought, this is not right."

Thomas Gutierrez was baffled by West's generosity, so he pulled his friend aside and politely expressed his misgivings about West.

"I had this bad feeling," Thomas Gutierrez said. "I told Howard, 'You know what? I'm glad for you, Howard. I'm glad you are getting straight. This might be what you need to get your feet on the ground.'

"But I said, 'Howard, what is she doing with you?'" he recalled. "Howard started laughing, and I started laughing, and I think he thought I was playing it off. But I said,

'Howard, look at you, and look at her. Is this really love, Howard?' And he goes, 'Yeah.'

"I said, 'Well, the best of luck to both of you, but if there's an insurance policy out there, you better be careful,'" Thomas Gutierrez said. "I was joking, but at the same time I wanted to put the thought in his head."

Tony Mercado was shocked by the relationship as well.

"I just said, 'Something is wrong here,'" he said.

Tyla Knotchapone was concerned, too. She was already wary of West due to her behavior at the AA meetings, and when she learned West was dating St. John, she literally feared for him.

"Howard had a potbelly, he had missing teeth, he had shabby hair, and she dressed him up," Knotchapone said. "I said, 'Howard, why is she doing this for you?'"

St. John told Knotchapone that West loved him and he loved her. He said he was especially captivated by West's sexuality—she was constantly teasing him with sex, and he loved it.

"Some of the statements Howard told me from Brooke were, 'Guess what I have on today? Fancy red lace underwear. It's pretty, like my nails,'" Knotchapone recalled. "That was what Brooke was saying to Howard, and we would tease Howard, saying, 'Geez, those words are hot for you?'

"But he was higher than a kite. He said, 'Oh, she is the woman of my life' and 'This is what I've been waiting for,'" Knotchapone recalled.

"I think the whole relationship revolved around sex," Knotchapone said. "There was no deep feeling from the heart. It was lust, sex and money. The Howard we used to know was never into that."

After about a month of dating, St. John told his friends he was taking West back to South Dakota to be married on the reservation. But when St. John called his father,

Sylvester told him not to bother—Howard was not welcome on the reservation. St. John and West then took a weekend trip to Reno and got married there. When they returned, the two told St. John's friends at the Native American Indian Center about the marriage, and West started showing off a huge diamond ring that she said St. John had paid $20,000 for.

Knotchapone laughed out loud at the idea of St. John's buying the ring. He, after all, was enrolled in the Four Winds program, and no one staying at the home on Rhodes Court could afford to pay their own rent, much less purchase a $20,000 wedding ring.

"The Four Winds program, that was the last stop," Knotchapone said. "The house they lived in, that was the last house on the block, as they say. Every Indian man you saw in there, they didn't have any kind of resources. Howard didn't have that kind of money.

"We used to tease Howard, and we'd tell him the ring was out of a bubble gum machine or a Cracker Jack box," Knotchapone said.

Knotchapone sensed a storm was brewing in Howard's life, and she repeatedly warned St. John that his new wife was no good for him. But there was no talking to St. John.

He was in love.

"We all told Howard, 'She scares us,'" Knotchapone said. "I was worried about Howard, and I told him, 'You are playing with fire, Howard. You are in the danger zone.'"

24

Mike Stoykovich and his wife, Crystal, are a couple of country bumpkins at heart. They each grew up in extremely rural areas—for Mike, it was Michigan's picturesque Upper Peninsula, and for Crystal, life began in the heart of Iowa. Their childhoods were spent in quiet, sleepy farming communities where everyone knew everyone, and their early years instilled in each a profound love of life in rural America.

But as is often the case, life rarely lets one pick and choose one's fate, and for the Stoykoviches, their time in the country was short-lived. The two married young, and a military career for Mike led him to Southern California. There, the couple had six children, and the economic demands of supporting such a large family mandated that the couple spend most of their time in the greater Los Angeles area, where Mike worked at the post office to pay the bills.

Yet Mike eighty-two, and Crystal, eighty, never gave up on their dream of returning to their rural roots, and in 1993 the Stoykoviches moved to the tiny farming community of Los Banos, California, on the western side of the San

Joaquin Valley. The Stoykoviches were charmed by the municipality of what was then 15,000 people.

"It is such a friendly town," Crystal Stoykovich said. "Everyone is nice, and no matter who you see, they wave to you. We felt like everyone was waiting for us with open arms."

The Stoykoviches were impressed by the natural beauty surrounding the city. There are flowing green farmlands, the Diablo mountain range and its ominous Pacheco Pass, which is a foggy, rocky escarpment travelers are forced to scale while driving to Los Banos on state Highway 152 from San Jose.

Los Banos is also adjacent to the pristine San Luis Reservoir. The series of lakes serves as a significant water source for the massive citrus, nut and cotton farms surrounding Los Banos.

The Stoykoviches scouted out new housing developments in Los Banos, and they settled on a planned community of one- and two-story houses on the outskirts of town called the Gardens. The Stoykoviches plunked down $125,000 for a new single-story home, and their residence was the first to be built on Fir Street.

"There was grass farmland in the back of our house, and we had jackrabbits running through our backyard," Crystal said. "It was beautiful."

But the Stoykoviches' return to the country came with one drawback. The neighbors from hell were about to move in across the street.

Brookey Lee West purchased a home on Fir Street in 1993, and at first the Stoykoviches were glad to have new neighbors. West moved in with her mother, Christine, and initially the two seemed like a normal, everyday mother and daughter. West was the first to introduce herself to the couple, explaining she was a technical writer in San Jose. West said she bought her house with a GI loan from her prior military service, and she told the Stoykoviches some fat lies about her nine-month military career.

"She told us she was a sergeant," Mike said.

"She told us she flew planes," Crystal recalled.

The Stoykoviches met Christine days later. She was thin and frail, and she always wore gray sweatpants and a gray sweatshirt. She had her hair wound in a long, dark braid stretching to the middle of her back, and the Stoykoviches—eager to make friends in their new neighborhood—invited Christine into their home.

"A very strange woman," Mike said. "She said, 'I'm Cherokee Indian, and I take no gump from nobody. I'll kill somebody if I have to, and we Cherokees don't stop at anything when we want revenge.' I didn't think she was Indian, but she claimed it."

Christine proceeded to tell the Stoykoviches a series of strange stories as she sat in their living room. She said she was born in Texas, and as a child growing up in rural Ennis, she spent time riding the rail lines with bums and hoboes.

"She said she used to ride the trains as a hobo, and she learned how to take care of herself in the boxcars," Mike Stoykovich said. "She said she was twelve, and when the bums got fresh with her, she would pull a knife out on them."

Christine said her nine-year-old granddaughter, Susie Alcantar, was kidnapped from a department store when she was five, and that West had hired a private investigator to find the child. Christine never discussed the real story behind West's separation from her daughter—that West gave the child away to her teachers at her Arizona boarding school.

"She had tears in her eyes when she was telling us this," Crystal said. "Christine still had a pair of the child's baby shoes, and she said, 'These were my granddaughter's shoes, and I miss her an awful lot.'"

The most shocking story Christine told the Stoykoviches, however, detailed her proudest moment in life. In her slow Texas drawl, she offered a grandiose, blow-by-blow account of blasting a hole in her lover with a shotgun in Bakersfield.

"She said, 'If I couldn't have him, neither could his wife,' so bang, she shot him," Crystal said. "You got the idea you'd better not cross Christine."

The Stoykoviches concluded Christine was certainly bizarre, and perhaps mentally ill, but she was also colorful and interesting. Christine was soon showing up every day at the Stoykoviches' front door, usually while the Stoykoviches were eating lunch or dinner. The Stoykoviches regularly invited Christine to eat with them out of pity. She was a very simple woman, and it seemed she was extremely lonely while her daughter was working in San Jose.

"She would make a point of showing up when we were eating, and I kind of felt sorry for her, really," Crystal Stoykovich said. "She was alone while her daughter was working, and I think she was really lonely."

"I don't think she was getting much to eat over there," Mike Stoykovich said. "She was very frail, and we didn't think she was eating at all."

Shortly before Christmas 1993, Christine invited Crystal over to her house to see a Christmas tree she had decorated. Crystal walked in West's home and noticed there was barely any furniture in the house, yet there were racks and racks of expensive clothing in West's bedroom, and the clothes still had the price tags on them. The amount of new clothing struck her as unusual.

"I started to wonder what kind of life they were leading," she said.

Christine brought Crystal a series of strange gifts in the coming weeks. One gift was an obnoxious, oversized scarf adorned with blue butterflies, and another was a pair of earrings carved out of a potato.

"She'd done it with a big potato," Crystal said. "She sliced it, carved the earrings, dried them and then she painted them. I said, 'Oh, how do you do that?' and she said, 'I'm not going to tell you the secret.' It was a nice thing to do, but people would look at you twice if they saw you wearing these potato earrings."

There came a time, however, when the Stoykoviches saw another side of Christine. The incident unfolded when Mike voiced an interest in buying a small Ford Tempo car owned by West. West and her mother offered the car for $6,500, but when Mike checked with the lender of the car, he found West owed only about $3,500 on the vehicle, and the car's book value was much less than the price West was asking.

"I said, 'Oh, boy, they're trying to double their money,'" Mike Stoykovich recalled.

He kindly told West he no longer wanted to buy the car, and Christine was enraged.

"The old lady was mad at us," Mike said. "She was furious."

Around the same time the car deal fell through, Christine delivered a pot of what she called "northern bean soup" to her neighbors. Mike Stoykovich took one taste of the soup and was aghast. The dish tasted like a bucket of salt.

"I tasted it, and it was all salt," Mike Stoykovich said. "I dumped it out in the garden."

Over time, the Stoykoviches recognized Christine was not normal, and they decided it was best to keep their distance.

"We were like, golly, who do we have living across the street?" Crystal said.

Sandy Corona has faced her fair share of obstacles in life. The pretty, sweet-natured Ohio native, now fifty-seven, was born with congenital progressive deafness, a disability that wasn't diagnosed until she was nine. But Corona's parents made it clear to their daughter that her disability was not going to hold her back in life, and as a child she faked several school-administered hearing tests to stay in a traditional school.

"My mom didn't want me to be abnormal, which she thought most deaf kids were because they were separated from so-called normal kids, so she instilled in me that I was a normal kid who couldn't hear well." It was the best thing she ever did for me, Corona said.

"I taught myself to lip-read well enough that I was actually the first handicapped student to integrate into the schools in Ohio," Corona said. "I remained in regular school, graduated with honors, and I was awarded several scholarships to Wright State University."

Corona completed three years of college before dropping out of Wright State to support her family. She eventually married her first husband, Dan, and Corona bore two lovely children. The relationship failed years later, and the marriage was dissolved.

Corona met her second husband, Al Corona, in Dayton, Ohio, in 1987. Al Corona was the love of Sandy's life, and the couple married, then moved to Gilroy, California, where Al Corona worked as a computer analyst. Life seemed to be going well for the Coronas, until tragedy shattered their world, in 1992, when Sandy's son, Gregory Douglas Turner, was brutally murdered in Ohio. Turner was shot and bludgeoned by a man jealous over a girl Turner was dating, and the loss of her only son devastated Sandy Corona. The killer was caught and sentenced to twenty years to life in prison, but the punishment was of little solace—life would never be the same again.

A year later, in June 1993, Sandy Corona felt it was time to move from Gilroy. The house she lived in reminded her of a visit her son made to California shortly before his death, and overwhelmed by grief, she felt it was time for a new environment.

"Prior to my son's death, he had visited us and stayed overnight at our house in Gilroy," Sandy Corona said. "The house had a lot of memories, I was distraught, and I didn't want to live there anymore."

The Coronas started looking for affordable new housing developments in rural California, and they found one in the Gardens community in Los Banos. The community offered quiet, peaceful country living in a neighborhood lined with farms and two-lane roads, and the Coronas were quickly sold on life in Los Banos. They purchased a two-story home on Fir Street, and they moved in the latter half of 1993, around the same time Brookey Lee West and her mother moved in to their home down the street.

Sandy Corona sensed Christine had experienced a lot of trials in her life.

"She was a thin, slightly built woman, and she had a lot of wrinkles," Sandy Corona said. "She looked like she had been through a lot. She was an older, weathered woman, and she told me she was part Indian."

Sandy Corona did share some similar interests with Christine. They both enjoyed crafts and making dolls, and Christine started to visit the Corona residence regularly.

"Chris said she didn't have a lot of friends, and she asked if she could come calling," Sandy Corona recalled. "My mother passed away when I was thirty-five, so I thought it would be nice to be friends with an older woman."

In turn, Christine invited Sandy over to her house, and during her single visit to West's residence, she noticed the racks of expensive clothing that Crystal Stoykovich had also observed.

"They had all this clothing, and I was shocked," Sandy said. "The clothing still had the plastic bags and the price tags on them, and there were boxes and boxes of shoes and hats. All sorts of brand-new things, like from Saks Fifth Avenue, Neiman Marcus—you know, all these really ritzy, expensive stores. All brand-new clothing."

After Christine visited the Corona residence on a few occasions, Sandy and Al Corona realized she was, well, strange. She told Sandy she could make a special potion to improve an individual's love life. On another occasion, Christine walked in the Corona home through a back door without ever knocking or letting her presence be known. When Sandy walked into her living room, she was startled to find Christine in her house, and the incident made Sandy Corona uneasy.

On yet another occasion, Sandy caught Christine secretly putting a note on the Coronas' front door.

"She'd written a note saying, 'Deaf woman lives here. Please call this number in order to get in the house,' and she'd written down her own phone number," Sandy said. "I told her I appreciated her concern, but such a note would endanger me rather than help. I told her I had taken care of myself for years, and I was capable of continuing to do so."

By late 1993, Christine was scaring Sandy Corona.

"Chris told me she had been on death row for a while," Sandy said. "I said, 'What in the world?' She said she married a police officer, had an affair with a married man and had gotten someone to kill her lover."

Strangely, Christine said the shooting unfolded in Texas—not Bakersfield—and she was spared from the execution chamber when the victim "came back to life," Al Corona said in a statement to police.

"Somehow he came back to life when he was in the morgue," Al Corona said. "It was real crazy talk . . . I just figured, you know, she is crazy. Nobody kills somebody, and all of a sudden the guy comes back to life in the morgue."

The Coronas questioned Christine how she could have ended up on death row for shooting a man who didn't die.

"That's Texas for you," Christine responded.

Christine seemed proud of her violent history, and her stories upset Sandy greatly. Her son had just been murdered two years earlier, and Sandy was keenly aware of the pain and misery caused by violent crime. She told Christine she was not impressed with her stories of violence and killing.

"I told her we were still going through some things [emotionally], and I was sorry, but I had serious problems about continuing a relationship with her if she'd been convicted of murder," Sandy said. "She said she believed in victims' rights, but she was being honest."

Christine, however, wasn't finished with her disturbing stories. She said her granddaughter was kidnapped from a department store when she was five, and that West had hired a private detective to find the girl.

"I was struck by the fact that this woman, who said she committed murder, had a missing grandchild," Sandy said. "She was frightening me, so I and my husband did not want her in the house anymore."

Sandy and Al Corona concluded Christine was someone they didn't want to associate with, and they started avoiding her like the plague.

The Stoykoviches and the Coronas weren't the only residents on Fir Street to realize they were living next to a couple of weirdoes. Laura Parra lived across the street from West and Christine, and she, too, was startled by her neighbors' strange habits.

"They were both weird," Laura Parra said. "Very odd."

Parra, forty-four, is an attractive, blond-haired mother of two children who moved to Los Banos in 1993 with her now ex-husband Fermin Parra. Laura is a vibrant, optimistic woman, and her glowing spirit gives no indication of her daily struggles with the potentially deadly disease of multiple sclerosis. She was diagnosed with MS as a young woman, and the disease has caused her an untold amount of pain and emotional difficulty. When her children were young, one of her hands frequently clenched up so tightly she had to change diapers with her teeth.

But with medication, her faith in God and a good attitude, she has persisted through the misery, and she now takes special pride in being an MS survivor.

"I have four friends, and their cause of death was MS," Laura said. "In my opinion, they gave in to the disease. They stopped fighting, and I believe God makes you stronger."

Laura Parra and her then-husband came to Los Banos from Gilroy, a city on the outskirts of San Jose, because the cost of living was much cheaper.

"We were paying $1,250 a month in rent in Gilroy, and this was ten years ago," Laura said. "Today, I'm paying about the same, I own my own home and I live in a very small, quiet town. I love it here."

Laura vividly remembers meeting West for the first time. West walked across Fir Street to introduce herself, and Parra sensed West was not quite normal.

"She was just a very different person," Laura said. "I thought she was a little creepy from the first moment I met her. She looked like she was on drugs or something. Odd."

Despite her first impression, though, Laura visited with West, and she, too, saw all the new clothing in West's home.

"I thought she might be a madam for a bunch of prostitutes," Laura said.

In her visits with West, Parra also recognized that West

and her mother were at odds with each other. On one occasion, Laura saw West screaming at her mother as they walked home from a grocery store.

"I was in front of my house one day, and Brooke and Christine were walking down the street," Laura recalled. "Brooke was just screaming at her. She was yelling at Christine in a way you'd never talk to your mother."

Days later, Laura was watering flowers in front of her home when she saw West yelling at her mother again.

"She called her a crazy bitch to her face," Laura said. "I was like, 'Oh, jeez, finish watering and get back in the house.'"

And on yet another occasion, West personally told Parra she disliked her mother.

"Brooke said her mom was a lunatic, she was driving her crazy and she didn't want her mom around," Laura said. "She was driving her crazy. She talked about what a pain in the ass her mother was, and her exact words were, 'She's a crazy bitch, and I can't wait to get her out.'"

25

On March 3, 1994, at 11:20 p.m., an anonymous caller dialed 911 in Milpitas, California, to report a car burning in an industrial area of the city's border with San Jose. A patrol officer with the Milpitas police department responded to the scene and found a 1989 Jaguar sedan smoldering on a dirt road just off Lundy Lane.

The car was a complete loss.

About fifty minutes later, the vehicle's owner, Brookey Lee West, called police in San Jose and reported the vehicle missing. West told the cops that on the night of March 3, she and her boyfriend—she did not identify him by name—went to dinner and a movie at a shopping complex at 3161 Olsen Drive in San Jose. After the Steven Seagal action flick was over, West and her boyfriend emerged from the theater near the city's historic Winchester Mystery House and discovered the Jaguar was gone. The vehicle, West said, had a common antitheft security device known as The Club on its steering wheel at the time it disappeared.

The white Jaguar, according to police records, was purchased by West just a month before it was stolen and torched. West bought the vehicle at a Buick dealership in Santa Clara in February 1994, by trading in a Toyota MR2 and putting down a $1,500 deposit. The deal required West pay a rather steep monthly payment of $554.

West's insurance company, AAA car insurance in California, cut a check of $18,897 to GMAC financing in Sunnyvale after the car was torched, and it must have seemed to West her financial liability for the car loan was over.

But unbeknown to West, the insurance company was suspicious. AAA directed the California Automobile Association to investigate, and the association, in turn, hired an investigative company called Lee S. Cole and Associates to conduct an inquiry. Cole and Associates investigator Dwight Bell, a retired thirty-year veteran of the California Highway Patrol, was assigned the case.

"We got this particular case . . . primarily because it was a Jaguar and because it was a vehicle fire, which is our area of expertise," Bell said in a statement to authorities.

Bell also found several aspects of the theft suspicious.

"In short, the 1989 Jaguar sedan was found on fire by the Milipitas police department before it was reported stolen," Bell wrote in a letter to the Automobile Association. "It was noted that the radio/stereo unit or speakers had not been removed from the Jaguar, and all wheels and tires were in place. . . . I thought it [also] interesting that the initial information came from an anonymous caller. I eliminated any mechanical, electrical or fuel source as the cause of the fire. In other words, there was no engine fire. There was no electrical fire, there wasn't a transmission fire, a battery fire, anything of that nature. The fire did not, in fact, start in the engine compartment. The fire pattern and the damage was definitely indicative of a fire starting in the passenger compartment. . . . I did not find a residue of flammable fluid, primarily because the fire had been set in the open, in the weather, so long before I got to it. [But] the metal distortion to the top of the doors definitely would indicate that the fire was from some type of flammable application."

Knowing the fire was not an accident, Bell then set out to contact the owner of the vehicle, but it took him multiple tries to get in touch with West, whose mailing address turned out to be a post office box in Santa Clara. Bell also called West's work phone number at the Syntex Pharmaceuticals building on Page Mill Road in Palo Alto, and he couldn't get in touch with her.

"My initial calls to the work number connected with an answering machine that disconnected before I could leave a message," Bell said.

Bell finally did get in touch with West, but he was calling from a pay phone, and a construction company happened to be running a jackhammer nearby. He said he would call West back, but he was never was able to get in touch with West again.

On May 9, 1994, Bell completed the first of two reports he prepared to summarize his investigation on the theft, and at the time he had few leads to work with.

But the investigation into West's burned-out car was about to heat up. Nearly three weeks later; on May 27, 1994, AAA insurance received a phone call from a man who claimed to be the arsonist, and his name was Howard Simon St. John.

26

Howard Simon St. John moved in to Brookey Lee West's Los Banos home in early 1994, and to his new neighbors it seemed as if the Tasmanian devil himself had just spun down Fir Street and invaded their peaceful community. St. John was drinking again, and the results were predictable— he was noisy and rude, and he was observed stumbling through the neighborhood drunk out of his mind on multiple occasions.

"He was basically a drunken Indian," Laura Parra said.

West introduced her new hubby to Parra shortly after St. John moved in, and Parra was astonished by West's choice for a husband.

"I thought, 'Wow, what a weird couple,' " Parra said. "He was a big guy who looked like an old-time biker. Sometimes he didn't wear a shirt, and he wore scraggily clothes. She had just met this guy, and then they got married, and I was like, 'What is she doing with this guy?' "

Sandy Corona said St. John had little regard for the sanctity of the neighborhood. "He yelled a lot, he always seemed to be slamming the front door, and he always looked a little disheveled," Corona said. "He was always acting like he was high, and it looked like he was drinking a lot. A lot of the neighbors on both sides of Brooke's house heard a lot of bottles breaking, and they heard cursing inside Brooke's house."

Mike Stoykovich met St. John in early 1994. At the time, St. John was working on a sleek white Corvette that Stoykovich had never seen parked in West's driveway before. Stoykovich, interested in making friends with his new neighbor, walked across the street and introduced himself.

"I walked over and I said, 'I'm Mike Stoykovich,' and he said, 'I'm Howard,'" Stoykovich recalled. "He didn't give me his last name. He said he had bought the car at a swap meet for $5,000, and I said, 'You know, that's a pretty good price.'"

About a week later, Stoykovich saw St. John in front of West's home again and yelled out a friendly hello. This time, St. John acted as if Stoykovich wasn't even there.

"He turned his back on me," Stoykovich said. "I told my wife, 'Howard's living with a wealthy woman, and he must be too good for us. If that's his way of living, we just won't bother with him. . . . I guess he thinks he's too good for the peons around here.'"

Days later, Stoykovich realized he hadn't seen West's new Jaguar in her driveway in weeks, so the next time he saw Christine, he asked about her daughter's car.

"I said, 'Where's the Jaguar?' and she says, 'Someone stole it, stripped it, and all they found was the burned shell,'" Stoykovich recalled.

Crystal Stoykovich said word soon surfaced that Christine and her new son-in-law were not getting along, and Christine's visits to the Stoykoviches' home were getting less and less frequent. And then, without any notice, Christine moved out of her daughter's house without telling anyone.

"The next thing we knew, she had moved back to Santa Clara," Crystal Stoykovich said. "She [Christine] really didn't say too much before then. All we heard from her was that she didn't think [the relationship between St. John and West] was going to work."

"Christine couldn't stand Howard," Parra said. "Brooke said the two fought like cats and dogs, and it was either her or him. She said one of them had to go."

West's stepmother Chloe Smith, said that when Christine moved out, West bought her mother a van and loaded up her belongings in it. West parked the van in the parking lot of a city park in Santa Clara, and left Christine there.

"She took the van, and she left it in a parking lot over in Palo Alto," Chloe Smith said. "She took her mother over there, dropped her off, and she said, 'This is yours, this is where you are living. Don't come see me anymore.' She just dropped her off and left her there. It was very strange."

Chloe questioned her husband, Leroy, about Christine's living in a van, and Leroy said West's decision to leave her mother in a van in a city park was consistent with the strained mother-daughter relationship.

"Leroy had always told me she hated her mother," Chloe said.

Christine's migration into homelessness coincided with a couple of other unusual events on Fir Street. Sandy Corona said a few homes on Fir Street were burglarized after St. John's arrival, and some started to wonder if West or St. John had anything to do with the break-ins.

"Whenever the houses were broken into, it was when the people were away, and it was as if somebody knew their habits," Corona said. "No one ever saw Howard go to work, and everyone seemed to think Brooke and him might have had something to do with it."

The break-ins prompted Corona to start a neighborhood watch program. She held a series of neighborhood watch meetings at her house, and the only residents of Fir Street who weren't invited were West and St. John. On May 21, 1994, Corona sponsored a particularly successful watch meeting attended by dozens of neighbors, and everyone present expressed optimism that the program would eventually deter the burglaries.

The next morning, Corona opened her front door and found a huge pile of ice on her front porch.

"It looked like someone had dumped a cooler of ice on the front porch," Corona said.

Corona looked down the street and saw St. John standing in front of West's residence. He was holding a drink in his hand, and he raised it toward Corona.

"He smiled, and I got the distinct impression he had done it," Corona said. "I didn't know what to make of it. The man just terrified me."

Her husband, Al, told his wife not to worry about the pile of ice on the front porch; but a neighbor later suggested the ice might be a warning to Sandy to mind her own business.

"This neighbor said, 'Don't you watch gangster movies?' " Sandy said. "When you ice someone, what you do is you murder them. This may be a warning. I was like, 'Oh, my God, we are having all these meetings at my house, and what are these people going to do next?"

By far, though, the most concerning aspect of St. John's move to Fir Street was the increased police presence in the neighborhood. Beyond the watch program, residents noticed officers with the Los Banos police department regularly driving up and down their street, and Parra said the police were called to West's home multiple times during the early-morning hours of 1994.

"There were more than a few incidents," Laura Parra said. "The police started showing up, and I would say it was at least four times. Honestly, the first time I thought it was stolen goods, because I knew Brooke had all these new clothes coming into her house. Then I thought, well, maybe it's drugs. She's all weird and stuff, so I thought she was dealing drugs. Plus, her husband was always either loaded or drunk, so I decided I wanted to stay away from all of them."

27

Thomas Gutierrez and his wife, Dana, don't believe their friend, Howard Simon St. John, was the menace his neighbors on Fir Street perceived him to be. More likely, St. John was drinking heavily, which made him ornery and depressed, and he probably ended up rubbing people the wrong way in a mostly white, middle-class neighborhood where he was out of his element.

"Howard would make you feel comfortable no matter where it was," Thomas Gutierrez said. "He got along with everybody."

In the spring of 1994, Thomas and Dana Gutierrez visited St. John to see how he was doing. The couple made the hourlong drive from San Jose across Pacheco Pass to Los Banos, and when they arrived, they found St. John living in the nicest place of his life. West's residence was an extremely clean single-story house with large picture windows, and St. John's new existence seemed to be a world away from his prior life of homelessness and destitution on the streets of San Jose.

But once again, within a few minutes of watching St.

John and West interact, Thomas and Dana Gutierrez got an eerie feeling about the relationship.

"Usually my gut instinct is very good, and I was very uncomfortable around her," Dana Gutierrez said. "When we went to their house, I was like, 'We're here, okay, let's go.' You know how you feel when you meet someone, and you don't even want to socialize with them? I didn't want to socialize with her at all."

Thomas Gutierrez felt the same way.

"I was trying to get in and out, because I didn't feel comfortable, either," Thomas Gutierrez said. "I wasn't comfortable because I felt like she was going to hurt my friend. I didn't necessarily think she was going to kill him or anything, but I felt she was playing with his heart and toying with his feelings. I would look at her, and I would look at him, and I was thinking there is no way they could love each other. If she really loved Howard, I would have sensed it."

The visit to West's house lasted less than an hour, and shortly before the couple left, St. John said something that startled the couple.

"He told me she was into witchcraft and stuff, and I didn't believe him," Thomas Gutierrez said. "I said, *'Yeeaah, right.'*"

But then St. John walked Thomas Gutierrez through the house and showed him a series of bizarre objects that he said West used to practice witchcraft. Strange trinkets. Handmade dolls. A shrunken head. A voodoo doll.

"I saw all these objects, witchcraft objects, voodoo dolls, and he was telling me what they were," Thomas Gutierrez said. "Then he said, 'She can put a spell on you.' Brooke was in the kitchen, she heard us talking, and she looked over and said, "Yeah, I can. I can put a spell on you.' I said, 'That's okay. I'm already married.'"

Everyone laughed at the crack, and Thomas Gutierrez

felt the conversation was lighthearted in nature. But at the same time, the topic matter was a little unnerving.

"I don't know the difference between good or bad with that stuff," he said. "I just know it was there. Handmade dolls and shrunken heads. Little ones."

"By and large, she was joking," Dana Gutierrez said. "It wasn't a threat or anything . . . but it was weird."

A few weeks after the visit to Los Banos, St. John showed up at Thomas Gutierrez's house in San Jose, and the two started to talk again about West. Thomas said that during the conversation St. John revealed West wanted him to burn her Jaguar in an insurance scam.

"He started telling me she can't make the payments on the Jaguar," Thomas said. "So he wanted me to help him, and I said, 'No way, I ain't getting involved in this, Howard.' He was like asking me for permission," Thomas said. "It was like, 'Do you think I should do it?' I said, 'No man, don't get involved. These days, they can lift finger-prints off anything, and you don't know who could see you. Do you know what is going to happen if you get caught?' I told him, 'Don't even do it,' and he said, 'Okay.'"

St. John's friend Tony Mercado said he visited his house around the same time, and during the visit, Mercado saw him hovering in his garage over a sawhorse. St. John had a hacksaw in his hand, and he was using it to cut through The Club vehicle antitheft device.

"He was cutting The Club, and I was like, 'What you are you doing?'" Mercado said. "He wouldn't tell me what he was doing, but something was clearly wrong."

On March 3, 1994—just days after Mercado witnessed this spectacle—West's Jaguar was found burned in Milpitas. St. John later confided in Mercado that he was the arsonist, and he said West's insurance company was suspicious.

"He told me about the Jaguar," Mercado said. "The insurance company was calling, and she [West] was getting nervous."

St. John told Thomas Gutierrez the car had vanished, but at first he didn't confess to being involved.

"He just said, 'The car is gone,'" Gutierrez said. "Then, the next thing I know, Howard comes driving up in a Corvette. He said, 'Brooke bought it for me. It's a wedding gift.' And again, I'm thinking, 'What is she doing spending this kind of money on Howard?' It was real suspicious."

Later, however, St. John told Gutierrez the truth about the Jaguar, and Gutierrez sensed his friend was in deep trouble. He'd married a woman he barely knew, and within a few weeks of the marriage, he was allegedly committing felonies for his new wife.

"He told me the story," Gutierrez said. "He said, 'The investigators are coming around asking questions, and Brooke is panicking. She is going to put the blame on me.' And, I was like, 'I told you, Howard.' He said, 'Things are getting out of hand. It's getting wild, and they are getting close.'

"He was scared. He thought they were going to get popped for it, and he said Brooke was getting nervous, too."

28

May 21, 1994 was a quiet, peaceful spring day in Los Banos. The sun was out, the temperature was hot for May and a light breeze was whisking its way across the community's farmlands and into the Fir Street neighborhood.

For Mike and Crystal Stoykovich, this was a perfect day for a drive to nearby Morgan Hill to visit family. The two hopped in their car around midmorning, and as they pulled out of their driveway, they noticed Brookey Lee West and Howard St. John embracing across the street.

"They were lovey-dovey," Mike Stoykovich said. "When we left, they were hugging and kissing in the garage."

Laura Parra and her husband, Fermin, noticed West and her husband in the garage, too.

"I was going to mow my lawn as I normally do on Saturdays . . . I could hear music playing, and I could see them dancing with each other," Fermin Parra said in a statement to police. "They were in an embrace."

Fermin Parra went about mowing his lawn, and it seemed as if it was going to be a nice, quiet weekend day. But a short time later, Fermin Parra was approached by

St. John, and he noticed St. John was intoxicated.

"He said, 'My name is Howard. What's your name?' " Fermin Parra told police. "And I told him my name, and it took him several tries to remember it. He introduced himself to me at least four times during the conversation, which was very typical of talking to somebody who was under the influence. . . . He had no short-term memory."

Fermin Parra said St. John was not threatening, but he questioned why everyone in the neighborhood was avoiding him. St. John said it was obvious everyone on Fir Street didn't like him, and St. John speculated that perhaps his neighbors were keeping their distance from him because of West's mother, Christine.

"He said, 'I'm not poison, you know,' " Fermin Parra said. " 'Nobody never says anything to us. They pretend like we're not here.' I told him, 'Hey, I'm talking to you now.' He mentioned that he knew Brooke's mother didn't get along with a lot of neighbors."

St. John gave Fermin Parra a strange feeling, so he went back inside his residence and told his wife and children to stay away from the couple across the street. Later that day, Fermin Parra's neighbor Raymond Delgado rang the Parras' doorbell, and Fermin Parra stepped outside to talk to his friend.

The two were talking for about twenty minutes when Fermin Parra heard a loud cracking noise coming from West's house.

"I thought I heard a door slam," Fermin Parra said.

Laura Parra was working in her garage, and she heard the noise, too. The noise sounded like a firecracker.

"But I knew it wasn't a firecracker," she said. "You heard some noise, and you heard some yelling."

What happened next shocked the Parras to the core. Laura Parra looked across the street and saw St. John stumbling out of West's garage. He was covered in blood, he was holding his neck and he was pacing back and forth like a wounded animal, screeching in agony.

"He yelled, 'She shot me!'" Laura Parra recalled. "He came out staggering with blood all over the place, and it was like a movie. He had a lot of blood on him, and I'm looking at him, thinking, 'No, that's not fake blood, she really did shoot him.'"

"What I remember him saying is, 'She's got a gun in there! A .357,'" Fermin Parra told police. Someone ran inside the Parra house to call 911—the Parras don't remember who. Almost simultaneously, Los Banos police officer Steve Goeken arrived at the scene and approached St. John in the driveway. Officer Goeken said St. John was bleeding badly, and he recorded in a police report what happened next:

I observed St. John walking out, bleeding from the right shoulder area. He immediately said, 'She's got a gun,' pointing toward his wife, who was later identified as Brookey [West]. I immediately grabbed Brookey, I patted her down, and she did not have a weapon. But she pointed towards a table where there was a .32-caliber revolver, which I then recovered. Howard said, 'She shot me,' and I observed his neck area, which did appear to have an entry wound on the right lower portion of his neck. Brookey then said, 'I did shoot him, but it was an accident. I didn't mean to.'

While waiting for my sergeant to arrive, I kept the two subjects separated. At one point, Howard stated, 'Bitch, you shot me. I'm going to kill you.' I then asked Brookey what happened, which she said, 'He was coming at me,' so she got a gun out of her purse and pointed it at him, but . . . it just went off. She said she set the gun down and she went and called 911.

Laura Parra, still standing in her driveway, watched a team of paramedics load St. John into an ambulance, and then West emerged flanked by two officers.

"They brought Brooke out in handcuffs, and I thought, 'Oh, shit,' " Laura Parra said.

Laura Parra was overwhelmed by the events across the street. She had moved to Los Banos get away from the trials of the greater San Jose area, and she was now living across the street from a bunch of lunatics. There was Christine— the ex-felon who talked regularly to her neighbors about shooting people. There was St. John—a drunk who looked like he just walked off the prison yard. And there was West—a woman who shot her husband in the neck.

"They were the neighbors from hell," Laura Parra said.

Brookey Lee West was transported in handcuffs to the tiny downtown headquarters of the Los Banos police department for questioning in her husband's shooting. Police were hopeful West would give a statement, and they got more than they ever hoped for when West decided to talk at length.

West told officer Goeken that St. John was drunk and was being extremely aggressive with her. She said the shooting was one of a series of domestic disputes initiated by St. John, and that the two had been cleaning the garage when St. John threatened to attack her.

The following are excerpts from West's interview with police:

GOEKEN: I just need you to basically go through and tell me just what happened between you and your husband, Howard St. John, tonight.

WEST: Well, I guess it started early this morning. He got mad at me because he thought that I washed his pants with his wallet in it. . . . He was real, real intense, and he took his fist, and he just banged the switch on the washer and broke the washer.

Later in the day, as the two were cleaning their garage, West said St. John seemed obsessed with the idea that she was going to leave him, and he snapped.

WEST: He grabbed a hold of me, and he was trying to kiss me and everything, and I said, 'Howard, I'm not leaving you. I don't know where you are getting this idea.' He said, 'Well, you said if I got drunk, that you would leave.' I said, 'I know how you are when you are drinking, okay,' but I said, 'I'm not leaving you.'

West said St. John then went off on a verbal tirade, calling West a "fucking cunt."

WEST: I was starting to shake because I knew what he was real capable of, and I didn't want to provoke him. I was just trying to be nice. I said, 'You need to calm down. I don't know how much you've had to drink, but you are pretty drunk.' He was real drunk, and so I walked away, and I started sweeping the floor.

So I started sweeping the floor . . . and he's like talking, like, 'No motherfucker is gonna get in my way.' Just talk like that. He wasn't even really addressing me, and I don't know what he was doing. I said, 'Look, Howard, what are you talking about? This is crazy, all right?' I kept sweeping, and he said, 'Come here and sit.' I said, 'Howard, I'm not a dog,' so then I sat on the side of him, and he was trying to kiss me and everything. He said, 'Take your clothes off. I want to make love to you.' I said, 'Howard, I don't want to. I don't want to take my clothes off here on the concrete. . . . I don't want to do it here.'

Then Howard got really, really nasty with me, and he says, 'You fucking bitch, you are trying to leave me.' He says, 'I know what you are going to do, Brooke.' I said, 'Look, Howard, I'm not going nowhere' [and] he sat up on the floor and he grabbed hold of my arm . . . and I twisted free of him, and I just said, 'Let go of me, dammit! Just leave me alone,' and he says, 'I'll show you, you fucking bitch. I'll show you exactly what I can do.' I said, 'Howard, don't do this, just don't,' and I guess I backed up into a corner because I had some things stacked there, and there were tables there.

My purse was sitting over there because I had sat it [there] earlier, on the table, and when he got up, I said, 'Howard, don't do this, get your control.' He said, 'I'll show you exactly what I'm fucking capable of, you fucking bitch!' He took [a] table and he just throws it. I mean, it just flips into the air. It's a pretty heavy table. He turns around, and he started for me, but when he threw the table, I just reached out and took the little thing where my purse is. I have this little thing that I carry that little pistol in, I just grabbed it, and I pointed it at him, and I said, 'Howard, you have to leave me alone. I'm not going to let you hurt me.' When he started at me, I just pulled the trigger. I didn't mean to hurt him. I didn't even mean to shoot him. But I wasn't going to let him beat me.

GOEKEN: Okay, has he ever beat you in the past?

WEST: I've never been with Howard when he's really been drunk. . . . He only did me that way one time, and he wasn't drinking.

GOEKEN: Do you normally carry your gun in your purse, or why was it in there?

WEST: Well, I had the gun in my purse. I had taken all of my guns to my dad's to be cleaned, and I put the big ones back in the closet. I have a small closet, and I had a locksmith put a deadbolt on there . . . because the law says you have to keep them locked up. Well, they are big, you know. One is a side-by-side shotgun and the other is a .357. I had put those up, but I hadn't put up the little gun. I don't know why. . . . The .32 is mine. They are all mine. I bought them legal, and they are all registered to me.

Goeken asked West what St. John said to her after he had been shot.

WEST: I said, 'Howard, just lay there. They'll be here in a few minutes.' He said, 'No, I know what you are doing. You're fucking trying to kill me. I know what you are trying to do.' I said, 'Howard, I'm not.'

Goeken asked West about St. John's history.

WEST: He has a long arrest record for assault, I know.

Police weren't necessarily buying West's account, and their investigation yielded a starkly different version of the shooting from St. John. Los Banos officer Terry Kirschman was dispatched to the emergency room of the Los Banos Community Hospital to try to get a statement from St. John. Luckily, the gravely wounded St. John was still conscious, and he gave a brief statement.

KIRSCHMAN: I asked St. John why he had gotten shot, and he stated that all she said was, 'I'm setting you up.' I asked St. John if there was any reason for this, and he stated, 'She's a crazy bitch.'

Upon reviewing the evidence in the case, Los Banos police and prosecutors felt there was enough evidence to file charges against West, and she was booked at the Merced County jail on charges of felony assault with a gun and corporal injury to a spouse. At first, it seemed to police like a pretty solid case. West admitted to the shooting; witnesses told police St. John emerged from the house screaming about his wife shooting him; the police had recovered the gun, which was a .32-caliber Colt revolver registered to West; and officers had a statement from the victim himself, and he was identifying West as the person who pulled the trigger.

29

Howard Simon St. John was one lucky son of a bitch on May 21, 1994. The .32-caliber projectile from his wife's gun shredded skin and tissue like a cannonball, tearing a huge, gaping hole in his neck. The bullet came to rest in his left shoulder, and it was the type of gunshot wound that would be deadly on ninety-nine out of one hundred occasions. But the Indian spirits must have been watching over St. John that night, because when he was flown by helicopter from Los Banos to Memorial Medical Center in Modesto, doctors discovered the bullet hadn't damaged any major arteries. The doctors decided to leave the bullet exactly where it was, giving St. John a lead token of his wife's love that he could keep with him forever.

The following day, on May 22, a still-groggy St. John picked up the phone in his room and called the AAA insurance office in San Jose. The company contacted its insurance fraud investigator, Dwight Bell, who called St. John at the hospital.

"I placed several telephone calls to Modesto, and the

hospital, and eventually, I got through to him," Bell said. "He was obviously under sedation, rather difficult to converse with, [but] at that time he said he had burned the car for her . . . for Brooke West, and she had bought a Corvette for him in payment."

It looked like a huge break for Bell's investigation. The investigator urged St. John to get some rest, and the two men agreed to meet in person once St. John got out of the hospital.

St. John was released from Memorial North hospital within the week, and he showed up at Tony Mercado's front doorstep in San Jose with a big bandage covering the opening in his neck. Teary eyed, St. John told Mercado and his mother, Angie Mercado, about the shooting and how West had ambushed him without warning in their garage.

"He said he was doing something in the yard, and she called him into the garage," Angie Mercado recalled. "She closed the garage door, and she said, 'I'm going to kill you because of the insurance. They are getting suspicious.'"

Thomas Gutierrez got the same story.

"Howard said he came inside the house. Brooke closed the door and said, 'Howard, I have to shoot you, and I'm going to burn the house down,'" Gutierrez recalled.

Meanwhile, in Los Banos, news about the shooting spread quickly through the community. A couple of days later, Mike and Crystal Stoykovich were in front of their home when a man in a pickup drove into West's driveway. The individual was an older, thin-framed gentleman with white hair and a thick, handlebar mustache. Mike Stoykovich walked over and introduced himself to the man, who said he was West's father, Leroy.

"Remember the book *Heidi*, with her grandpa in the Alps?" Crystal Stoykovich said. "That's what he looked like. He was an older man with a thick white beard."

Leroy talked to Mike Stoykovich about his daughter's troubles, and Leroy's voice seemed tinged with anguish as he talked about his disappointment over West's decision to marry St. John.

"He said he couldn't understand why a bright girl like Brooke would get involved with somebody who didn't have anything," Mike Stoykovich recalled. "He said, 'When Howard gets his Indian check [from the government] he probably buys a case of wine or something, and when it's gone, he waits for the next cheek.'"

Leroy said his daughter was housed at the Merced County jail on assault charges, and Leroy had no plans to get her out of jail until she calmed down.

"He said, 'A bail bondsman called me, and he wanted to know what I wanted to do about her bond,'" Mike Stoykovich said. "And [Leroy] says, 'Leave her there a couple of days until she cools off, and I'll go down and pick her up.'"

A couple of days later, West's neighbors watched in astonishment as Leroy dropped his daughter off at her house. She was released on her own recognizance by a Los Banos judge, and she was more than willing to tell the Stoykoviches and the Parras her version of the shooting. "The one thing she told us was Howard threw a table at her, a big banquet table with the folding legs," Stoykovich said. "She said when he threw that table, he was drunk, and she said, 'He probably would have killed me.' So she just pulled the gun out and winged him. She said, 'I didn't want to kill him, but I stopped him,' and then she went in and called the police.

"She said she had a restraining order because she didn't want him around the house, and she said she was going to keep a rottweiler in the house in case he'd come over, you know, and break in the house," Stoykovich said. "She was afraid of him. She was there all by herself, and her dad was gone."

"She was telling me it was completely self-defense, that he was coming after her," Laura Parra said. "I just kind of took it as, he was throwing all this stuff at her and she shot him. But I was wondering what she was doing with a loaded gun in her purse in the garage."

By all accounts, it appeared the relationship between West and St. John was over. West was talking about restraining orders, and St. John had reported his wife for insurance fraud. Everyone who lived on Fir Street suspected that their neighborhood would finally return to normal and that the volatile relationship between West and St. John had ended for good.

They were wrong.

Within a few weeks of St. John's shooting, the unthinkable happened—St. John was back at West's home on Fir Street.

"He said, 'She's trying to make it up to me, you know?'" Mike Stoykovich said.

His decision to return to West was a complete shock to those who knew him. "I said, 'Man, are you nuts?'" Thomas Gutierrez said. "'What is this?' I told him quite a few times, I said, 'Howard, I don't mean to break your heart, I don't mean to bust your balloon, but look at you and look at her. This woman is going to kill you.' And he said, 'Nah, we were just arguing and fighting.' He said, 'She just got a little scared.' I said, 'If that's how she acts when she's scared, I hate to see her when she's pissed off.'"

Tony Mercado warned his friend as well.

"I told him not to go back with her," Tony Mercado said. "I said, 'Otherwise, you are going to get killed, Howard.'"

But despite the hole in his neck, St. John wasn't listening. And to Dana Gutierrez, the decision was a sad commentary on St. John's status in life.

"I don't think Howard really had anyplace else to go," she said.

Angie Mercado said St. John told her West had promised to sign over all her worldly belongings if he came back.

"He said that she was going to sign over the Corvette to him because it was still in her name," Angie said. "And then I said, 'Howard, are you going to go back with her?' And he goes, 'Well, I don't know,' and right then I knew that he was. So then, I guess she contacted him again and said that she would sign over both cars and the house to him."

The couple was reunited even while felony assault charges were still pending against West. The reunion of St. John and West was a death knell for Dwight Bell's insurance fraud case. Bell repeatedly tried to contact St. John for more information about the burned-out Jaguar, but St. John was deliberately avoiding the private investigator.

Bell finally tracked down St. John outside the Valley Medical Center in San Jose on June 1, 1994. St. John was sitting on a park bench, waiting for a doctor's appointment to get treatment for his neck, when Bell approached. The investigator immediately realized St. John was very, very drunk.

"Well, as he sat down on a bench . . . he emptied a half pint, one of those small, half-pint bottles of tequila," Bell recalled. "I don't know how many of those little airline-type bottles he had in his pocket, but he drained one or two of those, and he followed that up with a can of Coke that he had in his hand."

St. John proceeded to recant everything he previously said about burning his wife's car, and he told Bell he made up the story about the insurance scam to get back at his wife because of his anger over the shooting.

The following is the tape-recorded statement St. John gave to Bell:

BELL: Howard, give me your full name.

ST. JOHN: Howard St. John.

BELL: Do you have a middle name?

ST. JOHN: Yeah.

BELL: What's that?

ST. JOHN: None of your business.

BELL: Okay, what's your date of birth?

ST. JOHN: 5/15/58.

BELL: And, ah, are you staying on Rhodes Court?

ST. JOHN: Not no more. I got kicked out.

BELL: Could I reach you at any of those telephone numbers?

ST. JOHN: Nope.

BELL: Okay, give me an idea about how much you've had to drink today?

ST. JOHN: About a pint. About six of those little bottles right there.

BELL: And that's tequila?

ST. JOHN: Yeah, tequila.

BELL: And what else have you taken?

ST. JOHN: Crank [crystal methamphetamine].

BELL: How much?'

ST. JOHN: Oh, about half a gram.

BELL: Do you smoke that?

ST. JOHN: No, snort it.

BELL: Snorted it . . . all right . . . tell me what happened on the night, ah, the Jaguar incident.

ST. JOHN: Well, all I know is, I and Brooke went out. She came by, and picked me up at home. At the Rhodes Court address.

BELL: Uh huh.

ST. JOHN: And when she picked me up, we went out to Flames, and from Flames we went to go see a movie. A movie, by uh—what's his name? Remember that there karate guy, Steven Seagal, or something like that.

BELL: Uh huh.

ST. JOHN: So we spent a total of time, oh, about four hours, five hours there, three hours—something like that. Hell, I got no idea. And then, and then when we came out of the movies, the whole fucking car was gone.

BELL: Okay. You, uh, you told, Mr. Vallejos of Triple A and also Mr. Walker that you had burned the car. Is that right?

ST. JOHN: No, I didn't burn it. The reason why I said that [was] 'cause I wanted to get back at her. The reason why I did that was because she fucking shot me, and I wanted to get back at her.

BELL: Okay, but let's not get ahead of ourselves. Okay, the car is gone from the parking lot that night?

ST. JOHN: Yeah.

BELL: And then what happened?

ST. JOHN: Then we, uh, we waited for the police for about a whole fucking hour it seemed like.

BELL: Well, you described over the telephone to me, a few days ago, the location where the car was burned. You said next to the railroad tracks.

ST. JOHN: Oh, yeah, because, uh, because . . . because . . . because the, uh, that there place that . . . towing . . . that the towing yard told us where exactly the car was picked up from. And then, and then, it was also written in the police report, so they, yeah, I fucking have it. Yeah, so, that's from reading the police report, and from what the towing company told us. So we went over there, and looked at the spot.

BELL: Oh, you went and found the spot?

ST. JOHN: Yeah.

BELL: All right.

ST. JOHN: Yeah, it was just obvious.

BELL: Uh huh.

ST. JOHN: You know.

BELL: You also told me over the telephone that you and Brooke got married?

ST. JOHN: Oh, yeah . . . in Reno, April thirtieth.

BELL: And, ah, where did you go live?

ST. JOHN: [I] went to go live with her [in] Los Banos. Fir. Sixteen-something. You know, I can't remember that fucking address.

BELL: Well, where does Brooke work?

ST. JOHN: She works at a company called [Syntex] . . . that's located off Page Mill Road.

BELL: Did you have a job?

ST. JOHN: No . . . because I got a hernia, so that stops me from my profession.

BELL: And, uh, the incident [the shooting] happened Saturday morning?

ST. JOHN: It happened Saturday night. I was drunk . . . I fucking tore up. I went over there and tore up her house. I slapped her around. And then, she was just . . . it was just common sense, you know? She didn't know what to do, you know. She panicked.

BELL: Uh huh.

ST. JOHN: You know, she fucking shot me, you know. Hey, you know, I deserve it. I mean, when somebody hits a woman, come on.

BELL: You're not supposed to do that?

ST. JOHN: I know that . . . I don't fucking blame her for fucking doing that shit.

BELL: She shot you in self-defense?

ST. JOHN: Yeah. I mean, it's fucking all there in the fucking police report. These fucking cops seen the house and everything. I'm just doing this so I can fucking try to get at her ass. The reason why I told you everything because I fucking seen the car, I read the police report, I seen where the car came from. I figured it out, put two and two together, and I was all fucking all high on fucking drugs anyway when I was in the hospital.

BELL: Uh huh.

ST. JOHN: So I just put two and two together. I mean, come on. Any fucking dummy can fucking make up something like that.

BELL: So you made up this story . . . of burning up the car?

Sᴛ. Jᴏʜɴ: Oh, yeah. Fuck, I had to, 'cause I'm trying to get her back.

Bᴇʟʟ: Does she know that you called [us]?

Sᴛ. Jᴏʜɴ: No, no, She don't fucking know nothing.

Bᴇʟʟ: Do you think she's contacted them about you?

Sᴛ. Jᴏʜɴ: I don't know. Probably . . . because she knows I'm crazy. Because, hey, I've been fucking put in the nut ward a few times.

Bᴇʟʟ: Where?

Sᴛ. Jᴏʜɴ: South Dakota. Here.

Bᴇʟʟ: What for?

Sᴛ. Jᴏʜɴ: 'Cause of my drinking, drugging problem. I got a whole fucking stack of fucking records.

Bᴇʟʟ: Uh huh.

Sᴛ. Jᴏʜɴ: You can fucking go in there [to the hospital]. I almost died here, twice—no, three times—for overdose. Drugs . . . alcohol.

Bᴇʟʟ: Okay, well, I appreciate your information.

30

Tyla Knotchapone learned of Howard Simon St. John's shooting and his miraculous survival from her friends at the Native American Indian Center in San Jose, and she was horrified. She wasn't, however, surprised. She had sensed a storm brewing in St. John's life two months earlier, and now that storm had come ashore with a fury.

In late May, Knotchapone sought out St. John, and she once again told her friend of her reservations about West.

"He mentioned he wanted a divorce, and that he felt very uncomfortable with her, and that he wanted his life back," Knotchapone said. "He said, 'You know, if I didn't meet her, this bullet wouldn't be in my neck.' He said, 'I just want to forget her. She is bad news. I think she is going to kill me.'

"He was in tears, actually," Knotchapone said. "He said, 'I can't believe I have this kind of problem in my life with a woman. This woman is dangerous, Tyla. I don't know how to go about divorcing her. It's like she's got me in a web, and I know the way out, but I'm scared. What could be next? I'm scared to find out.'"

Knotchapone wept during the conversation. She pleaded with St. John to leave his wife, and she offered him a bed in the small apartment she shared with her ten-year-old daughter in San Jose.

St. John didn't take up the offer.

" 'I don't want to put you and your daughter on the line, because she is a crazy lady, you know?' " St. John told Knotchapone.

St. John said he wasn't the only person who feared West—her mother did, too. He said West was abusive to Christine, and he actually witnessed acts of violence by West against her mother.

" 'She barely gets along with her mother,' " Knotchapone said, quoting St. John. " 'She even threatens her mother sometimes. The mother doesn't know how to even speak to her own daughter. She gets all scared because she's at the age where she's helpless.' He would hear [them] arguing," Knotchapone said, and West would tell her mother, " 'I wish you were dead, mother, you son of a bitch!' "

"She [West] would start throwing things around," Knotchapone said. "There goes her bottles of perfume all over the place. He [St. John] said she even picked her mother up and slammed her body against the dresser and told her, 'I wish you were dead. I'm so sick of you hanging around me. You're just getting old anyway. You should have just dropped dead when you were in prison. Why stay alive?'

"I mean, that is the way she talked to her mother when they were in a heated argument," Knotchapone said. "[That] is what he was telling me."

Knotchapone asked St. John why he had gone back to his wife, and St. John had no answer.

" 'I'm so stupid,' " St. John told Knotchapone. " 'I don't know why I went back with her.' "

31

Late on the night of June 2, several residents of Fir Street heard a commotion, looked out their front windows and saw something extremely strange. Brookey Lee West was running down the street like a commando carrying out a covert operation behind enemy lines.

"I looked out my window and I thought, 'Oh, my God,'" Laura Parra said. "Brooke was running around like a military person. She was crouching, hiding on the ground, going behind cars and stuff, and she was dressed in what looked like military clothes. I thought, 'What the hell is going on here?'"

West ran to the front doorstep of the home of Robert and Tara Fullington, who lived a few houses down on Fir Street. An officer wrote in a police report what the Fullingtons told authorities:

They were asleep at their residence when they heard someone beating on their front door. Robert Fullington opened the curtains next to the door, but he did not open the front door. At that time, he observed a female standing outside, who identified herself as Brookey West, who lives at an address down the street, and she requested that they call 911 immediately. She needed the police for immediate assistance. The Fullingtons advised that they would call the police, but they did not open the door to allow Brooke to enter their residence.

The Fullingtons then called 911 per Brooke's request, and they looked out the window as they waited for the police department's arrival. While looking out the window, they observed that Brooke took off running northbound down the street, and she hid in the front yards of several other residences.

Los Banos police arrived within a few minutes, and they located West standing in the middle of Fir Street. Officer Steve Goeken, who responded to the shooting that St. John had survived at West's house just thirteen days earlier, asked West what was going on, and she said St. John had threatened her because she'd misplaced a photo from their wedding in Reno.

She said she feared St. John was going to kill her.

Goeken memorialized the incident in a Los Banos police department report.

I responded to 1639 Fir Street on a report of a female requesting the neighbors call the police. When I arrived, I made contact with Brookey in the street. She advised me that she wanted me to go in the house to see if Howard was there. She said that he has been acting crazy because he is upset over a picture that he could not find of them when they got married in Reno. She said when they were coming down [Pacheco] Pass today, that he had slapped her twice because he was upset that he couldn't find it. She said when they got home, she was telling him that she was going to go look in the car to find it, but he did not want her to leave the house. She said that after she took a shower, she then went to the door, and he asked her what she was doing again. She told him she was going to the car to look for the picture, and he told her to shut the door. She said she then ran out the door and shut it behind her, and she hid until I got there. I then went in the house with Brookey, where I made contact with Howard, and I asked what the problem was. He said he was not angry anymore, and that he was mad about a picture of them together in Reno that they could not find. Brookey said she just wanted to leave, and that she went to get in her car, but Howard said it wasn't running. I asked him what was wrong, and he said he pulled the ignition wires off it. Brookey said she did not want me to have him removed from the house—that she would go stay with friends.

At West's request, Officer Cindy Hoskins gave West a ride to an all-night coffee shop in Los Banos, and West told the officer she wasn't going back home. She planned to divorce her husband.

Neighbors saw St. John coming and going from the residence in a panic the following morning, and he told neighbors West left the home the night prior and had not returned. Several times throughout the day, he jumped in West's car, peeled out of the driveway and then returned several hours later. He was frantically looking for West, and his search continued throughout Friday and into Saturday, June 4.

"We saw Howard driving Brooke's car wildly," Laura Parra said. "He would leave the house and speed somewhere, then come back speeding to the house. He was there by himself."

By Saturday afternoon, St. John concluded West had been kidnapped, so he called the Los Banos police department to report West missing. An officer filed a missing persons report for West that afternoon:

On June 4, 1994, at approximately 12 p.m., I contacted Howard St. John in regards to a missing persons report. Howard St. John stated that his wife, Brookey Lee, was missing from their residence, and she was last seen on June 2, 1994, at approximately 11 p.m. Howard St. John stated that on June 3, 1994, sometime in the evening, his wife, Brookey Lee, contacted him stating she was at a local motel, and she had gotten beat up, and she possibly broke her arm. Mr. St. John stated he did not feel she was missing voluntarily.

The missing person is Brookey Lee St. John, also known as Brookey Lee West. [She is] a white female, approximately 40, with hazel eyes. She is also known to wear contacts, and she has brown, shoulder-length, straight hair. Date of birth is June 28, 1953.

Mrs. West is missing from 1639 Fir Street. No possible destinations known. I note Mrs. West possibly has a mental condition, and she might be suicidal. Mrs. West has a brown birthmark on her right forearm, and she has two gold-capped teeth in the bottom left side of her mouth. Mrs. St. John was seen leaving the area in an unknown direction wearing a pink sweat top, pink sweatpants, black Reebok shoes, and a black purse.

I note that this couple has had a couple of serious altercations in the past few weeks where this department has had to respond for assistance. Brookey Lee West was seen on June 2, 1994, by officer Cindy Hoskins of the Los Banos Police Department, at which time Brookey Lee West stated to Officer Hoskins that she was not planning on returning. This would be an indication that Brookey Lee West is missing voluntarily.

Howard St. John gave me Brookey Lee West's father's phone number in the Bay area. Her father's name is Leroy Smith, and I [could not contact him]. At approximately 1:10 p.m. on June 4, 1994, Leroy Smith's wife, [Chloe],

contacted me at the department and gave me information
stating that she knew for a fact that Brookey Lee West was
not in the Los Banos area—that she is in the Bay area.
Santa Clara to be exact, staying at a motel for the time being. Leroy Smith's wife was unable to give me a number to
contact Brookey Lee West, but she stated she would talk to
her husband. She would have him try and get in contact
with Brookey and have her contact the department to clear
up this matter. Given the circumstances of the past few
weeks regarding different cases, in this officer's opinion,
Brookey Lee West is voluntarily missing, and it is possible
she is leaving her husband.

That night, on Saturday, June 4, St. John called West's
father, and Leroy could tell St. John was stone-cold drunk.
He slurred his words as he asked Leroy where his wife was,
and Leroy assured St. John that West was okay. But despite
the assurances, St. John kept calling Leroy Smith throughout the night, and the phone calls became so persistent,
Leroy finally unhooked his phone so he could get some
sleep.

That night, St. John also called Tony Mercado's mother,
Angie.

"He didn't know where she was, and the dad [Leroy]
had told him not to worry—that she was okay," Angie Mercado said. "I think right after that, Howard started drinking, and then he called me back, and he said that the dad
had said that she was there [at Leroy's]."

St. John made one other call on what would prove to be
the last night of his life. He phoned the Four Winds rehabilitation center on Rhodes Court, and he got in touch with
an old friend named Ernie Turtle. Turtle, a Native American man who was a member of the Four Winds program,
said St. John relayed how he and his wife were having
problems, and in a drunken rant St. John told Turtle he was

going to get even with his wife for running off on him.

"Well, he mentioned something about wanting to kill her, you know, and getting even," Turtle told authorities. "He was drunk, you know."

Sometime during the next twenty-four hours, someone shot St. John in the back, and his corpse was driven several hours away to Tulare County, where his killer dumped the remains like a piece of trash alongside the Tule River in Sequoia National Forest.

It was a sad, degrading end to a mostly sad existence for the Sioux Indian from South Dakota.

32

Where a crime is coolly premeditated, then the means of covering it are coolly premeditated also. I hope, therefore, that we are in the presence of a serious misconception.

—Sherlock Holmes, in Sir Arthur Cohan Doyle's "The Problem of Thor Bridge"

In the days following the discovery of Howard Simon St. John's corpse in the Sequoia National Forest, Tulare County homicide detective Daniel Haynes went into bulldog mode. He was dead-set on solving St. John's murder, and he wasn't going to let go of the case until St. John's killer was arrested, convicted and locked away in the California prison system for life.

The first lead of any significance came when St. John's father, Sylvester, told Haynes his son's wife had shot St. John in the neck just thirteen days earlier.

"He told me there had been some problems that landed Howard in the hospital," Haynes said. "We were on the road then to Los Banos. It was our best lead at the time.

"You've heard, 'Where there's smoke, there's fire'?" Haynes said. "When you don't have anything outside of what was going on there in Los Banos, then that's where you look, and I looked hard."

Haynes and his partner, Herman Martinez, drove out to

Los Banos on June 9. "A real nice guy," Haynes said of
Martinez. "A Vietnam vet, probably six feet two inches tall
or so, and he's very, very professional. A fairly quiet guy,
but he's someone you would definitely want on your side if
you are in a fight.

"He's very meticulous," Haynes said. "All work, no
play, and he comes in and does a straight, honest ten or
twenty hours of work for the day, and then he goes home.
He's a hard-core family man, and he has two sons who are
also in law enforcement."

The detectives' first stop in Los Banos was the police
department, where Sergeant Carey Reed briefed the Tulare
County investigators on all the problems at West's house
on Fir Street during the last two months: a shooting, a
handful of domestic violence calls and an insurance fraud
investigation in which her husband had reported her to the
authorities for the burning of her Jaguar.

"Los Banos police were very helpful, and the district attorney's office there was extremely helpful, too," Haynes
said. "It's very difficult to work a case out of town like that
when you are on strange turf, when you don't have the resources and when you don't have the knowledge of the
area. It's nice to find [a police department] that rolls out the
red carpet for you, and they did."

After the briefing from Los Banos police, Martinez and
Haynes drove a little more than two miles from Los Banos
police headquarters to West's home on Fir Street. They noticed in the driveway a small Chevrolet sedan belonging to
West and a white Corvette belonging to St. John. The detectives obtained a description of the residence, and they
returned to downtown Los Banos, where they met Merced
County deputy district attorney William C. Hunter at his
office. The detectives asked Hunter to pursue a search warrant for West's home, and the warrant was later signed by
local judge Phillip Castellucci.

The Tulare County detectives, accompanied by Sergeant Reed from Los Banos, then returned to West's home. The trio of investigators knocked on the door, and they were greeted by a frail, sweet-looking sixty-two-year-old woman with long, braided hair. Christine Smith introduced herself, invited the detectives inside and agreed to give the three men a taped statement.

"A little old lady," Haynes said. "Very nice. It was like talking to your grandma in her living room. She was friendly, and she'd answer any of your questions. How truthful? I don't know. You wouldn't immediately suspect her of being involved. It wasn't until much later on in the investigation when I got a different opinion of her."

The senior spoke in a thick Texas accent, and she proved to be a wealth of information for Martinez and Haynes. The Caucasian woman started off by claiming she was "part" Apache Indian and her daughter was "about 15 percent" Indian. She said she never did like St. John, a violent, temperamental drunk.

"He's a very violent man," she said in a taped statement. "He's got a record from here to Kansas City and back. Armed robbery and everything else. She really picked a thug . . . a hooter and a tooter. Crazier than a bedbug."

Christine frowned on the relationship between West and St. John, she said, in large part because St. John moved into West's house before they were married.

"I'm pretty churchly, and I don't go for the ways of modern young people," she said. "I don't go for that. I'm a Christian, and I don't go for it. To me, my home is sacred ground, and that's the way it is. I couldn't compromise, in other words."

The detectives asked Christine whether her daughter was a gun owner, and she said her daughter was fond of firearms.

"She takes her guns to her father [for cleaning], because, you know, it's like a collection," Christine said.

Christine also confirmed her daughter had shot her husband in the neck nearly two weeks earlier.

"She plugged him through the neck," she said. "Shootin'. 'Plug' is a Texas slang for it. I know that they were having trouble, and she was supposed to have shot him," Christine said. "He was insane drunk. He would have killed her if she hadn't of shot him with that little pistol. . . . He was a huge man, and compared to her, it'd be like a pissant coming up against an elephant. He was crazy. He was trying to get at her to kill her. She had no intentions of killing him. . . . She just wanted to stop him. He's a big, huge man, and when they get drunk, they go insane."

"So when you say 'they,' you're talking about a person like Howard?" Martinez asked.

"Indians," Christine said. "Indian people. All of them go crazy when they drink. I'm sure you heard the history. . . . Well, I know when I drink I ain't got no sense, so I don't drink. . . . Indians do that. They just go crazy when they drink that firewater. Just crazier than a loon."

But by far the most valuable information Christine provided to detectives was West's whereabouts on the weekend of St. John's shooting. On the evening of Thursday, June 2, Christine said St. John threatened her daughter's life in an argument over a missing photo from the couple's Reno wedding, and the threat prompted West to run to the neighbors, who called the police.

During the dispute, Christine said St. John tore the distributor out of West's car to prevent her from leaving.

"He didn't want her to go," Christine said. "He wanted her to stay here so he could beat the living hell out of her . . . he was souped de gooped . . . and no way was she going to buy that. She went to the people down here across the street, she banged on their door and she asked them to call the police."

Christine said the Los Banos police drove West to an

all-night coffee shop downtown to get her away from St. John on the night of June 2, and while at the coffee shop West met a truck driver. According to Christine, the truck driver gave West a ride over Pacheco Pass to San Jose, and the next morning, on Friday, June 3, West rented a car and got a hotel room there. That day, Christine said, her daughter went to work at Syntex Pharmaceuticals in nearby Palo Alto, where West was working on a freelance technical writing project.

After she was done working, West went to a do-it-yourself legal advice business in the San Jose area and filled out paperwork for a divorce. West then returned to her hotel room to get a good night's sleep.

The next day, Saturday, June 4, West picked up her mother from her van at a city park in Santa Clara, and the two went shopping all day. That night—the night authorities suspect St. John was slain—West dropped her mother off at the van, and West went back to work at Syntex Pharmaceuticals, where she worked all night. Christine told the Tulare County investigators that while her daughter was at work West received a call from St. John, and St. John cursed his wife for leaving him in Los Banos. During the phone call, St. John said his Corvette was in the shop for repairs, and he wanted West to go pay for the repairs, then get the Corvette back to the house immediately.

"See, I'm going to have to use some profanity, and it just hurts me," Christine said. "[But he said], 'Get your fuckin' ass over and pick up . . . the Corvette'."

Christine said her daughter also told her St. John had stumbled across about $3,000 in cash West had hidden in a kitchen drawer of her home before fleeing Los Banos in the domestic dispute. St. John told his wife over the phone he was taking the money and going to Reno with his "hometown boys."

"Who are you going with?" West supposedly asked her

husband, according to Christine. " 'None of your fucking business,' " she said St. John responded. " 'When I get back from Reno, that son of a bitchin' car, bitch, better be in the driveway.' That's what he said to her."

The next day, on Sunday, June 5, Christine told the detectives she and her daughter returned to Los Banos because they believed St. John had left for Reno. When they returned to the home on Fir Street, they found her house in shambles. "The whole house was completely turned upside down. Beer cans, tequila bottles," Christine said.

Christine and her daughter found two different types of cigarette butts in the home, which indicated to Christine someone else had been in the house with St. John prior to his departure to Reno. She said she and West cleaned the house all day Sunday, and West didn't learn of her husband's murder until a phone call came from St. John's mother, who had been in touch with the Tulare County authorities, which told her St. John had been murdered.

"She says, 'Well, you know, Howard's dead,' " Christine quoted St. John's mother as saying. "And Brookey said, 'No. Howard went to Reno, and he took $3,000,' which was her full income tax check."

St. John's father called a short time later and asked West to authorize the release of his son's body from the Tulare County coroner's office. Sylvester St. John told West he wanted his son's body returned to South Dakota for a proper burial on the Indian reservation.

"The father called and wanted to know if Brookey would sign the release papers to him so they could carry him back to the Dakotas to be buried on Indian ground in Indian style," Christine said. "And, uh, Brookey said, 'Well, I don't know how much money that would cost me to do that,' and he said, 'You don't have to pay. I'll do the paying through the Indians.'

"And, uh, he thanked her," Christine said. "He's a very nice person, and the mother's a very nice person, too. But, uh, Brookey said, 'It can't be, because Howard went to Reno, and I haven't heard from him.'"

St. John's father supposedly said to West during the phone conversation, "Well, he's had these type of things. He'll leave. We haven't seen him in fifteen years, and he'll leave and be gone maybe sometimes five years. We never knew where he was."

Christine then made a point of telling the detectives West should have receipts to prove her whereabouts in San Jose on the weekend of the shooting. When asked about her daughter's rental car, Christine said, "She had a rental car and, uh, I can't keep the story like it's supposed to be."

Moments later, during the middle of the interview with Christine, the phone rang. West was on the line. West said she was in nearby Gilroy, but she would hurry home to meet with the investigators. West arrived at the Los Banos residence shortly after six p.m., and she, too, agreed to give a taped statement to the Tulare County investigators.

Haynes' first impression of West was that she was a normal woman.

"Nothing out of the ordinary," Haynes said. "Quiet. Soft-spoken. Ordinary in appearance. She answered all of our questions."

Haynes is prevented from discussing specifically what West said to police, but her seventy-two-page taped statement documents her alibi for the murder. The following are excerpts.

MARTINEZ: This taped interview is being conducted at 1639 Fir Street in Los Banos. Today's date is 6/9/94. The time is 6:32 p.m. Present at this taped interview are myself, Detective Herman Martinez, Detective Daniel Haynes, Detective Carey

Reed of the Los Banos police department, and the subject is Brookey Lee West.

MARTINEZ: Brooke, for the purpose of this interview, what is your full name?

WEST: My full given name on my birth certificate is Brookey Lee Smith.

MARTINEZ: And you were married to whom on April 30?

WEST: Howard Simon St. John.

MARTINEZ: This individual's [body] was located in Tulare County. Are you familiar with Tulare County?

WEST: No. I've heard of it, you know, but I'm not like familiar . . . I couldn't say I've been there.

MARTINEZ: How have you heard about Tulare County?

WEST: Well, the Tule Indian Reservation is in Tulare County.

MARTINEZ: Have you ever been to Tulare County?

WEST: I've probably passed through it going to Los Angeles or something.

MARTINEZ: Do you know if Howard had gone specifically to the Tule Indian Reservation?

WEST: I don't know if he had ever been there . . .

MARTINEZ: Do you know of any specific person or persons that Howard associated with, who were from any of these reservations that we talked about?

WEST: No. He knows many full-bloods. My husband is Dakota Sioux. . . . There are six nations of Sioux.

MARTINEZ: Do you know which reservation in Dakota his Sioux tribe is from?

WEST: He's Wompton Saxton Sioux, but I'm not sure of the name of his reservation. He had showed me his papers, and he says he is registered Wompton Saxton.

MARTINEZ: Okay. Do you have any Indian heritage?

WEST: We're Mescalero Apache. I met Howard at the Four Winds Lodge. The Four Winds Lodge is a rehab center for Native Americans in San Jose. It's on Rhodes Court. Right around the corner from that is the Native American Indian Center in

San Jose. I used to [take my mother] there to the Four Winds Lodge on Friday evenings, mainly because they had open AA meetings. Open to the public. Even though . . . these are all male participants that go through rehab.

MARTINEZ: What was the reason for you going there?

WEST: My mother is an alcoholic, and I took her to meetings because she couldn't drive at the time.

MARTINEZ: When was it when you first met Howard St. John?

WEST: I didn't actually talk to Howard or meet Howard because Howard didn't want to meet me. [He] just wanted to watch me for maybe three or four months. When they [Indians] first see somebody they want, they are not like white people. They don't just introduce themselves. They have to watch you for a while, then they have to decide if, you know, what their approach is going to be.

MARTINEZ: So that's how you became acquainted with Howard? You saw him speaking at that AA meeting. And then?

WEST: Yes. I took my mom to the meetings on Friday, and . . . Howard was just there. He just turned around, I just turned around, and he was just right in front of me. And then he shook hands with me, and I said [unintelligible], and he said, "My name is Howard."

MARTINEZ: You spoke to him first?

WEST: Yeah. He was right in my face. I didn't know what else to do. I had asked him about that later, and he said, "Well, I decided that it was time to meet you." I had wanted to meet him.

MARTINEZ: So, basically, the people that were [at these meetings] were Indians?

WEST: Most of the time. I would say that it is very rare [for] white people . . . I don't know why. It just seems to be that way. You rarely see any white people there without [them] being married to [an Indian] or to have a half-breed . . .

MARTINEZ: So you and Howard eventually met. How did the relationship start with you guys as far as starting to socialize and that sort of thing?

WEST: Well, Howard had a problem. He had a hernia, and he was unable to work. Howard was an excellent mechanic, and he was unable to work because he couldn't lift, and he was very depressed. I spoke with him many times, and I thought I could help Howard because I had helped other Indians there. I would do things for them—get them shampoo for their hair. Especially the ones who wore their hair very long.

MARTINEZ: Where did he live at the time since he didn't have any money? How did he support himself?

WEST: Well, he was in the program. The Four Winds Lodge Native American program.

MARTINEZ: You guys eventually became girlfriend/boyfriend?

WEST: Well, I worked with Howard for a long time. I wanted him to be around me before anything happened like that because the way that American Indian males look at women is not the way white people [do]. You know, it's like they kind of have a [possessive] attitude. "Well, that's mine." Like a car, and so you have to have an attitude with him, that you [let them] know it's either this way or that way. So, for a long time, many months, we were just friends, and I helped him, and I bought the right groceries for him, and the right herbs, and the right teas, so he could start taking the weight off, and he did very well. He went from 304 pounds to 240.

MARTINEZ: How long did this go on?

WEST: Few months.

MARTINEZ: So how long did you guys go together, I mean—how long?

WEST: I did not change my relationship with Howard until about last year in October. I started seeing him as a man instead of just a friend.

MARTINEZ: Okay, who initiated that? That change of relationship, from being a friend where you were nurturing him to a relationship where you were seeing him as a man?

WEST: I think both of us did.

MARTINEZ: And whose house is this?

WEST: It's my house . . . I closed on September 30, 1993.

MARTINEZ: And you say in October was when your relationship changed with Howard?

WEST: Yeah.

MARTINEZ: So your house came first, and then Howard?

WEST: Yeah. I moved here, and my relationship with Howard changed.

MARTINEZ: Did Howard move in to the house then?

WEST: Yes.

MARTINEZ: I'm going to ask you some personal questions. Before February or March, did you and Howard have any sexual relationships?

WEST: Yes.

MARTINEZ: Did your family know about your relationship? That he was living here?

WEST: They didn't know anything about Howard until he moved in.

MARTINEZ: Did your family—I'm talking about your mother, your father—did they accept that relationship?

WEST: My father, you know, he just says, "You are an adult. You can make your own decisions." My mother was not happy about it because she felt he was trying to use me. We had originally planned to go back to the Sioux reservation in South Dakota [to get married]. Actually, we were supposed to leave tomorrow.

MARTINEZ: Did you guys go to South Dakota to get married?

WEST: No. We got married in Reno. He was very insistent, and he said, "Well, we can get married in Reno, and [then] we can get married on the reservation, too." We were going to go back [to South Dakota] and get married anyway, because he hadn't gone home in a number of years. I basically wanted to do the trip so he could see his family. And . . . he wanted a Corvette. I bought him his Corvette. The white one. I bought it after he moved in. Uh, I needed a second car, [and] he wanted to restore [it].

MARTINEZ: You guys came back from Reno. What was the atmosphere? What type of home life did you have?

WEST: After we came back from Reno, I think [he was] a different man than before . . . I don't understand what happened to him. He had a real attitude change. All I can say is that his attitude became nasty to me, like, I would ask him questions, [and] he'd say, "Shut up. It's none of your fucking business." Stuff like that . . . he just changed. Before, he treated me respectfully. He didn't cuss at me.

MARTINEZ: Was he physical with you? By that I mean, did he assault you? Did he hit you?

WEST: Just recently, he did do that. The very first time he actually hit me physically was when I had picked him up [after] he had gotten out of the hospital. This was on a Tuesday evening when I picked him up.

MARTINEZ: Why was he in the hospital?

WEST: Because he had a gunshot wound to his shoulder.

MARTINEZ: How did—how did he get shot?

WEST: I shot him.

MARTINEZ: Why is that?

WEST: Well, it wasn't deliberate. He got mad because he thought that I had washed his pants with his wallet in it—he was drunk. . . . I've had so much happen to me, but this is to the best of my recollection. I was sweeping [the garage], he laid down in the dog's bed, and he says, "Come here and sit." I looked at him, and I said, "Howard, I'm not the family dog, okay?" He said, "I know you're not the family dog. I told you, fucking bitch, get over here and sit down."

He went crazy, and he started calling me all kinds of names. He says, "You don't have nothing. You think you've got something? You fucking whore. You don't have nothing." And he got up off the floor, and he says, "I'm going to kick your ass."

He was screaming and ranting at me, and he got up, and he took this big, long table, and he just flipped it like it was a quarter. Just turned it in the air. He says, "I'm going to beat your ass." I couldn't run, and I knew I couldn't get away from him, and I seen my purse sitting there. I just reached out. I just unzipped [it]. I grabbed the pistol, and I was backing up, and he came at me. He said, "I'm going to beat your ass," and I said, "Howard, don't," and I was shaking.

I drew [the gun]. I wanted to run, but I couldn't. I didn't have enough room. I don't know why. I just grabbed it, and see, I thought maybe he would stop. I didn't want him to beat me. I didn't really even want to hurt him. I was shaking, you know, and he just kept coming at me, and I said, "Stop," I'm backed up against the wall, and I was shaking. I just shut my eyes. I said, "Stop," and I just pulled the trigger. I wasn't really trying to hurt him. I guess it caught him in the shoulder, or something, and he looked at me. He fell on the garage floor.

He said, "You fucking bitch, you just tried to kill me!" I said, "Howard, I didn't try to kill you. Let me call 911. Just lay back. I don't know how bad you are hurt." He kept reaching for me, and I wouldn't let him get ahold of me. I came in to call 911, and then I seen him run past me.

MARTINEZ: Did the police arrive?

WEST: Yeah, they did . . . [Howard] was in the driveway, and he's screaming, "That fucking bitch! Lock her up. She tried to kill me!" The officer asked me if I was armed, and I said, "No, sir." [He asked] where the gun was, and I said, "It's over there on the table," so he took it. He spoke with me for a few minutes, and he says, "Well, I have to arrest you." They put [Howard] on a stretcher, and they took him to the hospital.

MARTINEZ: So that was the incident that we're talking about where you shot him, and that's why you shot him. Did you guys ever go to court over that issue?

WEST: Well, I was in jail and everything, and then I'm supposed to go back on the twenty-fourth which I will do. I don't know what will happen. I gave a statement to the officer, and he taped it.

MARTINEZ: That's one incident. How long was he in the hospital?

WEST: He was in the hospital for a week, and I was in jail for a few days. I had asked to be released on the date of my arraignment, which was the following Monday, and the judge wasn't very sympathetic to me. I don't think the judge really realized I was the victim at that point. . . .

MARTINEZ: Who got out first? Your husband or you?

WEST: I did. And the judge . . . it took him a while to figure out if they were going to let me go, on [my own recognizance]. I told the judge, I said, "I'm the only one working. There is nobody to care for him," which was a fact. I said, "I have property . . . I need to be out working, if it's at all possible."

He [the judge] said, "I was unaware that your husband [was] very, very intoxicated, and he has a very long record for assault. . . . Based on these facts, if you promise me that you will not do anything to harass him or have any weapons, and show up in court, I will release you on [your] own recognizance."

MARTINEZ: Did they give you the gun back?

WEST: No.

MARTINEZ: Okay. What about the other guns? The .357, and a shotgun. What happened to them?

WEST: My father has them.

MARTINEZ: Did he own guns? Howard?

WEST: Howard told me he had a .38. He said he gave it to a [friend]. I had never seen Howard with a gun, okay? I never saw the gun, so I don't know if he was fabricating or not. Howard always told me that he carried a gun in his sleeve—in a jacket. But I never saw it. . . . I had [also] begun to suspect over the last couple of weeks that he had given the house keys to other people.

MARTINEZ: And who would that be?

WEST: I don't know. The reason is because he made a strange remark to me. He said, "I've got friends, and they are going to keep checking on me . . . they can come up here and check this place out at any time." I didn't understand. I said, "What do you mean, check it out?" And he wouldn't answer me.

MARTINEZ: Where did he say his friends were from?

WEST: He didn't.

MARTINEZ: You suspected he may have given the keys to somebody else?

WEST: Yeah. He became that secretive.

MARTINEZ: Did you notice if, in fact, there were any occasions that somebody else was coming into the house?

WEST: I didn't ever really know. Howard got to where he wouldn't let me have the car. Throughout the day, he was checking on me, and he would be very, very, very mad at me if I wasn't there [at work] to answer my phone.'

MARTINEZ: After Howard got out of the hospital, did he come straight to the house?

WEST: I didn't go to Howard, because I wasn't sure of his frame of mind. I wasn't sure of the medication he was taking. I wanted to give him a little bit of time before I made any contact with him. So I was released later in the evening, sometime on a Wednesday. Howard, I guess, was released on a Sunday. He went to a powwow. . . . I didn't know what to do. I didn't have anybody to talk to. I wasn't sure. I didn't know if he would retaliate against me.

MARTINEZ: When did you see Howard again?

WEST: I saw him the following Tuesday evening. He called me at my office, and he wanted to see me. I didn't know what he wanted in terms of, you know, like divorce. He seemed okay. He wanted to talk to me. I went to [Four Winds] at 109 Rhodes Court. . . . I seen him out on the street, and I stopped the car. I was driving the little Chevy. The other car was still in the shop. He just looked at me really strange and he took off running. And I thought, "What the hell is he running from?"

[He was] running away from me like he was afraid of me or something. So I . . . drove around the corner, which would have put me on East Santa Clara Street. It's just like a little corner, and I saw Howard coming across the street. I stopped, and I said, "Howard," and . . . he turned around, and he ran

back into a liquor store. I thought, "Well, I'm not going to
mess with this because I don't need to be arrested for something when I'm not really trying to harass him." So I just
drove off, and then I went to a phone booth in Santa Clara. I
called him there [at the Four Winds] and I said, "Howard, you
called me. You had to see me. I would like to see you. I know
we have so many problems. I don't know—I'm a nervous
wreck. I'd like to talk to you." He said, "Well, come over here
and pick me up on the corner where you just seen me fifteen
minutes ago."

So I drove up over there on the corner. He came out and
said, "Get out of the fucking car. I want to search you." He
was real belligerent.

MARTINEZ: He said he wanted to search you?

WEST: Yeah. He said, "Give me your fucking purse," so he
took my purse, and he searched me and checked my purse.

MARTINEZ: Did he say why he was searching you?

WEST: Who knows? He thought I wanted to hurt him. I
didn't want to hurt him to start with. I said, "Howard, I'm not
armed," and he said, "Get in the fucking car. I'm driving." So
we get into the car—we wanted to be able to talk privately—
and we went to a motel, and I rented a motel room at the Days
Inn there in Santa Clara in the name of Brooke West. He had
bought a six-pack of beer. We went into the room. He wasn't really violent to me, and I didn't really know what to expect. I just
sat down in a chair, and . . . he was calm at first. He took out a
beer, and he just drank it down, and then he got another one out,
and just drank that down. I said, "Howard, you shouldn't be
drinking, you know?" I didn't know what type of medicine he
was taking. I didn't know what to think. He took another [beer]
out, and he picked it up like he was going to hit me in the head
with it, and I flinched, you know? I jumped. I thought, "Well, I
had better get out of here." And, he says, "Honey, I'm not going
to hurt you." He put his arms around me, and he said, "I know
what I did. I know I caused this." And he drank another beer.

I asked Howard at the motel, "Would you be willing to go for counseling?" I didn't know what to think. I didn't really want to leave him, even though in some ways I was really scared of him. He said, "Yeah, you know, I'll do it." And then he got very, very mad at me. He pulled open his shirt [showing the gunshot wound to his neck], and he said, "You see what you did to me?" I said, "Howard, I didn't do it on purpose. I didn't mean to hurt you."

MARTINEZ: Was there a physical confrontation between you and Howard there at the motel room?

WEST: Yeah. He slapped me twice.

MARTINEZ: How come?

WEST: He was mad at me . . . he said that I was bragging that I hurt him.

MARTINEZ: So he slapped you a couple of times. Did he hurt you in any other way?

WEST: No. He could have really hurt me, you know, but he didn't. He just slapped me.

MARTINEZ: Where did you guys go?

WEST: I brought him here. . . . Now, before I go any further, I want to tell you that that day, on that Tuesday, I cashed my tax-return check for about $3,400, and I had all $100 bills. I still have a little paper from [the bank] because I guess they roll up $1,000 in division of $100 bills. I had cashed it, and I didn't make the deposit because I was anticipating going to go get the Corvette [out of the shop]. But Howard didn't know at that moment that I had all that money.

[Two days later, on], June 2, he dropped me off [at work] in the morning. He seemed okay. [Then] he called me up. He seemed really down and really depressed, and I said, "You don't sound like you feel very good."

MARTINEZ: Where was the [tax-return] money?

WEST: I hid it here in the house.

MARTINEZ: Where?

WEST: In a drawer in here, in the kitchen. . . . So he picked me up, and it was in the middle of the afternoon, and his attitude was very, very different. I smelled alcohol. I said to him, "You've been drinking," and he said, "No, that's cough syrup."

MARTINEZ: What are your normal working hours?

WEST: They are whatever I want. I have [a] twenty-four seven schedule. I have an access card that lets me in.

MARTINEZ: And by the way, where do you work?

WEST: Well, I'm a contractor. A job shop will hire me, and then they will send me to a job site, so I'll usually work at that job site even though I don't work for those people. . . . I write books. I can write anything, but my main living has been from the high-tech industry. I write manuals for their computers, and for their software. For example, if they want me to write a book that tells a person how to sit down and use their software application, I go there.

MARTINEZ: How long have you been doing this?

WEST: Thirteen years.

MARTINEZ: So Howard picked you up [on June 2] at work. Where did you guys go?

WEST: We went to a Walgreens pharmacy in Santa Clara to fill his painkiller prescription. [The pharmacist] said it was Vicodin, and that it was a very strong prescription. She said, "I want you to understand, Howard. You do not drink with this and you do not drive."

I wrote them a check for it, and we left. He drove part of the way [back to Los Banos]. There is a Chevron station at 152 East, so we stopped there, and we got a couple of sodas, and he said, "You drive because I need to take a couple of pain pills." So he took two of them, and I said, "You know, you really don't have to take two of them." And he said, "It's none of your fucking business how many I take, all right? I can take half this fucking bottle and I'd never even feel it." So I drove home.

MARTINEZ: What time did you get home?

WEST: I don't know. It was in the evening. Maybe six p.m. or seven p.m.

MARTINEZ: Anything happen when you got home?

WEST: He was just sort of laid-back. I don't remember . . . I think we rented a couple of movies . . . [and then] I was seriously thinking that this was all a mistake. He seemed fine, and he said, "Let's take a shower." I said, "Okay," so we went in and took a shower in the master shower. All of a sudden, he turns around and he looks at me rather strangely, and he gets this strange look across his face. He says, "Where is that fucking picture?"

I looked at him, and I said, "What? What picture?" I got out of the shower, and I thought, "Uh oh. Tantrum." There was a snapshot taken of us when we got married in Reno. That's the one he was looking for. I didn't know where the picture [was].

He says, "If I don't get that fucking picture by midnight, I'm going to tear this whole fucking house up, and I'm going to beat your ass." So I came in here, in the kitchen, and I went through some drawers and everything, and I made sure that the money [from the tax returns] was stuffed back there.

I said, "I know where I put it [the photo]. It's in the car. Let me go out there and look." What I was really trying to do was get away from him. So I went and I opened up the garage door, and I had my purse and my keys. I picked [them] up on the way out, and he didn't even notice, and he wasn't fully dressed. He had on his underwear and a T-shirt. He didn't even have his shoes or anything. He was tearing up things in the bedroom. . . . I just reached up, and I just grabbed the garage door, and I took off running. I hid in a field over here for a long time. I was just shaking. I didn't know what to do. I just shook. I just sat there until I could get my composure, and then I went to some neighbors over here on the corner. . . . I banged and banged on their door. The guy answered. He didn't open his door. He just peeked out of his blinds, and he

said, "Yeah, what can I do for you?" I said, "My name is St.
John, please call the police for me." He says, "I've got it." I
was just shaking. It wasn't very long after that a police officer
drove up, and then there was another lady [officer] who followed him up like three minutes or something. . . . And
Howard [told the police] "Well, I was looking for this picture,
you know, and she's just freaking out, and there's nothing
wrong." And . . . I said to this lady [officer], "I want to get the
car. I need the car."

MARTINEZ: Which car are you talking about?

WEST: The little Chevy. And Howard spoke up. He said,
"Well, you can't take it because I took the distributor out of it,
and I don't know what happened to it." And so the officer asked
him, "Why did you take the distributor out?" and Howard said,
"Because I didn't want her to leave. I wanted to keep her."

MARTINEZ: Did you suggest that you stay here or go or
what? What was the agreement?

WEST: I just said, "Look, Howard, you can stay, okay? I
don't know what I'm going to do right now." I was just a
wreck. I left with the police officer, and I asked the officer, "Is
there an all-night restaurant I can stay at?"

MARTINEZ: What's it called?

WEST: I don't know the name. . . . It starts with a B . . . but
it's down on Pacheco Boulevard.

REED: Grandy's.

WEST: Uh, [the officer] took me there.

MARTINEZ: To Grandy's?

WEST: Yeah. This little restaurant. And I had a cup of tea,
and I sat for a while. I didn't know what the hell to do. . . . I
didn't call my dad . . . I had some money on me, but . . .

MARTINEZ: How long were you there?

WEST: Maybe an hour.

MARTINEZ: Did you meet anybody there?

WEST: No.

MARTINEZ: Okay. What did you do? Did you stay there?

WEST: Uh, no. I stayed for a while. I just had a cup of tea, and then I got out, and [I] started walking . . . toward the Pacheco Pass.

MARTINEZ: Where were you going?

WEST: Um, I hitched a ride with a trucker.

MARTINEZ: You were walking at the time, and then you hitched a ride? Where was the trucker at when you hitched a ride?

WEST: Um, down here near this Shell station. I was just getting to that point.

MARTINEZ: Do you know who the trucker was?

WEST: He—he owned his own truck. The name of the truck was Delgado Trucking. He was from Fresno. Uh, he said his name was John, and, uh, he asked me, "Could I give you a lift?"

MARTINEZ: Oh. He asked you?

WEST: Yeah, and you see, he had gotten gas or something, and [he] pulled out, and he was checking his truck, and he noticed I was walking toward [Pacheco] Pass. I said, "Are you going to San Jose?" And he says, "Yeah, this is my regular route." He hauled paper . . . cardboard boxes.

MARTINEZ: Uh huh.

MARTINEZ: What date was this on?

WEST: This was on the evening of June 2 going into the morning of June 3. Thursday [night] to Friday morning. He took me all the way into San Jose, and he left me there where the Denny's is, near the airport. And I asked him to leave me there, because I went and rented a car from Dollar Rent A Car. I had to have transportation. I had to go to work. So I went to work that morning on Friday—about six or seven a.m. I was there very early.

MARTINEZ: Did you have any clothes with you?

WEST: All that I had was what I had on. I didn't even have any good clothes on.

MARTINEZ: And where did you stay?

WEST: Well, before I tell you where I stayed at . . . I had made several phone calls. I didn't know what to do. I thought, "I'm going to have to leave him, because I don't think I could deal with this fear." So I contacted a company—they go by the name of C&C Paralegals—I have their card. I can give it to you, show it to you. I went over there immediately, and I had them fill out papers for a restraining order and a divorce.

MARTINEZ: Who did you talk to there?

WEST: Um . . . I'll have to look his name up.

MARTINEZ: About what time was it when you were there?

WEST: In the morning time. Maybe ten or eleven a.m . . . something like that. I wrote them a check. $425. [They said we] have to have cash before we can start the process on the paperwork, so I went to the bank, and I cashed my payroll check that I've had from a couple of weeks ago.

MARTINEZ: Where was the $3,400?

WEST: Still here.

MARTINEZ: With Howard back at the house?

WEST: Yeah, still.

MARTINEZ: But Howard didn't know [about the money]?

WEST: No.

MARTINEZ: Then you went to work after that?

WEST: Um, I went to work. Yes. I went to work.

MARTINEZ: What happened after work?

WEST: I went shopping that evening way over on the East Bay. Um, I'll give you the receipts to what I got. I just bought some clothes and some personal things so I could take a shower, and then I came back to Santa Clara, and I checked into a place called the Budget Inn."

MARTINEZ: These items—were they purchased with cash, or were they purchased with a credit card?

WEST: I wrote a check for them.

MARTINEZ: Did they take your ID?

WEST: Yeah. They accepted them . . . I have the receipt. I

can show you. I think it was Mervyn's, and then I know I stopped at Wal-Mart drugstore to buy a blow dryer.

MARTINEZ: This would have been on Friday?

WEST: Friday afternoon. Actually, I didn't do the shopping until that evening.

MARTINEZ: About what time?

WEST: During the evening time. Maybe seven or eight p.m. Something like that.

MARTINEZ: Okay. You did some shopping. What happened then?

WEST: I came back to Santa Clara, and I checked into a place called the Budget Inn. Address is 2499 El Camino Real in Santa Clara. That was Friday evening when I checked in there.

MARTINEZ: How did you pay for that?

WEST: On the credit card. My Mastercard.

MARTINEZ: How long did you stay there?

WEST: Just that night.

MARTINEZ: What time did you check out?

WEST: Uh, at eleven a.m., Saturday.

MARTINEZ: Where did you go then?

WEST: I picked up my mom, and we did some errands . . . probably till about seven p.m., and then I took her back to her van, and I went back to work.

MARTINEZ: Seven . . . ?

WEST: In the evening. I stayed up with coffee.

MARTINEZ: Who works with you?

WEST: Oh, there's many people coming and going.

MARTINEZ: Where is that located?

WEST: Um, the assignment is at Syntex Pharmaceuticals company in Palo Alto . . . it's on [Hillview].

MARTINEZ: And who else works with you there in that office?

WEST: Oh, there are lots of people who come and go.

MARTINEZ: At seven p.m. at night?

WEST: Oh, there isn't anybody there. You have to use your card key to get in.

MARTINEZ: Is there some type of record that, when you use your card, there is some type of recording that would show that you were checked in that time?

WEST: Yeah. The computer logs in.

MARTINEZ: Who would have that?

WEST: Their security department, I suppose.

MARTINEZ: And that works merely by you running your card through it, so it can show them that you were there?

WEST: I guess so.

MARTINEZ: Even if you didn't go inside the building?

WEST: Um, yeah . . . think it would do that.

MARTINEZ: What time did you go in there?

WEST: During the evening.

MARTINEZ: So you checked in. How long were you there?

WEST: A long time. Several hours. I had lots of phone messages, and I had one from an officer at the police department here in Los Banos.

MARTINEZ: They called you there?

WEST: They said that my husband put a missing persons report on me. . . . Then I had messages from my father, and I called my father, and he said that Howard had been on the phone like every ten minutes. All night.

MARTINEZ: Howard was calling your father?

WEST: Yeah.

MARTINEZ: What was he saying when he was calling your father?

WEST: I don't really know. He was just real, real drunk . . . he just said it was a lot of drunk talk. You know, like, "I love her" and "She's just left." You know. That kind of stuff.

MARTINEZ: You said you made other phone calls or somebody talked to you [at work] on the phone besides the officer?

WEST: Howard called me.

MARTINEZ: What did he say?

WEST: He asked me to come home. He was sorry that he scared me. I said, "No Howard, I'm not coming home. I know you are drunk, and this is not a good idea right now."

MARTINEZ: Did he call collect, or did he call direct?

WEST: He just called. He called from home.

MARTINEZ: Okay. So that call would be recorded then as far as the bill? How long did you talk to him?

WEST: Just for a few minutes. I said, "Howard, no. I'm not coming home," and then he got real mad. He said, "Fuck you. You can come home if you want [because] I ain't going to be here when you get home." And I said, "Well, what are you going to do?" He says, "I'm leaving. I am going to Reno . . . I got the $3,400."

MARTINEZ: Did he say how he found it?

WEST: Probably just digging through the drawers, looking for something else, and he probably accidentally found it, which I was hoping he wouldn't, but he found it.

MARTINEZ: Was there anybody else in the house with him?

WEST: I don't know, because I haven't been here. These were his exact words: "I'm going to Reno. . . . One of my hometown boys is picking me up." I said, "With who?" He says, "It's none of your fucking business." But he didn't say when he was leaving, and he hung up on me. . . . All he said was, "One of my hometown boys is picking me up." That's all he said.

MARTINEZ: If he took the $3,400, why wouldn't he take the car also?

WEST: I don't know.

MARTINEZ: Did you come home?

WEST: I didn't come home until the next day [Sunday, June 5] around eleven a.m. I called my father, I brought my mom. I stopped and I picked her up.

MARTINEZ: Weren't you afraid that Howard was going to be home?

WEST: Not with the $3,400. No, because he liked to gamble.

MARTINEZ: And you were coming home to see if, in fact, he'd taken the money?

WEST: Uh, I knew he had the money. He [hadn't] known about the money, so I knew he had found it. I came home, and I asked my mom to wait outside.

MARTINEZ: What did you find?

WEST: The house was a complete pigsty with bottles. You know, tequila bottles, and a lot of beer cans. There's still beer in the refrigerator.

MARTINEZ: Did it look like just Howard [had been] here at the house?

WEST: There was somebody else here, too, because there were [two types of] cigarettes—a brand he did not smoke. Howard smoked Camel. There were Camels, and then there was a pack of Marlboro. There were cigarette butts put out in beer cans. There were empty brandy bottles. Empty tequila bottles. I just sacked it all.

MARTINEZ: Where did you take it?

WEST: I took it over there, and [I] threw it in a Dumpster.

HAYNES: What Dumpster was that?

WEST: Just a Dumpster behind one of those places over there, and I just threw it out. I didn't want to leave it here.

MARTINEZ: Would it still be there?

WEST: I don't know. I just tossed it.

MARTINEZ: So this would have been on . . . ?

WEST: Monday afternoon.

MARTINEZ: Uh, you got back . . . ?

WEST: Sunday afternoon [June] 5.

MARTINEZ: You picked up your mother at her home at about eleven a.m. at her van?

WEST: Yeah . . . I got here about eleven a.m.

MARTINEZ: What day was that?

WEST: Sunday.

MARTINEZ: Sunday. And then, uh, so you cleaned up all day Sunday, and then Monday you got rid of all that stuff?

WEST: I still had more to clean up. . . . There were drawers dragged. There was paper all over. I told my mom. "We'll just stuff everything back in the drawers," and we left midday, and then we went to the valley.

MARTINEZ: The valley. Where at?

WEST: Over in San Jose. And I took my mom to the bank. She withdrew some money for me. I had to borrow some money from her to pay for the Corvette. And I picked up my mail, because I have a mail drop there, and then we had dinner at Denny's. And I called my dad.

MARTINEZ: Did you go to Tulare County yesterday?

WEST: No. I didn't.

MARTINEZ: What do you think might have happened to Howard?

WEST: I don't know. I have no idea what happened that day. I can tell you based on what I've been told, he was very belligerent. I don't know what happened to Howard. I don't know where he went. I know he had money. . . . But I was getting ready to have papers for the restraining order and the divorce.

He said, "One of my hometown boys is picking me up." I said, "Who?" And he said, "It's none of your fucking business."

MARTINEZ: I don't have any other questions.

WEST: Wait. Wait. Can you please tell me what happened?

MARTINEZ: He died as a result of gunshot wounds, and that's all we'll talk about the case—as a result of gunshot wounds. This will be the end of the taped interview.

Once the interview with West was complete, Haynes and Martinez told West they wanted to search her home and vehicles, and she consented to the search. The detectives scoured through the house for more than an hour, and they collected a number of items. They included a twelve-pack of Budweiser beer left behind by St. John; a box of white plastic garbage bags; a cigarette lighter with the words DAKOTA CASINO SIOUX on it; a roll of plastic tape; a bottle of carpet stain cleaner; a box for a Savage shotgun; a leather handbag containing 12-gauge shotgun shells; and two letters to West from Christine and St. John.

The letter from Christine to her daughter read:

Dear Brooke:
I wish you would come and see me. I love you Brooke, no matter what you do or did . . . You need me, and I need you . . . I will always love you . . . You [are] the only one in this world who loves me, and it doesn't matter . . . know I'm with you. Love you.

Your mother.

The second letter was from St. John. It read:

To my baby.
Wish this would have never happened tonight. Sweetheart. I told you that I will never hurt you, and I mean that . . . What I say, I mean. Haven't I always kept my word to you? I know what we are going through is hard. I always thought that my shit don't stink, but, when it comes to you, I hurt so hard. Like, right now, I don't know what to do . . . I don't know if I should just cash in my chips and let you go on with life, and leave you alone. Brookey, my baby, I love you. I wish I could always be with [you] forever. You know, when I was in the hospital, all I ever thought of was you. What I'm trying to say is, I love you. What has happened between us? I hope we can always be together forever. Well, if you leave me, there is only one way out. I have 20 of them. You know what I mean, so good bye. I love you.

Haynes, Martinez and Reed left West's house around midnight, and the two agreed that portions of West's story weren't adding up. She said that on June 2—the night of the domestic dispute—she had gotten a ride from the police to an all-night coffee shop, and then she started hitch-hiking toward San Jose. The very premise of her hitchhiking late at night over the ominous Pacheco Pass, a remote stretch of mountainous, winding highway, seemed preposterous. No one in her right mind would try to cross the pass on foot in the middle of the night.

Also, West seemed to be deliberately trying to document her whereabouts during the entire weekend in which St. John was slain. It seemed as if she was going out of her way to formulate an alibi.

"I can't talk about anything she actually said, but I think there were things probably said in her statements that didn't make sense in my mind," Haynes said.

Still, Martinez and Haynes were not going to jump to any conclusions. St. John, after all, was no saint, and there were plenty of possible scenarios in which he could have been murdered. Maybe he did leave the house with friends and with West's tax money and was then murdered and transported to Tulare County by some unknown suspect.

"We have to approach it with the idea that every stone needs to be overturned," Haynes said. "Howard had been around. He had been in rehab. There were too many unanswered questions at that point to form any opinion."

But the detectives were suspicious of West. She had shot her husband nearly two weeks earlier. There was an insurance fraud inquiry pending, and her husband had ratted her out to the insurance investigator.

There was certainly a potential motive to want St. John dead.

"I would not have eliminated her as a lead when I left her house," Haynes said.

33

Laura Parra was driving down Fir Street a few weeks after Howard Simon St. John's murder when she witnessed one of the strangest sights of her life. Brookey Lee West was walking on the side the road, and she was dressed like a witch. Her hair, her pants, her shirt and her shoes were all black.

"She had a thick white powder caked all over her face," Parra said. "There was no color in any of her hair or clothing. I didn't even know it was her. It was very, very weird, and she looked like a forty-year-old lady trying to be goth. It was like she thought she was a witch."

On June 10, 1994, Daniel Haynes and Herman Martinez drove to San Jose to contact West's father. They met Leroy and his wife, Chloe Smith, at their front doorstep, and the couple invited the Tulare County detectives inside.

During their interview of Leroy, it quickly became apparent to the detectives that Leroy was the person West sought out whenever she was in a bind. He was the one who picked his daughter up from the Merced County jail after she shot her husband in the neck, he was the one who took possession of his daughter's guns to prevent her from violating a judge's order not to possess weapons and he was the person West called in San Jose on the weekend of St. John's murder.

"My impression was that Brooke's contact with her father took place when Brooke was in trouble, and daddy had to help her get out of it," Haynes said.

In a taped statement, Leroy told the detectives his daughter's alibi for the slaying. The detectives then asked Leroy if he had any guns, and Leroy produced an arsenal of firearms. There was a loaded gun behind a couch, another in a nightstand, and other firearms in a locked cabinet. The guns included a .38-caliber Smith & Wesson revolver, a German Mauser pistol, a .38-caliber Derringer, several rifles, a Ruger pistol and a 12-gauge shotgun.

The detectives took the guns to the Tulare County crime lab to be examined by a forensics firearms expert. The weapons could not be linked to St. John's murder.

The crime lab was, however, able to examine the bullets plucked from St. John's body during autopsy, and the ballistics indicated a .38-caliber handgun was probably the murder weapon. The gun used to kill St. John was likely a Colt or a Miroku make, and the description was similar to the weapon Wayne Ike saw in West's possession the night West threatened to shoot him.

The actual murder weapon was never found.

After their interview with Leroy, Haynes and Martinez spent the next several days in Los Banos talking to West's neighbors. The neighbors recounted the bizarre events at 1639 Fir Street, and they gave the detectives a far different picture of West's mother, noting that Christine Smith bragged about killing a man and being on death row.

"The neighbors all took Christine in," Haynes said. "She was the sweet little old lady who lived around the corner. They welcomed her into their home, and in very short order they had to run her off their property.

"I suspect anyone who was around Christine or Brooke had similar experiences. They couldn't keep friends, and these people saw something in these two they didn't want around. I got to know the whole neighborhood," Haynes said. "That was an interesting street. My impression was they were all scared."

Mike Stoykovich provided a valuable clue to the detectives. He told police that on the night of the slaying he never saw anyone other than St. John at West's house, and there were no loud parties. The account contradicted West's claim that someone else was at the house partying with St. John the night he was slain.

Armed with the witness accounts of Christine bragging about shooting someone, the detectives ran a background check and learned of her assault conviction from Bakersfield in 1961. The detectives then returned to West's home to interview Christine about her criminal history.

SMITH: Assault with a deadly weapon with intent to commit murder is what they booked me on. I shot him. He was a man I was going with, and, uh, it was one of those triangles you get involved in. I'll admit, it was premeditated. . . . He was a boyfriend. Maybe you all better listen to this because you might learn something. He handled the breakup from me in the wrong manner. Are you with me?
MARTINEZ: So you were intending to . . . ?
SMITH: Kill him. Do [I] have any sympathy? Am [I] feeling sorry? Hell, no.

"I was quite surprised," Haynes said. "You wouldn't see it by looking at her. Of course, the shooting had been many, many years before, but when asked, she had nothing to hide."

Next, the detectives spent weeks interviewing St. John's friends at the Native American Indian Center and the Four Winds Lodge.

"That was not the friendliest setting," Haynes said. "They don't welcome you. When you go into a rehab center like that, it's like you are still on the frontier, and you are the white man. Their [attitude is] 'I can't talk to you.' It took some time convincing some of those people I was there to avenge Howard's death. I had to tell them, 'You know, if Howard were here, he'd tell you to talk to me.'"

Gradually, St. John's friends warmed up to Haynes and Martinez. One especially helpful witness was Knotchapone, who told the detectives about West's spewing venom about her ex-husband at the AA meetings. Knotchapone also relayed how St. John once told her he feared West might kill him.

"She was very open," Haynes said. "She was a wealth of information. She was extremely close to Howard emotionally, and his death really tore at her. More than anyone else, she wanted to see justice."

Thomas Gutierrez and Anthony Mercado told the detectives West hired St. John to burn her Jaguar. Interviews with officials from AAA insurance and investigator Dwight Bell revealed West collected more than $18,000 in insurance for the burned-out Jaguar, and Bell told the detectives St. John had revealed the insurance fraud scheme to him, then recanted.

The detectives also learned St. John's white Corvette was in a Milpitas repair shop at the time of the slaying. The owner of the auto shop, Mark Morales, said that one or two days after St. John was found dead, West showed up at his auto shop in Milpitas to pick up the Corvette.

West appeared disheveled and extremely exhausted.

"On that day, he noticed Brooke was extremely unkempt," Haynes wrote in a police report. "She was out of it,
as though she had been up all night or had not slept. . . . She
was having a lot of trouble, and he assumed she was having
trouble because she had not slept in quite some time."

The account of West's exhaustion coincided with the
detectives' theory of the case—that West had killed her
husband on the evening of June 4 and drove all night to Tulare County to dump the body. The scenario of West's being up all night might account for West's sleep-deprived
state at the auto repair shop a day or two later.

Haynes and Martinez tracked down the rental car West
drove on the weekend St. John disappeared. West told the
detectives she drove the car from San Jose to Los Banos,
but paperwork from the rental car company showed West
racked up more than 1,000 miles on the vehicle. The
mileage was hundreds more than what should have been on
the rental car's odometer, according to police reports. The
detectives suspected it was possible West accumulated the
mileage driving to the Sequoia National Forest in Tulare
County to dispose of St. John's corpse.

But by the time the detectives tracked down the rental
car, it had already been rented twice by other customers.
The vehicle had been cleaned each time it was rented, and
there were no valuable clues inside. No bloodstains. No
fibers. No bullet holes.

The Tulare County investigators spent several more
months checking West's alibi, including West's claim that
two nights before the slaying a trucker gave her ride from
Los Banos to San Jose as she hitchhiked over Pacheco
Pass. West said the truck driver, named John, worked for a
company called Delgado Trucking, so with the help of the
California Highway Patrol, the detectives obtained a list of
every Delgado Trucking in the state. None had drivers in

Los Banos or surrounding areas that night, according to police reports.

West provided receipts to the detectives showing a number of purchases in San Jose on the weekend of the murder. The receipts placed her in San Jose on the actual day of the slaying, but they did not, however, account for her exact whereabouts on the evening of June 4 or the early morning hours of June 5.

To check West's alibi further, Haynes and Martinez contacted a security supervisor for Syntex Pharmaceuticals. West said she was at the business working on the night of June 4, and the detectives were told by the supervisor that time cards filled out by West placed her at the business that evening. A computer security system also showed West used her company-issued identification badge to access the business that night, but there was no way of documenting exactly when West left Syntex. This meant West was unaccounted for the entire night of the slaying and the morning hours of June 5.

"Her coworkers knew exactly nothing about her," Haynes said.

Haynes and Martinez sought out West's brother, Travis, for questioning, but they couldn't find him. The detectives knew Travis was once committed to the Atascadero state prison for the criminally insane, and they knew Travis lived on the streets of San Jose, but an extensive, days-long search for Travis at homeless shelters and on the streets of San Jose turned up nothing.

"To this day, the brother exists by name only," Haynes said. "The information I was given back then was he was homeless. He was living under bridges. No one had seen him for some time. When they did see him, it was because someone [in West's family] was driving by, and they happened to see him alongside the road, and they stopped. It wasn't like he was coming home and having Thanksgiving dinner.

"It seemed like, for the most part, he was pretty much written off," Haynes said. "I certainly never could find him, nor could anyone else find him."

Search warrants were served by Martinez and Haynes on West's bank records, phone records and credit card accounts. The records showed West was in San Jose on the weekend of the murder, and they confirmed the phone calls she said she made.

Gradually, Haynes and Martinez pieced together a portrait of a successful, intelligent businesswoman known by no one.

"Brooke gets close to no one," Haynes said. "She has no real friends—at least not anyone I could identify as someone she buddied around with. Brookey would never list an address other than a drop box or a post office box. I don't care if it's the vehicle registration or the phone or water bill—you'll never find a physical mailing address for her.

"Your average, reasonable, prudent individual wouldn't do something like that," Haynes said. "If you are out in the middle of nowhere and the corner store was the only place available for a drop box, okay. But she lived her life that way. Brooke never wanted to be found by anybody, ever, for any reason. I've never ran into someone like that. I've never ran into anyone else who lived a life like Brooke did. It's almost a life of cover—someone who doesn't want to be found."

Over time, the inconsistencies in West's statement made the detectives more and more suspicious. Her alibi could not be confirmed, and try as they might, the detectives could never identify any other suspects in the slaying of St. John.

"In my opinion, without going into any reason, I believe Brooke was responsible for his death," Haynes said. "She's the only suspect I ever developed. Often, in a case like this, you can have a multitude of suspects, and you have to figure out which one. Not only did things point to her as the best possible suspect—there was no one else."

Haynes also entertained the possibility West's mother and father were involved. Of Christine, he said, "She was capable of the crime. It was something to consider. It's not something that can be overlooked, as opposed to your grandma, who's never done anything wrong in her life. It's something that's got to be looked at."

Of Leroy, Haynes said, "There was absolutely nothing to lead to him as a potential suspect in this case, other than he's the father of Brooke West, which doesn't make him a murderer. Is he someone who may know what is going on? Yes. Looking back, is he someone who is capable of helping in the aftermath of an event like this? Yes.

"My personal opinion is this family was in and out of a lot of things, and I think more than one thing has been covered up in their lives," Haynes said. "I think any one of them is capable of getting into a mess, and the others would come in and bail them out. That's my impression. Brooke, her mother, her father, her long lost brother. . . . I think that was their life.

"If Brook was responsible, I think the mother could have been part of getting the body out there. Anyone can shoot somebody, and we know she [Christine Smith] can, because she's done it in the past. From interviews, she shows no remorse for it. That tells you a lot about a person," Haynes said.

Haynes, Martinez and their colleagues at the Tulare County sheriff's department spent nine years investigating West in the slaying of her husband. They interviewed every witness several times over, and they produced an investigative case file nearly 2,000 pages long.

The detectives consulted with the Tulare County district attorney's office to determine if West should be charged, but prosecutors felt they didn't have enough to go on. There was circumstantial evidence for sure—a questionable alibi for West, and she had shot her husband two weeks prior to his murder. She had a potential motive as well. Her husband reported her to authorities for insurance fraud, and if he was dead, any potential fraud charges would evaporate.

But the detectives were told by the Tulare County district attorney's office that if a prosecutor was going to stand in front of a Tulare County jury and ask them to convict West of murder, they had to have more evidence linking her to the crime.

The murder of Howard Simon St. John remains among the unsolved files at the Tulare County sheriff's office to this day.

"When you work something that hard for so long, it's hard to get rid of," Haynes said. "It's even harder to realize someone got away with it, whether it's Brooke or not. Somebody got away with it, and it just so happens, I believe Brooke's responsible.

"You never forget a case. I don't lie awake at night and worry about it anymore, but it's the type of case you'll think about the rest of your life. I don't really know what else I would do. We put in thousands of hours."

34

For much of their twenty-year marriage, Leroy Smith was a kind and loving husband to his wife Chloe. But in 1995, a series of events unfolded that caused Chloe Smith to realize she had married into a spider web.

The events started with tragedy. Leroy was diagnosed with terminal brain cancer in late 1995.

"He came home one night and he told me, 'This is the hardest thing I've ever done in my life, but I have to tell you, I'm dying,'" Chloe Smith said. "It was devastating."

Terribly distraught, Chloe Smith was forced to contemplate life without Leroy. He was the one who always took care of her, and he was the one who made sure she was safe in life. Leroy was also the one who paid the bills, and as Chloe Smith waded through her grief, she realized she had to begin to take control of the couple's finances. She started to look into her husband's management of their money, and she was mortified at what she found. Throughout 1995, Leroy had forged Chloe Smith's signature on about twenty-five credit card applications, and he took out nearly $250,000 in cash advances without ever telling her.

Chloe Smith suspects the money went to Leroy's daughter, but there is no proof this is true.

"Brookey told me he was gambling it all away," Chloe recalled. "I told her, 'That's bullshit.'"

Chloe Smith also started to question whether West was meddling in her father's finances to secure his belongings after his death. The suspicion was bolstered during a trip Chloe and West took to meet with a San Jose doctor about Leroy's prognosis in early 1996. During the drive, West said Leroy was financially destitute and owed thousands to Asian bookies. To pay off the debt, Leroy gave the bookies his prized gun collection.

"She said he owed these gambling debts to these Chinese bookies, they were threatening to do harm to Brooke, and who knew what they were going to do," Chloe Smith said. "She said, 'We had to come up with some money, so we gave them all the guns.' She put the guns in a big white cotton bag and dropped the guns off on some street corner."

West said the Asian bookies were threatening to make West "work in their whorehouse" if the debt wasn't paid.

"I told her, 'This is ridiculous,'" Chloe said. "I said, 'Brooke, what are they going to do? You are forty years old. All they'd have you do [in a whorehouse] is sweep the floors.'"

Simultaneous to the bizarre story, Chloe noticed Leroy was getting more and more distant. Leroy was spending all of his time with West—not Chloe—and when Leroy suffered a ministroke because of the cancer in 1996, Leroy forbid his wife from visiting him at a temporary inpatient care facility.

"Brookey spent day and night there," Chloe said. "He asked me to please not show up, and I'd show up anyway, and he really didn't like it. Finally, he got so mad at me that he just screamed and yelled at me for coming."

Still, Chloe loved her husband, and she assigned his

meanness to his disease. It wasn't until several weeks later, on February 26, 1996, that Leroy's dark side emerged in full fury.

On that day, Chloe was organizing the couple's finances, and she asked West about the whereabouts of six titles to vehicles owned by Leroy and Chloe Smith. West informed her the titles were probably at a San Jose apartment Leroy was using in between chemotherapy treatments. Chloe and West drove to the residence to get the titles, and they found Leroy resting in bed. Chloe and West then started looking for the vehicle titles, all the while trying not to wake Leroy.

"I was trying to get paperwork together," Chloe said. "I was trying to pay a couple of bills, and I was trying to get everything in line. So Brooke told me she thought her dad had brought some stuff to the apartment, and maybe it would be there. She said, 'I think I saw my dad sticking a box under the bed.'"

Chloe walked to the bed Leroy was sleeping on, got down on her knees to search under it, and within seconds heard a large crackling sound behind her. The noise sounded like a bug zapper.

"Brooke came up behind me with a stun gun," Chloe said. "I was under the bed, and she tried to hit me with it. It was one of those real powerful ones, like 200,000 volts or whatever. She tried to hit me on the side of the neck, but for some reason she didn't get me. She got the bed covers. I knew the sound, and I pulled out from under the bed. I turned around and said, 'What the hell are you doing?'"

Leroy sprang up in bed and started screaming in a bloodcurdling pitch.

"You troublemaking bitch!" he said. "This is all your fault!"

Chloe darted for the door like a deer. Her head spinning from fright, she scampered down a flight of stairs and into the apartment complex parking lot, where she called the police on her cell phone. West was trailing her, screaming at her in a rage.

"She had her hand behind her back, and I'm on the phone talking to 911, telling them, 'I think they are going to kill me,'" Chloe said. "Brookey's yelling at me, 'You troublemaking bitch! Get off that phone! You are nothing but a troublemaking bitch!' Just before the police got there, she [West] jumped in her car and drove off with the stun gun."

The San Jose police believed Chloe Smith's account, but they had no evidence to make an arrest. West and the stun gun were already gone, and Leroy told the police his wife was lying about the entire incident.

"Leroy came out and told the police it was all a big lie, and he said no one tried to hurt me," Chloe recalled.

"The police told me I ought to start carrying a gun," she said. "Can you imagine?"

To this day, Chloe Smith is convinced West was trying to murder her. West, she suspects, wanted to kill her so she would be able to take control of her father's assets after he died.

But there was a bigger prize, too. An insurance policy Chloe took out at work dictated that if she died before her husband, Leroy stood to inherit about $250,000.

"If I had predeceased him at that time, I had about a quarter million dollars worth of life insurance," Chloe said. "So if I died, she [West] would have been next in line for that, and Leroy knew this.

"I think she would have killed me," Chloe said. "What was she going to do, stun me, let me lie on the floor and say, 'Gee, I'm sorry, it was a mistake?'

"Just another body," she said. "I don't know what makes her tick."

Leroy Smith died from brain cancer in Los Banos two months later.

MOTHER

35

Las Vegas is a city of last chance—a place where the nation's rebels, misfits and downtrodden come for salvation from financial ruin, a broken marriage or a life filled with mistakes. Vegas offers a fresh start, a new beginning, a chance at being a born-again American.

At least that is what one is led to believe.

The reality of the city, however, is far different from the reputation. Vegas can be a cold, hard place for the undisciplined. Drinking, drugging and gambling can quickly lead to homelessness, and most who end up on the city's streets rarely escape its death grip.

There is no better demonstration of this than the leagues of homeless men who line Bonanza Road in the downtown corridor of the city every morning. Unshaven and dirty, they stand on the street corners and flag down pickups in the hope they can land a few hours of manual labor in the valley's construction industry. The jobs usually pay for another beer, another hit of methamphetamine, a nightly stay at a weekly rent motel, or a few more minutes on the gaming tables. America's city of last chance—a repetitive, desperate cycle of substance abuse, sin, poverty and lonely death.

Christine Merle Smith got her last chance in life in 1997, at the age of sixty-five, when her daughter, Brookey Lee West, drove her to Las Vegas and set her up at an apartment complex on Sahara Avenue known as the Orange Door apartments. The two-story, low-income flats sit just west of Interstate 15 in a once classic Vegas neighborhood long ago destroyed by poverty and gangbangers. Christine, however, had no reservations about living at the Orange Door apartments. In fact, she thrived there, and she quickly became close friends with several of her neighbors. One was Alice Wilsey, a sweet-hearted, sixty-six-year-old Utah native who worked as a bookkeeper at the 7-Eleven convenience store headquarters for Las Vegas. Out of kindness, Wilsey served as Christine's caretaker at the Orange Door. She made sure Christine had food, she took her to the bank to use the ATM and she took her to run basic errands for prescriptions or medical appointments.

"We were good friends, and I looked out for her when her daughter Brooke was in California," Wilsey said. "Christine had a very serious case of osteoporosis. She was kind of bent over, and it caused her abdominal pain. Christine also had a hard time taking a shower. She had to have a shower seat . . . and she couldn't remember my phone number. She couldn't even remember her own address. I'm pretty sure she was getting Alzheimer's."

Another woman who Christine befriended at the Orange Door apartments was Judy Chang, seventy-four. The white-haired woman with a soft voice and an even softer temperament was born in Illinois but lived much of her life in Texas, and she became friends with Christine in short order.

"Christine was a lot of fun," Chang said. "Our day would start at seven thirty to eight a.m. Christine would come and look in my apartment window, looking to see if I was up yet so I could come out and sit and talk. Her daughter would be out in California, and she would be in her little apartment all alone, and she would get bored. So we would go out by the pool (of the apartments) and we would have lunch out there, and we'd sit out there all day long."

Christine told Chang and Wilsey her daughter was a technical writer in San Jose, and her son, Travis, was homeless in the Bay Area.

"She told me that he was a street person, that he was an alcoholic, that he drank a lot, and he didn't have a place to live," Wilsey said. "He apparently took drugs, as well."

Christine was a conservative Pentecostal, she said, and she prayed daily to a wood-burned picture of Jesus on the wall of her apartment.

"Sometimes she would break into a strange voice, and she would talk in this thick tongue, and you couldn't understand what she was saying," Chang said. "It would go on for a few minutes, and then it would be over, and she'd say the Holy Ghost got her."

Christine also bragged to her friends about her Indian heritage—even though she was white—and she bragged that she was once on death row for shooting a man. She said she escaped the electric chair in Texas when her victim didn't die.

"It was one of the first things she told me," Wilsey said. "Chris loved to tell this story. It was a big thing in her life."

Chang recalled, "She told me she was on death row in the penitentiary, and I said, 'Well, what happened?' She said she had shot a man, and I said, 'You shot a man? What did you do that for?' And she said, 'Oh, well, he was acting the fool.' I was thinking, 'You don't get on death row unless the person died.'"

Around the same time that they met Christine, Wilsey and Chang also met Christine's daughter, and they both liked West. West stayed at her mother's apartment every few weeks in between her commutes to work in San Jose, and in late 1997 West moved into her mother's apartment.

"I understood they both loved each other very much," Wilsey said. "They showed me a picture of Brooke always taking care of her mother and giving her mother things. But later on, I discovered that wasn't true."

West often took Chang out to lunch or dinner, and she occasionally studied tarot cards with Wilsey.

"Brooke was very good at the tarot cards," Wilsey said. "Excellent. She was an excellent reader. And I know a little bit about it because I have tried some of it. I have a tarot card program on my computer, and every time Brooke would come over, she'd want me to read the cards for her. But I'm not really versed in it like Brooke was.

"Brooke is really psychic," Chang said. "She believed in it, and her mother told me Brooke once helped the cops in California find a little girl who was kidnapped and molested. This child was hidden away in some guy's garage, and Christine said Brooke helped the police find her."

Near the end of 1997, West and Wilsey took Christine to a pet store in Las Vegas to get a dog, and Christine picked out a little brown Chihuahua she named Chi Chi. Chi Chi followed Christine everywhere over the next several months, and the dog became the most cherished thing in Christine's existence.

"He was so sweet, and I know Christine loved that dog," Wilsey said.

But a couple of months later, sometime in January or February of 1998, Judy Chang visited Christine at her apartment, and when she arrived, she found Christine on the tail end of a bitter argument with her daughter over Chi Chi.

"Christine was on the couch, and she had her little bitsy

dog, and Brooke was [on the phone] trying to give her dog to somebody," Chang said. "Christine said, 'No! You are not giving my Chi Chi away!' And Brooke looked at her kind of funny. I said a few words to Chris, and then I said, 'Okay, Chris, I'm going to go ahead and go. I'll see you in a couple of days.'"

Alice Wilsey had a similar odd encounter with West and Christine around the same time. She stopped by Christine's apartment and found her in bed, and it appeared to Wilsey that Christine was very ill.

"She was not able to get out of bed alone by herself," Wilsey said. "She was sort of—, almost like she was drugged, or she was just extremely tired. I saw Brooke give her what she said was aspirin twice. Chris had to go to the restroom, and so I helped her to the restroom. It was an ordeal because she just couldn't [move] by herself. I have no idea what her illness was at that time, but she appeared to be ill."

Two days later, Chang went back to Christine's apartment, and West said her mother had suddenly moved to San Jose to live with her brother, Travis.

"I said, 'Hi, where's Chris?'" Chang recalled. "Brooke said, 'Oh, I took her to my brother's to stay.' Brooke said, 'I gave her three choices. She either goes to a home for older people, she goes to my brother's, or I'm leaving and I'm not coming back anymore.'"

West told Chang she gave her mother about an hour in the middle of the night to decide whether she wanted to live with her brother, reside in the old folks home or never see her again. According to West, Christine decided to go live with Travis, a person Chang and Wilsey knew to be a street person.

"So she [West] said, 'I just jumped up and got some bags and started throwing Christine's belongings in a bag,'" Chang said, quoting West.

West went on to say that she drove Christine to West's brother's house in San Jose in the middle of the night.

"She told her mother, 'We're going right now,' " Chang quoted West as saying.

" 'Well, can't we wait until the morning?' Christine said," Chang recalled.

" 'No, I don't want you to change your mind,' " West said she told her mother. "So she grabbed up the bags and things and left with her.

"She didn't even stop to say good-bye," Chang said. "That wasn't like Christine."

Wilsey got a similar story from West. Christine, West claimed, went to live with her homeless son.

"I saw Brooke, and she said that she had taken her mother in the middle of the night. She had packed up her mother and took her to San Jose," Wilsey said. "She said that her mother was staying with Christine's son, Travis, and he had a girlfriend. She moved Christine into the apartment with Travis and his girlfriend."

Christine Smith was never seen alive again.

Natalie Hanke was working as a technical writing supervisor for a Silicon Valley computer company called Hybrid Networks in 1997 when Brookey Lee West applied for a job at the company, and almost immediately Hanke was impressed with West's resume, intellect and talent.

"I hired Brooke, and I got to know her on a daily basis," Hanke said. "We worked together, and I enjoyed Brooke's company. She's very bright, and she's fun."

Hanke, an attractive forty-year-old woman with blond hair, struck up a casual friendship with West, and during the next three years Hanke became one of the few people who ever really got to know West. She and West occasionally went to dinner after work or talked once or twice a week on the phone, and during their conversations, West confided in Hanke some of the most intimate details of her life.

"She admitted to me that she was on some medication, that she was manic-depressive, and sometimes she got a little moody," Hanke said.

"Her mother was quite strange, from everything I heard at the time," Hanke said. "[West] was raised by people who walked around with shotguns."

"She said her mom was a Satan worshipper and that her mom was crazy," Hanke said. "Brooke had told me such horrific stories about her childhood that they just tore my heart out. It just made me think, 'Jeez, this is one of those times in your life where you meet someone who needs a hand, so you give them a hand.'"

Hanke sort of felt sorry for West given her turbulent childhood, and at the same time she saw West as an extremely talented woman. West was personable and clever, and she was very good at taking complex information about computers and condensing it into manuals people could understand. The talents landed West jobs at some of the Silicon Valley's highest-paying computer companies, including Cisco and Hybrid.

"She was so good at this job, and so many people are not," Hanke said. "You have to have a detail-oriented mind, a disciplined mind, and you have to be very bright. She is all that."

But despite West's talents, she never seemed to reach her potential. She wore worn-out clothes to work even though she was making $60 to $70 an hour, and she could be abrasive. Many of West's coworkers labeled her "strange," and they avoided her. In 1997, the workplace strangeness culminated in West disappearing from her job at Hybrid without calling anyone. Fearing the worst, Hanke filed a missing persons report with the sheriff's department in Santa Clara County.

"I had no idea where she was," Hanke said. "I didn't know if she'd been kidnapped or what."

The police called Hanke a few days later to let her know West was safe, and within a few more days Hanke learned West had checked herself into the psychiatric wing of the Veterans Administration hospital in Las Vegas.

"She had a problem with her medication, and I guess she had some sort of episodic event, which caused her to be in the hospital for a month or so," Hanke said. "We sent her a beautiful bouquet of flowers that said, 'Get well soon.' I told people at work she got in a car accident and she's in the hospital. I thought it was stress induced."

After West got out of the hospital, she seemed even more willing to talk to Hanke about her past, and she started to reveal her deepest, darkest secrets. She detailed for Hanke the shoplifting scams West carried out with her mother.

"She told me about this big burglary ring where you'd go and you'd steal a bunch of clothes professionally," Hanke said. "She said she had been arrested for over $100,000 worth of stealing in Los Angeles."

West told Hanke she possessed special psychic powers.

"She can hold an object and tell you who owned it or what have you," Hanke said. "And she actually did that for me once. She's never been to my parents' house, and yet she described my parents' living room and this china cabinet where this sugar bowl [was]. So, you know, it was something interesting to me. I make no judgment."

West said her dad was a witch, and he handed down the craft to his daughter.

"She said, 'It's historical—my family's been in witchcraft for generations,'" Hanke recalled.

"She said her dad was a very powerful warlock, and that he was the source of her psychic power. Her dad would do incantations, and her dad would put evil hexes on people.

She said he taught her spells, and he taught her hexes, and she also said he's extremely dangerous when crossed."

West went on to reveal that her husband, Howard Simon St. John, was a murder victim.

"I said, 'Oh, come on, Brooke. You didn't have anything to do with that,' " Hanke said. "And she said, 'Um, well, I won't say that I wouldn't have done it. Someone beat me to it.' "

But of all the strange things West told Hanke, the thing that stuck out in Hanke's mind was the way West talked about her own mother. West, it seemed, hated her mother. She constantly vented to Hanke during their phone calls about financial problems her mother was causing her, and she repeatedly said her mother was a "psychopath" who couldn't be trusted.

"Increasing problems with her mom," Hanke said. "It was a regular event. Every phone call . . . it was her mom was crazy, a sociopath, and all this stuff. And I said, 'Well, Brooke, you know, you moved into your mom's place. Why don't you just leave?' And she said, no, her mom should be the one to leave. She's crazy like her brother, [Travis]. She said her brother was a sociopath, and she was gonna send her mother to go live with her brother.

"It was a love-hate thing with her mother," Hanke said. "It seemed like a thing of dominance. There was a need to dominate her mother. Somewhere, psychologically along the way, she had been damaged by her mother."

36

In mid-February of 1998—just two days after Christine Smith disappeared from the Orange Door apartments—Alice Wilsey was walking through the courtyard of the apartments when she saw a homeless man pulling a blanket out of a Dumpster. It was a blanket Wilsey immediately recognized as Christine's, one she had given Christine as a gift.

"It was a green blanket that I had given to Christine, and I saw a street person take that very blanket out of our Dumpster and walk away," Wilsey said.

Seeing the blanket in the trash made Wilsey suspicious. It certainly didn't seem likely that Christine would have just thrown it in the trash before departing to San Jose, and Wilsey was starting to doubt Brookey Lee West's story that Christine had moved to live with West's homeless brother.

"A lot of what she told us just didn't make sense," Wilsey said. "I was thinking about the possibility of foul play."

That same day, Wilsey went to Christine's old apartment and encountered West cleaning. Wilsey noticed

Christine's white scarf was still in the apartment, her painting of Jesus still on the wall.

"She wore [the scarf] even in the summertime," Wilsey said. "The painting—she almost worshipped it. The face of Christ. Christine would have never left that picture behind."

West then offered to give Wilsey all her mother's groceries.

"I said, 'What if Chris comes back?' " Wilsey recalled. " 'Isn't she gonna want these things?' "

"Well, she's not gonna come back," West told Wilsey.

"How do you know?" Wilsey asked.

"Because I threatened to put her in a home if she comes back," West said.

Wilsey wasn't the only one suspicious of West's story. A few days after Christine's middle-of-the-night departure, Chang visited Christine's old apartment, and she, too, noticed Christine's most cherished possessions still in the apartment. Among them were Christine's arts and crafts and a set of handmade dolls Christine had showed off to her friends.

"I looked way up on a shelf, and I saw a little bitsy box, and there was a ring in that box," Chang said. "It was a ring that I saw Chris wear the first time I met her. It looked like an opal stone and a turquoise stone."

Chang asked why Christine's ring was still in the apartment if she'd moved to San Jose to live with her son.

"That wasn't my mother's ring," West said. "I asked her so many times where it was, and she couldn't remember where she put it."

Chang asked West how Christine was doing.

"She said, 'Oh, she's doing fine,' " Chang recalled. "She said they [Christine and Travis] were talking about moving to Bakersfield."

In the fall of 1998, another incident unfolded that made Wilsey even more suspicious. Wilsey and West were using

Wilsey's tarot card computer program, and Wilsey decided to call up tarot cards on the computer screen while she thought of Christine.

The first card?

Death card.

The second card?

Death card.

The third card?

Death card.

The fourth card?

Death card.

Four death cards in a row.

"I read the tarot cards in my computer for Chris, with Chris in mind when I did it, and every time, the death card came up," Wilsey said. "I told that to Brooke, and Brooke said, 'What?' She tried to show that she didn't believe it."

By November 11, 1998, Wilsey decided to tell the police about her suspicions that West had murdered her mother. Wilsey sat down at her computer and wrote a lengthy letter to police detailing all the odd circumstances surrounding Christine's supposed trip to San Jose to live with her homeless son. In it, she wrote:

I am concerned about the possible demise of Christine M. Smith, born Feb. 15, 1932, in El Paso, Texas. Christine and her wonderful dog are gone. I have many reasons to disbelieve the story that Christine is with her son:

1—Her son is an alcoholic, a heavy drug user and is a street person.

2—Since Christine has been gone, I have discovered that some of her treasured things are still with West.

3—Christine was heavy into religion and had a picture of Jesus Christ. That picture is now in the possession of West.

4—West threw away many of Christine's things.

5—No one in the neighborhood has talked to Christine since the day she left.

6—West said that Christine has called her a few times and said to say hello to her friends. I don't believe her.

I have discovered that West has times when she is violent in nature because of her mental disability. Since her doctor told her that she must get away from her mother, I feel that she killed her mother in a rage and left her someplace where she wouldn't be found.

Is it possible to check Christine's doctor and bank accounts to see if they are still being used? If her Social Security is still being deposited in her account, and if so, what location is the money being taken from? West has access to Christine's account as she helped her set it up. I believe it is with Nevada State Bank.

My name is Alice Kay Wilsey and I live at the Orange Door apartments. I would appreciate it if West would not be told about the possible investigation as she would know who is responsible for the inquiry. If she did dispose of her mother, my life would be in danger.

Wilsey printed out the letter and drove to the Las Vegas police substation on Fourth Street in downtown Las Vegas. Wilsey asked to see a detective, but the detectives were unavailable, and Wilsey was asked to return a few days later.

Wilsey left the police station with the letter in hand, but she never went back because she doubted whether the police would believe her. She also questioned whether her suspicions about West were accurate.

Christine spent the next twenty-seven months rotting in a garbage can at the Canyon Gate Mini Storage on West Sahara Avenue.

* * *

In 1998, Brookey Lee West announced to her friend Natalie Hanke that she had finally solved the biggest dilemma of her life—what to do with her pain-in-the-ass mother.

"She said she had sent her mother away to live with her brother," Hanke said. "She said, 'They deserve each other.'"

Over the next three years, West called Hanke on the phone several times, and during many of those calls West told Hanke her mother was living with her brother, Travis, in San Jose. In one call that Hanke remembers well, "She said she had just gotten off the phone with her mother, and her mother was driving her crazy," Hanke said. "Her mother needs some money, and she needs money a lot. She goes, 'Natalie, I can't visit them. I can't stand being around them.'"

Hanke said there was nothing in West's tone or demeanor to suggest what was really going on—that her mother was already dead.

"There was nothing at all," Hanke said. "She acted as if her mother was alive and well."

In 1998, West attended Hanke's fortieth birthday party at a local restaurant in Foster City, California, and during the party, West produced an expensive birthday present. It was a small box containing a diamond ring, and to Hanke, the ring looked like it had been worn before.

"She made a big speech about what a great friend I was," Hanke said. "The only person who ever gave anything to her without expecting anything in return. It was obviously a ring that had been worn, and it was just inappropriate all the way around.

"I tried to give the ring back to her the next day, and a week later, and a month later, and she said no each time," Hanke said.

Hanke started to suspect the ring belonged to West's mother, and she persisted in trying to give back the gift.

"Finally, she goes, 'Natalie, that ring is possessed. I don't want anything to do with it,'" Hanke said.

"I said, 'Well, why did you give me a ring that's possessed?' " Hanke said.

"Well, it's only possessed for me," West said.

Months later, in 1998, Hanke went on vacation in Las Vegas, and during the trip Hanke agreed to get together with West to see how she was doing. As soon as Hanke arrived, West insisted Hanke come visit her mother's old apartment at the Orange Door. The apartment was small and cramped, and Hanke immediately noticed the residence was decorated with dark, occult-themed artwork and statues.

There was a disturbing gargoyle statue inside, and a bloodied picture of Christ on the wall.

"There was a religious painting, and it looked like it had been stolen from a church or something," Hanke said. "Christ on the cross. And it looked to me like blood had been added to it. I remember animal bones being on a table there, and there was just this feeling of weirdness. Books on Satan [and] witchcraft. I said, 'That's a little weird, Brooke,' " Hanke recalled. " 'Why do you have animal bones in your living room?' "Oh, that's my mom," West responded. "She's crazy. She reads them or something."

Hanke felt like she needed to leave the apartment as soon as possible, so she faked illness and rushed back to her hotel room. She was freaked out by the incident and decided to slowly distance herself from West, but there was one more time when Hanke ran into her.

In 1999, Hanke happened to return to Las Vegas on another vacation, and she reluctantly agreed to meet with West again. But this time, she made it clear that she had no intentions of going back to West's apartment. Instead, she met West for lunch, and during the meal at a Strip casino, West told Hanke she had a new boyfriend named David.*

"She looked at me in this very strange way, which I've never forgotten, and [she said], 'David and I want you to come to the storage locker,' " Hanke recalled.

Hanke said the invitation seemed extremely strange. It was a hot summer day in Vegas, and no one in her right mind would head out to a storage shed unless they absolutely had to.

"It's like 110 degrees out, and she's trying to get me to go to the storage locker," Hanke said.

"My gut instinct was like, 'No, this isn't going to happen.'"

Hanke believes West was plotting to kill her and steal her identity.

"I don't know for certain that she was going to do me in, but nothing else seems to make sense given the patterns of behavior and given that she wanted me to go to the storage locker," Hanke said. "Especially now [it makes sense] because I know that her dead mother was in that storage locker. She had already been decomposing for a year or two."

37

Any professional gambler in Vegas will tell you that good luck comes in streaks. When the good luck comes, you ride it like a wave, but when the good luck goes bad, you never ride it out. You pocket your chips and run for the casino door as quickly as you can.

Up until 2001, Brookey Lee West's good luck streak was especially long. In 1985, she'd been in an explosive custody dispute that ended with her boyfriend's grandmother being shot in the chest.

No one ever suspected West or her father in the shooting.

That same year, she was arrested for felony theft in a shoplifting scam with her mother, and the two got off with probation.

In 1994, West was the prime suspect in the killing of her husband in Tulare County, but she was never charged.

And in 1996, she was suspected of using a stun gun on her mother in law in San Jose.

Again, she was never charged.

It was a hell of a run.

But on February 8, 2001, West's luck officially went

cold, and there was no more running away from her mother's murder.

"We felt like we had a case, so I decided I was going to go ahead and arrest her in the death of her mother," Las Vegas homicide detective Dave Mesinar said.

To Mesinar, the evidence supporting West's arrest on a murder charge was overwhelming. Christine Smith's body was in a garbage can in a storage shed rented in West's name; a search of West's apartment had turned up a key matching the lock on the storage shed on the door of unit #317 at Canyon Gate; financial records from West's apartment indicated West's mother was continuing to receive Social Security checks long after she was dead; and the checks were being direct deposited into an active bank account that West had access to.

But to arrest West, Mesinar had to find her. He started his search by telling all of West's neighbors at the San Croix condominiums—where West now lived—to be on the lookout for her. One of West's neighbors there called Mesinar on the night of February 8 and told him she was back at her apartment. Mesinar raced back to the condominium complex, but he was just minutes late. West had apparently discovered a business card left by the homicide detective on her front door, and she fled.

Mesinar started to drive back home, and within a mile or two he got an extremely lucky break. He stumbled across West's pickup in a convenience store parking lot on Rainbow Boulevard.

"Dumb luck," Mesinar said. "We knew what kind of truck she had, we had the license plate number, and there it was, parked in front of a 7-Eleven at Rainbow Boulevard and Sahara Avenue. I was like, 'Oh, my god, I see her in there. She's buying a cup of coffee.' I waited until she came out, and then I called in the black-and-whites to stop her."

Patrol units stopped West's pickup on Rainbow Boulevard in Las Vegas. West got out of her car, was handcuffed and was driven to the Las Vegas police Homicide Detail on West Charleston Boulevard.

Mesinar then called Sergeant Kevin Manning, and the two met up just before midnight at the office to confront West about killing her mother.

Manning quickly took notice of how normal looking their suspect was.

"Nothing unique about her, and nothing sinister," Manning said. "The type of person you'd pass on the street and you'd never even take notice of. She looked normal. But to us, that is not what matters. It is what you can't see that is significant. It's not the outward package.

"We brought her into an interview room. I had a tape recorder, and I told her about her Miranda rights," Mesinar said. "Sergeant Manning was there, along with myself, and she appeared calm. Very matter of fact. The first thing I did was tell her that her mother was dead. For all I know, I don't even know if she knew, but when I told her, all she said was, 'My mother died a natural death, and I want to talk to an attorney.' We were in the room just a minute."

West's response to the news that her mother was dead was very telling. West wasn't stunned with shock when told her mother was in a garbage can, she wasn't teary eyed, and she wasn't outraged. It was clear to the detectives that West already knew her mother was dead.

"There was never, ever any signs of grieving," Manning said. "There was never any kind of feeling of loss."

There would be no lengthy statement to police like the one given to Tulare County homicide detective Daniel Haynes in the slaying of Howard Simon St. John. This time, West was silent.

"I think she realized things were not good for her," Manning said.

West was led in handcuffs to Manning's sport utility vehicle and then driven to the Clark County Detention Center
in downtown Las Vegas for booking on a murder charge.
During the brief, ten-minute drive, West asked Manning
how she could take care of an outstanding traffic ticket.

"She had a traffic ticket, she was going to court and she
was worried about a warrant being issued for this traffic
ticket," Manning said.

"I told her, 'That's the least of your worries,'" Manning said.

"I've got nothing to worry about," West said.

38

On February 9, 2001, the television news stations in Las Vegas were in a frenzy over the arrest of Brookey Lee West. All of the three local stations in Vegas led their broadcasts with stories about the woman charged with murdering her mother and stuffing her in a can to rot.

"Is it a murder mystery now solved, or the most bizarre sort of burial?" a gorgeous blond news anchor asked on television station KVBC Channel 3.

In the story dubbed "Mini Storage Murder," Channel 3 reporter Kim Capozzo aired the first interview with the suspected killer at the Clark County detention center. West looked pale and heavy on television—she was at least forty pounds overweight—and her brown hair was cut short at the shoulders.

"At most, I'm guilty of not reporting my mother's death," West told the reporter through a Plexiglas window at the jail.

"You put your mother in the storage shed?" Capozzo asked.

"I did," West said.

"But you did not murder her?" Capozzo asked.

"That's correct."

"My mother wasn't murdered at all," West told journalist Cindy Cesare of KLAS Channel 8 television station. "My mother died of natural causes."

"Why didn't you bury her?" Cesare asked.

"These are some very interesting answers that people would like to have," West said. "They will get them, but I can't give them to you in this particular filming because this is stuff I have to give to my attorney."

Las Vegas homicide detective Dave Mesinar watched the television interviews with glee. West was squawking before she'd been appointed an attorney, and in the interviews she admitted she put her mother in the storage shed. The admission made Mesinar's job much easier because he no longer had to investigate other possible suspects.

"She still never said, 'Oh, my god, my mother's dead,' " Mesinar said. "There was no emotion at all, and I'm thinking, 'This lady killed her mother.' It was valuable to me just to see her nonreactions and her nonemotions on TV. I honestly think she was enjoying the attention."

Hours later, Mesinar got another surprise. His phone rang, and on the line was former Tulare County homicide detective Daniel Haynes, who now worked for the Porterville, California, police department. Haynes heard about West's arrest from his former partner, Herman Martinez, and he called Mesinar to let him know about Howard Simon St. John's murder.

"My thoughts?" Haynes said. "I wasn't surprised, and honestly I was relieved. At least she was caught for something.

"They weren't aware of Howard's murder, so I said, 'Man, have I got a story to tell you,' " Haynes recalled. "I said, 'Here's the case number, here's your contacts, and you are going to be quite pleased to find a lot of your background work is already done for you.' "

St. John's murder, the shooting of Ray Alcantar's grandmother in Palo Alto, the stun gun attack on Chloe Smith, West's missing brother and the details of West's crazy family were all valuable facts for Mesinar because it reaffirmed his belief that West was capable of killing.

"It showed me Brooke has some deep-rooted psychological problems, and that she is unstable," Mesinar said. "She isn't all there."

One particular fact from St. John's murder captivated Mesinar. St. John was found in the Sequoia National Forest with a plastic bag partially on his face. Christine had a bag tied tightly on her face, and Mesinar was optimistic the details of the bag on St. John's face could be used against West in a Las Vegas courtroom.

"We had similarities with plastic bags around or near their heads," Mesinar said. "There has got to be some significance to that."

Mesinar and another homicide detective, Darlene Falvey, traveled to Los Banos and interviewed all of West's old neighbors. With the help of Nevada prosecutor Frank Coumou, they tracked down Natalie Hanke, they interviewed West's stepmother, Chloe Smith, and they tracked down Christine's neighbors at the Orange Door, Judy Chang and Alice Wilsey.

"Brooke told everyone her mom was in California living with her brother, so we decided we had to try and find her brother, Travis," Mesinar said.

Mesinar, Falvey and Clark County district attorney's office investigators Pat Malone and Pete Baldonado spent weeks looking for Travis Smith, but like Haynes, they never found him.

"We checked the welfare rolls in California," Mesinar said. "We got Travis' prints from the FBI, and we sent them to all the coroner's offices with unidentified dead bodies. We never found him. We put in hours and hours looking for him, and all we came up with were dead ends everywhere we looked."

There was, however, one fascinating clue uncovered during the search for Travis. Around the time Travis was last seen alive, West wrote a letter to the Social Security Administration asking the agency to deposit her brother's Social Security checks in a bank account West had access to. Mesinar considered the possibility that West had murdered her mother, her husband and her brother, and if that was true, he'd apprehended a female serial killer.

"The more we dig, the more people we find who are shot, killed or missing," Mesinar said. "At some point, it becomes more than a coincidence."

But despite the suspicions, Mesinar still had one major problem with his case against West. West was claiming her mother died a natural death, so Mesinar went to Clark County medical examiner Gary Telgenhoff to affirm Telgenhoff's suspicions that Christine Smith was murdered. Telgenhoff, however, shocked Mesinar, telling him the cause of death for Christine was undetermined—not murder. The medical examiner decided Christine's body was too decomposed to determine a cause of death.

"I didn't make the decision lightly," Telgenhoff said. "I agonized over this. I stayed up at night, and I thought about it a lot. But if I was going to say she was murdered, then I could envision three other pathologists questioning the decision," Telgenhoff said. "They would say, 'On which basis did you decide she was killed?'

"I could say she was in a garbage can and she had a plastic bag around her mouth," Telgenhoff said. And then they would say, 'Yeah, but what was the mechanism that killed her? Demonstrate that to me.' And I couldn't. There was nothing left of her body to see. No marks. No hemorrhages. No bruises were left. There were no bullets or stab wounds.

"I could see myself being on *60 Minutes* when it comes out later that somebody else killed her, and this woman [West] didn't know what had happened; then I'm out there with my dick in the wind," Telgenhoff said. "I didn't make a lot of friends in the police department that day."

Mesinar was mortified. The detective's seemingly solid case now had a huge, gaping hole in it, and if the county's medical examiner couldn't say Christine Smith was murdered, how could a jury?

39

Justice, and only justice, you shall pursue.

—The Bible

Clark County prosecutor Frank Coumou was taught early on in life that rules were made to be followed—not broken. He was born to an authoritative Dutch ship captain named Bram Coumou, who demanded his children always respect the rules.

"With my dad the captain of a ship, you just didn't question him," Coumou said.

A prosecutor in Las Vegas for thirteen years, Coumou was also taught another very important life lesson as a child—respect your mother. The lesson was driven home to Coumou as a child growing up in South America's Dutch Guiana, which is now called Suriname. Suriname and its dense jungle landscape was a stopping point on Bram Coumou's shipping route, and settling his family there allowed the cargo ship captain to see his wife and children once a week or so. But when Bram Coumou was out to sea, the Coumou family paid a price. The Coumous, who are white, were targeted by the country's black majority.

"My mom went through hell because, when my father was away, we had bad things happen to us," Coumou said. "Our house was totally burglarized. One time we came home, and someone had broken in and defecated inside the house. Another time, our car was turned over. They were trying to get us to leave."

The experience left Coumou with a profound respect for his mother's courage, and he never forgot how she got the family through those difficult times.

"Your mother is someone you treat with respect and dignity—not put in a garbage can," Coumou said.

Coumou was assigned to prosecute the case of Brookey Lee West in February of 2001, and he was horrified by the crime.

"I remember going back to my office with the case file, going through it, and then I got to the pictures," Coumou said. "When I saw the pictures of Christine in that can and how her body had liquefied, I was shocked. It was gross and nasty, and then there was a plastic bag tied over her face. It was like the night of the living dead. Who does that to her own mother?

"You are charging the daughter with killing the mom, stuffing her in the garbage can and taking great efforts to seal the garbage can with the duct tape," Coumou said. "Then the body is stored with all these books about Satanism and witchcraft, and I was like, 'Whoa, this is not the gangbanger shooting the gangbanger. This is something way different.' "

Coumou was assigned to prosecute West with veteran prosecutor Scott Mitchell of the Clark County district attorney's office. Mitchell is a quiet, reserved father of seven and a bishop in the Church of Jesus Christ of Latter-day Saints, and when he reviewed the contents of the West case file and the details of Howard Simon St. John's slaying, he saw an obvious pattern in West's behavior. Instead of just separating herself from the people who became problems in her life, West killed them like a black widow preying on her bloodline.

"Howard Simon St. John became inconvenient to Brookey West," Mitchell said. "He appeared to be a weight around her neck. He was someone who couldn't support her or himself, he was threatening to squeal on the insurance fraud, so it appeared to me that she took his life.

"It looked like that is what happened here in Las Vegas with her mother, too," Mitchell said. "Her mother became a weight around her neck. She didn't want to be making trips back and forth from Las Vegas to San Jose, so to rid her life of one more inconvenience, she took her life.

"And it appeared that she did the same thing with the brother, although we can't prove that because we never found the brother," Mitchell said. "But the suggestion was there that he met the same fate, and that he disappeared off the face of the earth.

"We are probably dealing with a serial killer, and we are only scratching the surface," Coumou said. "Everywhere she goes, people turn up dead or missing, and I think she got caught because she got sloppy. I think she got caught because she killed somebody who was too close to home, and she couldn't cover up for that one."

After receiving the case file, Coumou set out to determine whether Christine Smith's Social Security checks were a motive for her slaying. Social Security records showed that in December 1997, just two months before she disappeared, Christine asked the Social Security Administration to begin depositing her checks directly into a Nevada State Bank account. Although West was not named on the account, prosecutors learned from Christine's friends at the Orange Door that West helped her mother establish the account. This, the prosecutors believe, allowed West to learn the account's personal identification number.

Coumou charted the Social Security deposits to Christine's bank accounts after Christine was last seen alive, and he charted the withdrawals as well. The financial records showed $1,000-a-month deposits were being made from 1998, when Christine disappeared, until the discovery of her body in 2001, and throughout those years, more than two dozen withdrawals were repeatedly made at ATMs where no video surveillance was in place. Most of the withdrawals were made in San Jose or Las Vegas, and an examination of West's banking records showed withdrawals were often made from her accounts at the same time from the same ATM machines.

Coumou and Mesinar were unable to say definitely that West made the withdrawals from her mother's account, but such a scenario certainly seemed likely.

"This woman was decomposed and in a garbage can, so it's obviously impossible for Christine to be going to all these areas and withdrawing the money from her account," Coumou said. "I think Brooke thought she was entitled to the money. In her mind, she thinks, 'I still have mom, and nobody is ever going to find out about it.' She thought she was going to get away with it. No one was asking any questions for three years, and that money kept on getting deposited, so she kept spending it."

Coumou also pursued the possibility that the method of death for Christine was part of a Satanic ritual. The premise was based on the books found at the crime scene, and it was only furthered by the letter sent to Ray Alcantar by West's father days after Alcantar's grandmother was shot in Palo Alto.

Coumou meticulously scoured through *The Satanic Bible* and *The Geography of Witchcraft* in search of a reference to killing someone and tying a bag tightly over his face. He found vague reference to killing victims and keeping them from telling secrets in the afterlife. Coumou believes there was a connection between Satanism and the way Christine's body was disposed of.

"If you read *The Satanic Bible*, it talks a lot about doing things to people who have wronged you," Coumou said. "Maybe West thought in her mind, 'My mother has kept me trapped all my life.' I don't think it is too far-fetched."

Mitchell and Coumou ultimately decided, however, not to pursue the Satanic angle at West's murder trial, because they worried if they were to get a murder conviction of West, the Nevada Supreme Court would find the Satanism theory too inflammatory and overturn West's conviction.

"I stayed away from it because I didn't want the media spectacle, with headlines about Satanism and witchcraft, and then have it blow up in my face later," Coumou said. "Ultimately, that is not the only motivating factor as to why she killed her mother, either. She killed Christine because she hated her mom and she wanted to get rid of her."

The prosecutors felt they had a strong case. There was no disputing West put her mother in the can—she'd already admitted it; she had a financial motive to kill her mother; and witnesses told how Christine had become a burden to her daughter. To make their case even stronger, the prosecutors asked jail officials to monitor West's phone calls, and in a call West made to a male friend in Northern California, West said, "No one knows" where her brother is.

That would directly contradict what West told everyone—that she had sent her mother to live with her brother in 1998. If West walked into court and continued to maintain that she did, in fact, take Christine to live with her brother and then put her mother in the can at a later date, the jailhouse tape recording would destroy such a claim. To Mitchell, the tape showed West lied about the whereabouts of her mother from the very beginning, and the call also showed West likely knew no one was ever going to find her brother.

"She had to know Travis was not going to be found to be able to say that with confidence," Mitchell said.

But the prosecutors had one very big problem. There

was no cause of death for Christine, and without a medical examiner willing to say Christine was murdered, West could tell the jury her mother died a natural death, and the jury might just believe her.

Coumou decided to try something different. He consulted a forensic entomologist to see if an examination of the insects found on Christine's body could yield any clues about when she died and the circumstances surrounding the disposal of her corpse.

It was an extremely wise move.

40

On his rural farm in Rensselaer, Indiana, Dr. Neal Haskell gets up most mornings, cooks his breakfast, reads the paper and he heads out to his grassy farmlands to pluck bugs off decaying pig flesh.

"I enjoy collecting insects," said Haskell, a burly, bearded man with a big belly and even larger personality. "Entomology is like going on a treasure hunt. There are just so many different specimens collected, and every time you go to a different habitat, there is something new. Plus, it's been a damned good excuse to travel throughout my life. Hey, it's too cold, so I've got to go to Florida or the Yucatan Peninsula to collect bugs."

Haskell is a forensic entomologist and professor at St. Joseph's College in Rensselaer. He has spent decades studying insects, and he is an expert on the role bugs play in the decomposition process of bodies. The way bugs consume a corpse or animal is pretty much an exact science, he said. As soon as the body dies, there are certain insects that show up like clockwork, and the bugs on the body go through specific, discernible life cycles while feeding on the flesh.

By examining whether an insect is in egg form or is a maggot, cocoon or fly, Haskell can often make observations about the time of death for the victim.

"In certain cases, we may also be able to show the geographical location where a body has originated from based on a particular [insect] species," Haskell said. "We can also do drug testing on maggots and larvae that have been feeding on human remains. . . . And then there is a new application. It is the recovery of human DNA from the blood meals of insects that feed on humans such as lice, bed bugs, fleas and mosquitoes."

Haskell's understanding of the role insects play in the decomposition of the human body has led him to be a much-sought-after expert in criminal cases across the United States. He has testified in or consulted on five hundred different cases, and he is a consultant for numerous criminal forensics television shows, including HBO's *Autopsy*.

In 1999, he examined the bodies of four Anasazi Indians found in a grave in Farmington, New Mexico. The four Indians were bludgeoned to death, and forensic science determined the deaths unfolded sometime around A.D. 750. By examining the insect remains on the ancient corpses, Haskell could say the victims were likely killed in the summertime.

"It was most likely summer, and the individuals were held above ground before they were buried for a considerable period of time because they had a good amount of fly puparia or cocoon stage [on them]," Haskell said.

In the spring of 2001, Haskell was contacted by Clark County prosecutor Frank Coumou and Las Vegas homicide detective Dave Mesinar to see if he could determine a time of death for Christine Smith. He was also asked to see if he could make any findings about the circumstances in which Christine's corpse was stuffed into the garbage can.

Haskell examined the insect specimens collected at Christine's autopsy under a microscope, fully expecting to find a fly species that is commonly referred to as the blowfly. The blowfly is easily recognized by the metallic green and blue coloration of its body, and it is usually the first bug to find a body after an individual's death.

"I've seen [blowflies] find dead animals within fifteen to twenty seconds after death. . . . These blowflies can detect a dead animal from over a mile to a mile and a half away," Haskell said. "So they have very strong chemical receptors that will key in and then follow, primarily, upwind. They will fly upwind, trace the odors upwind and access the remains.

"The blowflies will be among the very first colonizers," he said. "The quicker [an insect] can get to that food and start utilizing it, the greater [its] chance for survivability."

But when Haskell examined the insects from Christine's body, he was shocked to find no blowflies at all, which told him Christine's body was placed in the garbage can almost immediately after death.

"The absence of any of these early colonizers [blowflies] tells me that this body, these remains, had to have been purposely placed in such a way as to exclude the early colonizers," Haskell said.

Instead of blowflies on Christine's body, Haskell found an insect species known as humpback flies. The gnatlike flies, also known as coffin flies, are notorious for being able to access dead bodies in confined spaces such as coffins or mausoleums.

"These flies are so tenacious, they've been found to burrow down three to four feet through soil to coffins," Haskell said. "They are very tenacious at getting into any small crack or opening, particularly when we have the remains in an advanced decompositional state. So a garbage can, I wouldn't think, would be much of an obstacle."

Haskell's findings were extremely important to Coumou because they showed Christine's murder was premeditated. Since there were no blowflies on the body, West must have already had the garbage can ready at the moment her mother died, and she immediately stuffed the body into the can, preventing the blowflies from finding the remains.

"If Christine was killed, then Brooke must have already had the tools ready—the garbage can, the cellophane, the duct tape, the wrap, the plastic bags," Coumou said. "Had mom died of natural causes, and then Brookey goes out and gets a garbage can, you are going to find blowflies. But we never found them. So that tells me she got all the tools she needed to put her mom's body in there.

"I think West probably drugged her mom, put the plastic bag over her face, and she realized the bag wasn't quite doing the trick, so she got the garbage can," Coumou said.

Haskell also raised a much more sinister possibility for the manner in which Christine was killed. Perhaps the blowflies never found Christine's remains because she was still breathing when she went into the can.

"It's possible West put her mom in there while she was still alive," Coumou said.

41

There are certain cases that are referred to as "bad fact" cases in the world of criminal defense attorneys. Your defendant's DNA is found at the crime scene, the victim's blood is found on your client's clothes, the assailant was captured committing the crime on videotape, or the suspect confessed on camera. They are the type of cases that beg for a plea deal—not a jury trial.

To Clark County deputy public defender Scott Coffee, Brookey Lee West's murder case was not a "bad fact" case. In fact, when Coffee was assigned to defend West in court in the spring of 2001, he was convinced West had a good chance of being acquitted of first-degree murder.

"I thought the case had potential," Coffee said. "It's not your normal case, of course. A daughter is charged with killing her mother. But you ask yourself, 'What can they prove?' And the fact that a body is in a shed someplace, even if it has been there a long time, doesn't prove murder to me."

Coffee is not your stereotypical defense attorney. He is tall, somewhat portly and down-to-earth. He has an aura of confidence but not arrogance. Adopted as a child to a logger and a stay-at-home mom in Red Bluff, California, Coffee worked his way through high school and then went on to college in Oregon for an undergraduate degree in philosophy.

"Where do you find a job in philosophy?" Coffee said. "Driving cabs."

Instead of driving a cab, Coffee cut firewood for a year with his dad after college. His first wife had family in Las Vegas, so Coffee moved to Southern Nevada and took a job managing a fast-food joint.

"Raley's Hamburgers," Coffee said. "A little fast-food place, seven hundred square feet, and we had up to twenty-eight people working there at a time. Hang and bang."

He quickly realized the burger business wasn't for him, so he enrolled in officer training school for the U.S. Marines. He dropped out of officer school just two days before he was commissioned.

"They didn't like me and I didn't like them," Coffee said. "They were probably going to drum me out anyway, and it just wasn't the right fit. I'm more the type to stick my thumb in authority's eye than follow their rules."

Coffee went to law school next, and it was there that Coffee found his calling. He hired on with the Clark County public defender's office in Southern Nevada in 1995, and he honed his skills as a trial lawyer over the next six years with a simple, down-home approach that connects with Las Vegas juries. At thirty-nine, Coffee is now recognized as a shining star in the public defender's office.

In 2004, Coffee won what many thought was an unwinnable case as the defense attorney for a slaying suspect named Michael Kane, who plunged a knife in another young man while on an LSD trip in Vegas. At Kane's trial, Coffee presented evidence that Kane was mentally ill and that he didn't know what he was doing at the time of the killing. A jury agreed and returned a verdict of not guilty by reason of insanity—the first jury verdict of its kind in Nevada in a decade.

"The jury recognized that Mike was mentally ill, and the best thing to do was to put him in a mental institution," Coffee said.

In West's case, Coffee knew he needed help in court because of the magnitude of the case and the media attention, so he asked fellow deputy public defender Lynn Avants to assist in crafting West's courtroom defense. Avants, the son of veteran Las Vegas police homicide investigator Beecher Avants, jumped at the chance.

"I was fascinated by the case," Avants said. "This whole garbage can thing in a storage shed was interesting. But as a defense attorney, I was thinking, 'How do you know she committed murder?' "

Coffee and Avants were impressed with West's intellect. Unlike many defendants, she was sharp, well spoken and logical.

"I like Brooke," Coffee said. "Brooke's very intelligent, she's a likeable person and, unlike a lot of defendants I encounter, she's bright. A lot of defendants have psychological problems or other issues such as a lack of education, but that's not the case with Brooke. She's self-taught."

West was adamant she was not guilty of murder. She told her attorneys her mother died a natural death, she panicked, and she put the body in a garbage can.

"She said she was traveling back from San Jose after picking her mother up [from her brother's], that her mother was sick, her mother had gotten the chills, and she died in bed," Coffee said. "She panicked. She had a garbage can full of books, so she dumped out the books, put her mother's body in the can, and then hid it because she was scared.

"Who put the body in the storage shed was never much of a question in this case," Coffee said. "The prints were on the plastic wrap, the name was on the storage shed rental sheet and there was no question who put the body there. She admitted it."

Coffee found West's account believable, and with the Clark County coroner's office labeling the cause of death for Christine Smith undetermined, Coffee liked his chances with a jury.

"No signs of a struggle," Coffee said. "Christine's nails weren't broken, her bones weren't broken. I know the body was badly decomposed, but there were a lot of good things Dr. Telgenhoff had to say from the defense perspective as to cause of death. There was no evidence of drugs in the system, no poisons, no gunshots, no stabbing. For all we know, Christine could have died of natural causes."

But Coffee and Avants are not dummies. They recognized that if West was going to be acquitted, they were going to have to overcome some huge obstacles in court.

"The problem is, you've got a daughter charged with killing her mother, and the mom is in a trash can, and she's rotted there for almost four years," Avants said. "People don't like that. And then you've got this theft problem with the mother's Social Security, so people were not going to be happy with Brooke. I was really concerned about that. The case doesn't have a lot of jury appeal because people are going to be fixated with the fact that the daughter is accused of killing mom."

Another huge problem were the books found at the crime scene. The news media learned of the books, *The Satanic Bible*, *The Geography of Witchcraft*, and *Necronomicon*, in April of 2001 during a preliminary hearing for West in the courtroom of Las Vegas justice of the peace William Jansen. Reporters grilled Coffee about the books afterward, and Coffee recognized the chum was in the water for the news media. West was no longer just a woman accused of killing her mother and stuffing her in a can. She was also a suspected Satanist and witch.

"We had witch hunts in Salem several hundred years ago," Coffee told the *Las Vegas Review-Journal*. "This shouldn't turn into one."

The next day, the *Review-Journal* ran a section-front story about the books at the crime scene and the suspicions that West was involved in witchcraft. Coffee knew if a jury heard about those books, West didn't stand a chance in hell of being acquitted.

"When we first heard about the case, we heard a lot about devil worship and things like that. That stuff really doesn't have a place in a court of law," Coffee said.

"There are all kinds of First Amendment problems as well," Coffee said. "Let's just say, for the sake of argument, she was a devil worshipper. Doesn't mean she's guilty of anything. Or lets say she is a witch. Doesn't mean she's guilty of anything.

"You want to talk about prejudicial," Coffee said. "Witches? Devil worshippers? You are automatically going to put the jury in the mind-set that she must be guilty, and it is not necessarily the truth. And Brooke's got a First Amendment right to practice whatever religions she wants."

Travis Smith's missing status was another big dilemma. They suspected prosecutors were going to imply Travis was murdered by his sister, and Coffee and Avants' hands were tied in diffusing those suspicions, because they didn't know where he was, either.

"I don't know how you prove a negative," Coffee said.

Perhaps the most troublesome aspect of West's case was her prior history. West was a suspect in her dead husband's shooting; she had a mother-in-law who was stun-gunned; she had an ex-boyfriend who believed West had shot his elderly grandmother; she had a felony grand larceny conviction; she had a missing brother; and she had a father who was a practicing devil worshipper.

"I know a lot about West," Coffee said. "I know she has been institutionalized, and I know the state is going to try to dig into that. I know they are going to try and dig into witchcraft, whether it is legitimate or not. I know they are searching San Francisco covens and things, trying to look for something to tie in the witchcraft, and they'll try to find anything and throw it against the wall to see if it will stick."

With this in mind, Coffee invoked West's right to a speedy trial, meaning prosecutors had to present their case to a jury within sixty days of arraignment or the charges would be dismissed.

"The whole idea was to push the state forward with what they had," Coffee said. "We wanted to try this case on the body in the storage facility and nothing else. The state was digging, and this was becoming more and more about West's past than it was what they had against her. The less time they had to scramble and investigate, the better off we were."

Coffee got his wish. West was arraigned on May 1 in the courtroom of District Judge Donald Mosley. She entered a not guilty plea, and her trial was scheduled for July 2, 2001.

Brookey Lee West's fate would soon be in the hands of a jury.

42

District Judge Donald Mosley is a man who presides over his courtroom with an iron fist. Known as one of the toughest sentencers at the Clark County courthouse in Las Vegas, he is admired as a judge willing to give a defendant every benefit of the doubt when it comes to making sure he or she gets a fair trial. But once you are convicted in Mosley's courtroom, look out. If you are a convicted murderer, rapist or child molester and you appear before Mosley for sentencing, you might as well kiss your ass good-bye and resign yourself to spending your remaining days looking out an eight-inch-wide window from a jail cell in the Nevada penitentiary.

"I know I have that reputation," Mosley said. "I'm a firm believer that you ought to work for what you get, and there ought to be consequences for what you do, right or wrong. You do something good, you ought to be rewarded. If you do something screwy, you ought to be punished."

The tall-wiry, cowboylike figure with grayish-brown hair hails from Tulsa originally, and he comes across as a mix between Midwestern cowboy and Southern good old boy. A sportsman to the core, he loves to talk about hunting buck, ducks or other wild game in Northern Nevada and other hunting hot spots across the United States.

"That's what I do," Mosley said. "I hunt and fish. Most people understand being outdoors, you know, like hikers and bird-watchers. But to me, to go to all that effort and all that time and not have a gun in your hand makes no sense to me at all."

Mosley, during the last quarter century as a judge in Las Vegas, has found himself to be a lightning rod for controversy. He says what he thinks, critics be damned.

"A lot of judges are spineless," he says without flinching.

He's not afraid to mix it up, either, if necessary. During one verbal exchange with a motorist in rural White Pine County, Nevada, Mosley punched a man out in the middle of the road like a prizefighter felling a tomato can has-been in the boxing ring.

"The fact of the matter is, he attacked me and I dropped him on his butt in the street," Mosley told the newspapers in Las Vegas at the time.

In 2002, Mosley got in hot water with state judicial regulators amid allegations that he used his position as a judge to gain an advantage in his own child custody dispute. The Nevada Commission on Judicial Discipline fined Mosley $5,000 and gave him a public censure, but Mosley has always said he did nothing wrong. Mosley denies the allegations to this day, and despite the professional setback, voters, reelected him to the bench overwhelmingly in 2003.

"Someone once said, 'Mosley never dodges a bullet,'" Mosley said as he puffs on a big fat cigar in his county office, where smoking is supposedly banned.

It was in Mosley's courtroom that Brookey Lee West found herself in the legal battle of her life on July 2, 2001. Upon her arrival in court for jury selection, onlookers noticed West looked much different from her prior court appearances. She had shed a lot of weight, and she was dressed like June Cleaver. She wore frilly tops, her hair was in a curly bob and she looked like a librarian. Prosecutor Frank Coumou would later label West a chameleon who was trying to invoke sympathy from the jury.

"West is so good at creating this aura of 'Poor me,' when she's really not," Coumou said. "She's a criminal."

"She had a bookworm look," Mosley said.

True to his reputation as a fair judge, Mosley did everything he could to make sure jurors in the West case heard only what they needed to—no inflammatory facts that might prejudice their ability to be fair. He ordered that prosecutors not present details of any of West's prior encounters with the police to the jury. This meant the jury would not hear about Howard Simon St. John's murder, the stun-gunning of Chloe Smith, the shooting of Ray Alcantar's grandmother or even West's prior felony conviction.

He limited the number of autopsy photos the jury would see of Christine's melted body in a can. And although prosecutors weren't going to pursue the issue anyway, Mosley ordered there was to be no mention of Satanism or witchcraft during the trial.

"To a large degree, most of the rulings by the judge leading up to the trial were in favor of the defense," Coumou said.

Mosley did, however, give prosecutors some leeway in presenting to the jury evidence about the missing status of West's brother, Travis Smith. To Mosley, the information was relevant because West had told so many witnesses she had taken her mother to live with her brother.

Throughout jury selection, Mosley took notice of how at ease the defendant was. West was on trial for charges that could land her in prison for life, yet she seemed completely at peace with her circumstance.

"She was confident—almost smug," Mosley said. "I actually think she deluded herself into thinking she was going to walk. . . . Nothing seemed to bother her. It looked to me like she was going down the pike here, and she didn't seem to care."

West's behavior seemed so cavalier, at one point during jury selection, Mosley warned her.

"There has been an indication that throughout at least a portion of this process, the defendant was making eye contact with prospective jurors, mouthing certain words, smiling," the judge said. "I want to admonish the defendant that we will not have any more of that kind of thing."

A jury of six men and six women was picked in four days. The jury was a slice of middle-class America. Two jurors were teachers. One was a salesman. Two others were retired. One juror was a stay-at-home mother with kids.

West remained optimistic she would be acquitted of murder because, she says, she didn't kill her mother. She admits, however, that she had visions of a guilty verdict.

"I knew something bad was coming," West said. "Prosecutors? That's their job. To prosecute. What was it someone told me? It doesn't have to be true. It just has to work."

The police?

"I hate police," West said. "I do not trust police at all. . . . My dad always told me, 'Brookey, never trust the cops. They are dirty.'"

Opening statements in West's trial unfolded on July 6 in front of a packed courtroom, and both Coumou and Coffee started out strong in their remarks to the jury. Coumou recounted the gruesome details of Christine Smith's fate and presented his case: the fact that her body was in a storage shed rented by her daughter; how the key to the storage shed lock was in West's apartment; the bevy of witnesses who said West said her mother was alive when she was dead; the financial motive of stealing her mother's Social

Security checks; the bag tied tightly over Christine's face; and the unabashed hatred West had for her mom.

"From the outside looking in, it appeared like it was a normal relationship between mother and daughter," Coumou told the jury. "When you actually start looking and hearing the testimony of people who were close to the defendant, you will find the relationship was far from normal. She would make statements, 'My mom is a sociopath. My brother is a sociopath. They should be happy together,' " Coumou said.

Coumou told the jury West's statement that her mother was with her brother was a three-year-long lie concocted to cover up a heinous murder.

"There is no record of Travis Smith Jr.," Coumou said. "The idea of saying mom is going to go live with the brother and then maintaining that story would turn out to be just a big deception. [The] motive for this killing was hatred," Coumou said. "In addition to that [there] is the finance from her mom's Social Security money. . . . These are classic reasons [to kill], and the state intends to prove the defendant is guilty of murder."

Coffee conceded in his opening remarks to the jury that West stuffed her mother in the can.

"The body of Ms. West's mother was placed inside a garbage can in a storage facility," Coffee told the jury. "Of that, there is no question."

But he said West didn't kill her mother, and she wasn't the monster prosecutors were painting her as. She took her mother to the doctor, she helped pay her bills and, most important, she loved her mother.

"Ms. West also took care of her mother," Coffee said. "The state didn't mention that. She helped pay the rent. She took her to the doctor. She did the normal things that a daughter would do for a mother."

Coffee told the jury Christine was sixty-five years old,

and given her age, it was certainly possible she died a natural death.

"I can with confidence say one thing—it's doubtful she [Christine] would like to see her daughter wrongfully prosecuted for a murder that didn't happen," Coffee said.

"Dr. Telgenhoff is going to tell you that a lot of things can't be ruled out," Coffee said. "A heart attack can't be ruled out as a possibility. A stroke can't be ruled out. Christine Smith was asthmatic. Her lung capacity was low. The day before she left [the Orange Door apartments] her friend Alice Wilsey said she was as sick as she had never seen her before," Coffee said. "She didn't feel well.

"The mother was taken to live with the brother," the defense attorney said. "At some point, the mother comes back to Las Vegas. She dies. She dies from what we will learn were likely natural causes."

Coffee said that after her mother's death West panicked and put the body in the garbage can.

"Brooke West did do some things wrong," Coffee said. "When her mother dies, Brooke panics. She doesn't handle stress very well, as you will hear from a number of witnesses. She puts her mother in a storage facility. At that point, a lot of things become too late," he said. "Too late to call the authorities. Too late to report the death. Too late to tell anybody where mom is because of fear. This is motivated by stress.

"I will concede that Ms. West misused her mother's Social Security. . . . There's no question. She probably figured, 'Who's going to know?' "

And with that, the trial of West was under way. Little did Coffee know he would soon be fighting off a bombshell of a development that threatened to sink his client before he'd even called a single witness.

43

It never fails. Everytime a high-profile murder case begins in Las Vegas, an inmate at Las Vegas' dungeon of a jail—the Clark County Detention Center—comes forward to say the defendant confessed to him while behind bars. Brookey Lee West's trial was no exception. The jailhouse snitch in West's case was a pretty young woman named Heather Hearall, and Hearall was in custody on allegations she'd violated her probation in the winter of 2001 when she met West.

Hearall told authorities she was talking to another inmate about West's case at the jail when West walked up and started volunteering information.

"Without provocation, she told us that whatever happened between her and her mother, that her mother had forgiven her, and God had forgiven her, too," Hearall said. "That was my first interaction with Brookey West."

In another instance, Hearall said she overheard West talking to another inmate about her brother, Travis, and that during the conversation West detailed the method she used to cash her brother's Social Security checks.

"She talked about impersonating her brother," Hearall said. "That's the only way she could cash the check. She talked about having to dress as her brother. 'That's the only way I can cash the checks.'"

Prosecutors were elated with the potential bombshell witness. In the middle of West's trial, Hearall was brought into Mosley's courtroom where she repeated the same information she had told authorities. Mitchell and Coumou both agreed that Hearall's testimony sounded true.

"She said, 'Oh, yeah, Brooke was telling me how she had tried to disguise herself as her brother to try and get the Social Security money, so we seized on that," Coumou said. "I thought, 'We've got it. We've got proof of financial motive.'"

But Coffee argued to the judge that Hearall was lying to curry favor in her pending probation revocation proceeding.

"She's a jailhouse snitch with every motivation in the world to better her position," Coffee said. "What she said wasn't credible."

With Mosley on the verge of deciding whether Hearall should testify, Coffee announced he would seek a delay in the trial if she was called to the witness stand. He told the judge he would need time to try to disprove what Hearall was saying. This, in turn, alarmed the prosecutors, because the state had already spent the money to take the case to trial, and if a delay was announced, the state would have to start over again. Feeling that they had a strong case already and slightly worried that the jury might view Hearall's testimony with skepticism anyway, they decided not to put her on the stand.

As a result, the jury never heard what Hearall had to say.

44

The Heather Hearall fire was quickly squelched by Scott Coffee, but a bigger blaze was starting to burn in Donald Mosley's courtroom. Namely, a parade of witnesses was walking into court and portraying West as an unstable lunatic.

When the first of these witnesses, George Burnett, arrived in Mosley's courtroom on the afternoon of July 6, it seemed as if the ghost of Howard Simon St. John had just walked through the courtroom doors. Burnett, a Native American with flowing black hair running down to the middle of his back, took the witness stand and told the jury he was West's fourth and final husband. He said he met West in November 1996 at the Stardust casino on the Las Vegas Strip when West walked up to him and started the conversation.

It was the same way West had met St. John in San Jose nearly three years earlier.

"She walked up to me and asked me a few questions about my [Indian] heritage, and we started speaking," Burnett said. "I told her generally I was a loner out here [in

Vegas]. I really didn't have anyone to spend Thanksgiving with."

Burnett ended up spending Thanksgiving day with West, and a passionate, whirlwind romance ensued. The two were married on January 5, 1997, in a little chapel on the Vegas Strip, and the two then headed to the San Jose area, where Burnett planned to spend the rest of his life with his new bride.

But within a day of arriving in San Jose, West suddenly said she had to go back to Las Vegas to be with her mother.

"She said she had a problem with her mother being sick, and as I recall, she said that her mother wouldn't let her go," Burnett said. "She said she had to go back immediately to Las Vegas to help her mother out. 'She's just really kind of fucking up my life more or less,' she said."

Stunned, Burnett asked her, "What is this? What is happening? We come all the way out here, and all of a sudden, it's just like a total change of mind? The next thing I knew, her car was gone, and she was no longer there," he said.

After West left him, Burnett decided he wasn't going to give up on his new bride so easily, so he drove all the way back to Vegas and stopped by West's mother's apartment at the Orange Door. He identified himself as West's new husband, and he was surprised to learn Christine knew nothing of her daughter's marriage.

Christine quickly ran to the phone and called West, who denied the marriage to her mother.

"She told her mother she didn't know what she was talking about, [that] she didn't get married," Burnett said.

The marriage was annulled within a few months, and that was the last Burnett heard from his bride until her arrest in Las Vegas on a murder charge. Burnett's testimony, however, should have been an omen for West and her defense team, because the painting of West as an oddball by witnesses would continue pretty much nonstop for the next two weeks.

Natalie Hanke took the witness stand, and in what was perhaps the most dramatic moment of the trial, she tearfully told how West repeatedly claimed her mother was alive when she was really dead.

" 'Mom's a bitch. A sociopath. All she wants is money,' " Hanke quoted West as saying. " 'She never did a thing for me in her whole life.

" 'She's got to go, Natalie. She's got to go,' " Hanke said West told her in late 1997 or early 1998.

Coffee questioned Hanke's value as a friend, but the damage was done. The aura surrounding West in the courtroom was one of strangeness—a freakish lady who was a liar and therefore capable of murder.

"They painted Brooke as an oddball," Coffee said. "The insinuation was, be scared. If she could do this to her mother, what could she do to you?"

Clark County prosecutor Frank Coumou strongly disagrees. He said portraying West as an oddball wasn't a strategy—it was a matter of fact detailed by witness testimony and evidence. And providing the jury witnesses who observed West's strange behavior wasn't the only thing prosecutors did well at trial. They also laid out a case for murder.

Dr. Gary Telgenhoff walked jurors through the autopsy and how Christine's body rolled out onto the autopsy gurney like a waxy, cheesy ball.

"The first thing that was most noteworthy other than the body being in a trash can—which is something you don't see everyday—[was] there was a white plastic bag around the nose and mouth tied tightly behind the head," Telgenhoff said. "It certainly must have been tight before decomposition occurred."

Telgenhoff told the jury the cause of death was undetermined, but he gave prosecutors a tidbit of optimism when asked about the cause of death.

"Would [the circumstances] be consistent with the belief that this victim died of suffocation?" Coumou asked.

"Yes," the medical examiner responded.

On cross-examination, Coffee and Avants fought back, getting Telgenhoff to concede the circumstances of Christine's burial could also be consistent with a natural death.

Joe Matvay told the jury how the crime scene was processed and how West's fingerprint was recovered from the cellophane wrap on the can. He showed the jurors the grisly crime scene photos and the images of Christine up to her neck in a soupy mix of decomposition and insects.

"I observed a human form or human figure at the bottom of the can," Matvay said. "The human form was in an advanced state of decomposition, and I could discern there was a head with hair present."

Several jurors appeared aghast.

Dr. Neal Haskell told about the life cycle of blowflies. Using a large chart with a picture of a massive blowfly on it, he narrated for the jury how the flies lay their eggs on bodies, the eggs turn into maggots, and then eventually the maggots form a cocoon.

"And after a few days in this form, the adult flies will eventually hatch out both male and female," Haskell said. "It will take a few days to reach sexual maturity, they'll mate, then the fly is off doing the next generation."

"Landing on your hamburger?" Coumou asked.

"We hope not," Haskell said.

Haskell told the jury he believed the blowflies were prevented from finding Christine's body immediately after death, and that putting the body in a garbage can would explain the lack of blowflies on the body.

"And within your findings, is it also consistent with the theory that the victim could have been placed alive into this garbage can?" Coumou asked.

"I suppose it would be possible shortly after death, but

definitely into the period after death," Haskell said. "It would be definitely possible for any of that to have occurred."

Coffee was angered by the jury hearing the premise that Christine went into the can while she was still breathing.

"That just scares the hell out of you, doesn't it?" Coffee said. "Isn't that what you want [as a prosecutor]. It scares the heebie-jeebies out of you. She could have been put in there alive. We don't have any evidence of it, but it could have happened. What the hell is that?"

But Coumou and Mitchell continued with the assault. Three different bank employees and Dave Mesinar offered testimony indicating that withdrawals were made from Christine's bank account after she was dead. A Social Security investigator said West had written a letter to the administration asking it to deposit her brother's Social Security checks in a bank account. The implication was clear—West wasn't just stealing her mother's money, but her brother's, too.

A Las Vegas Valley nurse practitioner, Judy Zito-Pry, said she treated Christine on numerous occasions for minor ailments ranging from toenail fungus to urinary tract infections, and that West once expressed to Zito-Pry concerns about Christine losing her mental facilities.

"She was concerned about her mother's memory," Zito-Pry said. "She thought she'd developed Alzheimer's. She was quite concerned."

Zito-Pry said Christine had a history of asthma, and a test showed her lungs were in bad shape. Christine's lungs had the efficiency of a 132-year-old, the nurse practitioner said, leading Coffee to say Christine could have died of lung failure, old age or an asthma-related reaction to her asthma inhalers.

"Her health was basically stable," Zito-Pry countered.

But the most powerful witnesses for the prosecution were Judy Chang and Alice Wilsey. The senior citizens shuffled into court, took the witness stand and proceeded to humanize Christine for the jury with their emotional testimony. They painted Christine as a sweet little old lady who didn't deserve what she got. Chang described the last time she saw Christine alive.

"I walked down to the apartment to see her, and she was lying on the couch with a little dog, the little Chihuahua we called Chi Chi," Chang said. "All of a sudden, I heard Chris say, 'You are not giving my Chi Chi away!' Brooke looked at her kind of hard and weird like."

Chang told the jury that after Christine disappeared, Christine's belongings were still in the apartment at the Orange Door.

" 'Oh, she will forget all about them,' " Chang quoted West as saying. " 'She won't even remember them.' "

Wilsey told the jury Christine was ill the night of her disappearance, and that West was giving her "so-called aspirin."

" 'Here, honey, take this. It's aspirin,' " Wilsey quoted West as saying to her mother. " 'It will make you feel better.' She came in several times. She [West] told me that she could no longer live with her mother, and that she found a way to make a place for her," Wilsey said. "That she wouldn't have to be bothered anymore."

Under cross-examination, Wilsey and Chang acknowledged they liked West, and they continued to associate with her after Christine's disappearance despite their suspicions. Once again, though, the damage was done. West was perceived as a coldhearted killer.

"Alice was golden," Coumou said, crediting Wilsey for her courage in describing for the jury what really happened. "Her mind was so sharp, and she remembered everything. Suddenly, Christine was gone, and Brooke is giving away all the stuff that belonged to her mom."

The defense case, in comparison, was quick. One witness, Steven Michael Cornett, was a resident of the Orange Door apartments, and he said he actually saw West moving her mother out of the apartments. The testimony seemed to contradict prosecutors' contention that West had murdered her mother the night Wilsey last saw Christine.

A medical expert, Dr. James Anthony, told the jury he had treated hundreds of asthma patients, and that 5,000 people a year die from asthma. His testimony furthered Coffee's premise that Christine could have died because of a rare reaction from an asthma inhaler, and he said Christine's lung age of 132 was a significant health concern.

"That's very bad," Anthony said. "That's severe lung disease."

Closing arguments were delivered on July 18, and both Mitchell and Coumou rehashed their evidence one more time for the jury. Coumou emphasized the most crucial piece of physical evidence—the bag tied tightly to Christine's face.

"It's the one piece of evidence that cannot be explained," Coumou said.

Coffee told the jury that perhaps the bag was placed over Christine's face to preserve her dignity in death.

"It's a shroud placed over the face," Coffee said. "When people are in the hospital [and die], they have sheets pulled over their faces."

But it was too late—the jury was convinced Christine was murdered. After just a couple of hours of deliberation, on July 19 the jury returned a unanimous guilty verdict on a charge of first-degree murder. West showed no reaction, but for Coumou, Mitchell and Mesinar, the guilty verdict was an incredibly rewarding moment. They'd taken off the street a stone-cold killer who left a trail of missing and dead people in her wake, and justice had been served for Christine Smith, regardless of all her faults in life.

"There has been no one here to speak for Christine

Smith," Mesinar told the *Las Vegas Review-Journal*. "This verdict speaks for her."

Two months later, during her sentencing hearing, Mosley hammered West. He committed her to life in prison without any chance of parole.

"Ms. West is not being sentenced this morning for anything other than what occurred to this elderly woman," Mosley said. "Since the jury has made the determination of guilty, I have thought about this case on many occasions. And in each instance, I am left with one very nagging point of confusion. How did this white, plastic, kitchen garbage bag ever find itself around the nose and mouth of the decedent?

"We've heard two possible explanations. One is that it was a shroud, a sort of a covering of the face in deference to the decedent's status. And of course, we've heard the other suggestion—that it was, in essence, what killed her by virtue of suffocating.

"I have to tell you, Ms. West, that the latter is more likely in my view. She was overpowered, this item placed around her face, tied tightly, and she was placed into this garbage container, presumably to suffocate her. Now that doesn't paint a very pleasant picture.

"And while I think everyone would agree putting someone's mother in a garbage can to bury her is bizarre, placing her in there conscious to suffocate her is not only bizarre—it's criminal. You are sentenced to life without the possibility of parole. That's all."

45

The Southern Nevada Women's Correctional Center is located on the outskirts of the Las Vegas Valley along Interstate 15. It is a maze of hallways, cells, bars and barbed wire expressly built to house Nevada's female lawbreakers. Everyone from murderers to ordinary thieves in Las Vegas call the women's correctional center home.

Brookey Lee West is scheduled to spend the rest of her life at the prison, yet by all accounts she is a model inmate. She leads a Bible study class, she teaches other inmates art and she is an advocate for raising money for Nevada's wild horses, which are becoming more and more scarce in the natural landscape surrounding Las Vegas.

"While I'm in here, I don't do anything bad," West said. "I've never even had any kind of disciplinary action. I teach other inmates. I do an art program. I collect all this money to get people to participate [in the wild horses benefit program]. It's my job, but I don't get money for it. When the money is raised for these horses, the ultimate good is for these animals. They are created, just like we are, and they have a place, and they are losing that place. They need medical care. They need a lot."

West, in fact, seems to be making the best of her predicament in prison. She said that throughout her life she has suffered from a serious mental health condition—she is bipolar—and in prison she has gotten the treatment she needs to be a stable, productive person.

"I don't even see myself in a bad situation," West said. "I see everything as a learning experience. I came here, and I wasn't in good shape. I'm in good shape now. I'm meditating again. My diet is right. I'm starting to lose the weight I need to lose to be the right size. The shrink they've got here is really, really good. I get my medication. I see my mental health person, and she said I have a borderline personality, but she said that is a learned behavior and that I've made so many changes that I'm not really sick.

"[Being in prison] has really gotten me back on track, and I've been able to get the rest I needed," West said.

But just because West is in prison doesn't mean she admits to murdering her mother or anyone else, and she denies committing any crime other than shoplifting.

She denies having anything to do with Howard Simon St. John's murder.

"We were only married for six weeks. West said. It wasn't like there was some reason that I would want him dead," West said, denying there was a plot to kill her husband in order to quell the insurance fraud investigation for her burned-out Jaguar.

"The car was stolen. I know that Howard got mad at me because I didn't go to the hospital [when he was shot the first time]. He didn't know that I was under a restraining order, so he got pissed off, he called up the insurance company and he made up this story. When he realized what he had done—after the asshole got sober and off his medication, he told me, 'Do you think they are going to lock me up for it?' I said, 'Why? You didn't do anything.' So that's when he called them again. I guess he met them somewhere, and that's when he told them he made the story up.

"The second time he told the story, he told the truth," West said. "The first time, he made the story up, he fabricated it, and I had nothing to do with it. All of that happened before he was dead. Why would I have killed him over something that wasn't going anywhere?"

West said she cooperated with the police in Tulare County.

"You think I killed him?" West said. "Well, go ahead and charge me. Try it. That's the way I feel about it. The reason I wasn't charged is because I wasn't involved in it. I told these people the truth. I sat for hours with those two cops. No lawyers or nothing. . . . They asked me everything in the book. Short of asking me how I liked him in bed, they asked me everything else."

West denies stun-gunning Chloe Smith.

"No," West said. "She thought that if she could get me arrested and get me out of her hair as opposed to putting my father in a rest home, she could do what she wanted. And I was like, 'No, we'll go to court over this. I'm not going to allow it.'"

West said she had nothing to do with the shooting of Ray Alcantar's grandmother, although she acknowledges her father sent the Satanic letter to Alcantar after the shooting.

"He said, 'You pray to your God; I think my God is just as good as your God.' He [my father] had the seal of his cult club on it. He didn't give a damn. He said, 'That's my God,' and Ray was freaked out about it from then on. . . . He blamed me for things I really didn't have any control over. I don't know what happened."

West said she is not a practicing witch or Satanist, although she has studied all kinds of religions.

"Well, that sells," West said. "It sells papers. It sells news. Who wants to read, 'Well, she's a really nice person, she just has a few problems.' That's not interesting."

West said her brother, Travis, will eventually surface, and she will be vindicated from allegations that she somehow killed him.

"He'll turn up," West said. "Mark my words. He will."

And, perhaps most important, West denies killing her own mother.

She said she took her mother to live with her brother in San Jose in 1998, and in 1999 she went back to San Jose to bring her mother back to Las Vegas. On the drive home, she said, her mother died in a hotel room, West panicked, so she placed her mother in the garbage can.

"We were traveling, I'm not going to tell you where, what state, but she was complaining that she was feeling bad, she was real, real tired, and she wanted to get a place to stay," West said.

"She went to bed. I got up the next morning, and she was dead. But I wasn't coping, I wasn't handling things very well, and I just freaked out. I couldn't handle her death. This is too much, too many deaths, too close together. And not only that, I wasn't really medicated.

"I already had the can. It was full of books. . . . I stood there for a few minutes, and I had her purse, which was that sack [plastic bag] she carried. I grabbed it, I dumped everything out of it and I just tied it behind her head," West said.

"I kept her, and I had to have her in something," she said. "But once I set her there [in the storage shed], I never, ever moved her again. I did nothing to even touch that. I kept it nice and clean there for her.

"If I had of been then like I am now, I would have nev-er've done that. When you have the kind of condition I have, people don't understand," she said.

"I look at it the same way I looked at Howard's death," West said. "I knew I hadn't killed her, but I did keep her, and that's why I said on the news that I did put her there. Maybe that was the wrong thing to do, but I did put her there. But I didn't kill her, and I said I didn't kill her. Nobody killed her. She just died. And that's the way that it was."

West said she is confident someday she'll get out of prison despite her sentence of life without parole.

"There are a lot of people who go to the pardons board," West said. "They were all sentenced to life without parole."

In 2003, the Nevada Supreme Court denied Brookey Lee West's appeal on her murder conviction. She is still vow-ing to pursue the matter in both state and federal courts, claiming she is innocent. Nevada police and prosecutors say she is a dangerous woman who was convicted of a hor-rifying murder, and she deserves to remain in prison until she dies.

In the fall of 2004, West got a glimmer of hope for her appeals. A man identifying himself as Travis Smith went into a medical clinic in San Jose for treatment, and he used the same name and Social Security number as West's brother. The development sent a shock wave through Las Vegas—West's brother may actually be alive.

Defense attorney Scott Coffee sent an investigator to San Jose to see if Travis Smith could be found, but the in-vestigator was unable to track him down. There were ru-mors that the individual identifying himself as Travis was becoming a nuisance in a well-to-do neighborhood in San

Jose, so the cops bought the homeless man a bus ticket to
Florida to get him out of the city for good.

To this day, Travis Smith's whereabouts remain a mystery.

Born in 1970, **Glenn Puit** is an award-winning journalist and investigative reporter. He has spent his entire career writing about the criminal justice system. He was the district court beat reporter for the *Las Vegas Review-Journal*, which is Nevada's largest newspaper. Previously, Puit worked at the Florence, South Carolina, *Morning News*, where he was the first reporter in the nation to document the federal government's theory regarding the identity of John Doe #2 in the Oklahoma City bombing. Puit also worked at the *Leader-Herald* in Gloversville, New York, and has a degree in journalism from Indiana State University in Terre Haute, Indiana. A native of Lansing, New York, Puit lives in Michigan and is a father of three.